The
Case of
the
Murdered
Muckraker

A Daisy Dalrymple Mystery

CAROLA DUNN

Constable • London

CONSTABLE

First published in the US in 2002 by St Martin's Press, New York

First published in Great Britain in 2011 by Robinson,
an imprint of Constable & Robinson Ltd

Reprinted in 2015 by Constable

3 5 7 9 10 8 6 4

A CIP catalogue record for this book
is available from the British Library.

ISBN 978-1-84901-705-3 (B-format paperback)
ISBN 978-1-84901-843-2 (ebook)

Printed and bound by Clays Ltd, Elcograf S.p.A.

Papers used by Constable are from well-managed forests
and other responsible sources

MIX
Paper from
responsible sources
FSC   FSC® C104740
www.fsc.org

Constable
is an imprint of
Little, Brown Book Group
Carmelite House
50 Victoria Embankment
London EC4Y 0DZ

An Hachette UK Company
www.hachette.co.uk

www.littlebrown.co.uk

To all the readers in Eugene
who have asked me over the years,
'When are you going to set a book here?'

ACKNOWLEDGEMENTS

My thanks to Sue Stone, Keith Kahla and Therese Theophano for their help with New York research; and to Mr Stanley Bard and his staff for their willingness to answer questions about the Hotel Chelsea.

All errors, omissions, additions and alterations for artistic purposes are all my own.

AUTHOR'S NOTE

A number of real people have sneaked into this story. Needless to say, their activities herein, inspired by meeting Daisy, are entirely imaginary.

CHAPTER 1

Voices raised in anger: in the quiet when the clacking of the typewriter keys ceased, as Daisy reached the bottom of a page, the muffled sound came through the wall from the room next door.

It was not the first time. Apparently her neighbour was not of a conciliatory nature. This time there were two men and a woman, Daisy was pretty sure, but try as she might, she could not make out the words. None of her business, she told herself firmly, and turned her attention back to her work.

Squealing, the Remington reluctantly released the two sheets of paper and the carbon between. Daisy used them to fan herself. Not yet accustomed to the indoor temperature preferred by New Yorkers, and bred as she was to an age-old tradition of roaring fires tempered by icy draughts, she found the hotel room stifling. Her battle with the baulky radiator had been less successful than that with the typewriter provided by the management.

She looked longingly at the French windows, surrounded by elaborate rosewood carvings, then scowled at the typewriter. The Hotel Chelsea was a noted haven for writers and catered to their needs, but the Remington was on its last legs. Daisy suspected it had stood on this very desk for forty years, ever since the place was built in 1883, pounded daily by fingers expert and inexpert. It creaked and groaned at every touch and strongly objected to demands for capital letters. The prospect of resuming her battle with the beastly machine made her feel hotter than ever.

Beside the typewriter, the piles of paper were growing. Mr Thorwald had requested few changes in her article about the transatlantic voyage. It was all typed, ready to be delivered tomorrow. The article on her first impressions of America was coming along nicely. She had time to spare.

Stepping out on to the balcony, she shivered in the biting chill of a wintry breeze. The yellow-grey sky threatened rain, or even snow, though it was not quite November yet. Petrol – gasoline – fumes drifted up from West Twenty-third Street, mingled with dust, but the tang of sooty coal smoke was not as predominant as in faraway London.

Daisy leant on the flowery wrought-iron rail to watch a tram rattle and clang past seven storeys below. Not a tram, a streetcar. She wondered why Americans insisted that they spoke English, when they might just as well call their language American. The oddest thing was that people kept telling her, an Englishwoman speaking the King's English, that she had a quaint accent!

An unmistakably American voice interrupted Daisy's musing. The window of the next room was open a few inches. The woman whom Daisy had heard indistinctly before was now clear as a bell – no mellow church bell, no tinkling harness bell, but the shrillest of shrill electric bells.

'You bastard!' she cried venomously. 'I wouldn't come back to you for a million dollars.'

'If I had a million dollars,' retorted a biting male voice, more sarcastic than irate, 'you still wouldn't squeeze one red cent out of me.'

A different man said something indistinguishable in a soothing, rather nervous tone. A moment later a door slammed.

Guiltily aware that curiosity as much as overheating had driven her outside, Daisy ducked back into her room. She hoped she had not been spotted eavesdropping on the balcony. Rather than sit there awaiting an indignant knock on her door, she decided to go in search of a cup of tea.

It was, after all, past four o'clock. Prohibition had led some Americans to rethink the Boston Tea Party and agree that the British custom of afternoon tea was worth adopting. True, other Americans appeared to obtain alcoholic drinks without the least difficulty. Despite its bohemian clientele, however, the Chelsea was a respectable hostelry, not to be compared to a speakeasy. With any luck, a pot of tea and perhaps even a few biscuits – cookies – might be available below.

Why on earth *speakeasy*? Daisy wondered, making for the lifts. No one she had asked had the foggiest.

As she approached the nearer lift, the outer gate of the farther one clanked shut. She hurried, but when she arrived, the inner gate had also closed and the lift was already moving down the shaft with a rattle and whine of aged machinery. It left behind a whiff of mingled bay rum, expensive cigars, and still more expensive perfume. Daisy caught a glimpse of the top of the lift boy's livery cap, and beyond him a man's head, thin on top, and a scarlet cloche hat with a spray of white egret feathers.

'Missed it!' she exclaimed. 'Blast!' On the other hand, if

that was the couple who had been quarrelling in the room next door to hers, she was quite glad not to be boxed in with them.

She walked back to the other lift and pushed the button to summon it.

A young chambermaid popped out of a linen room just down the passage, her arms full of towels. ''Tis a long wait ye'll be having of it, I'm thinkin', miss,' she remarked in an Irish brogue thick enough to spread on soda bread. Her carroty hair and freckled face reminded Daisy of her stepdaughter, Belinda. A pang of homesickness struck, unexpectedly strong.

She smiled at the girl, who was probably just as homesick, with far more reason. 'Is this one out of order?' she asked.

'The elevator boy's a bold young limb o' Satan, ma'am. This time o' day he'll likely be off creating 'stead o' minding his duties.'

'I dare say this is a slack time and it must be frightfully boring going up and down in a cage all day.'

The girl beamed at her. ''Tis me little brother, ma'am. He's been on since six this morning. Sure, 'tis hard on a lively lad, but he's his bread to earn and lucky to have a job.'

'I shan't tell tales,' Daisy promised. 'I'm in no hurry. I suppose I could always take the stairs, at that.'

'Oh no, ma'am, 'tis a desp'rate long way down. The other elevator'll be back in a minute, if our Kevin don't come.'

In fact, the groan and clatter of cables and ratchets announced the imminent arrival of the maligned Kevin. Daisy had only to wait while his lift made its laborious way aloft, but during that interval a man came along the passage to join her.

At the sight of him, the chambermaid turned pink and ducked hurriedly back into her linen room.

He didn't look at all bohemian – in his forties at a guess, dressed in a medium grey tweed suit, with a black homburg and tan leather gloves in one hand, an attaché case in the other. Stocky, slightly bowlegged, he walked with a swagger. His jaw had an aggressive thrust, and his nose was long and inquisitive above a narrow moustache. His glance at Daisy was bold, impertinent even, with a sort of cynical dismissiveness which at once raised her hackles.

At the same time, she wondered if he was the man next door, if he had seen her on the balcony, and whether she was blushing like the Irish girl. She hoped not. She despised blushing as too, too Victorian. She gave him a haughty, withering look worthy of her mother, the Dowager Viscountess Dalrymple, but the bounder had already turned away.

He punched the call button, quite unnecessarily as the cage's rackety approach was obvious. Impatiently he opened the gate on to the empty shaft, where loops of cable performed their mysterious trigonometrical functions. Unless it was calculus Daisy was thinking of – her girls' school had not plumbed such mathematical depths, but she remembered looking over Gervaise's shoulder while he groaned over holiday cramming.

All that cramming for nothing, she thought mournfully. Her brother had gone off to the war instead of to university, and all his maths had not saved him from death in the Flanders trenches.

Maths would not save her impatient fellow-resident, either, if he plumbed the depths of the lift shaft, as he seemed in imminent danger of doing. However, he pulled his head back safely. The lift arrived, piloted by a youth of fourteen or so, whose carroty hair and freckles proclaimed him to be Kevin, while his watering eyes and scarlet ear suggested misconduct chastised.

Nonetheless, he gave Daisy a cocky, snaggle-toothed grin and enquired, 'Going down, ma'am?'

Perhaps his words recalled the impatient man to a sense of common courtesy. He was already stepping forward, but he drew back and, with an ironical half bow, allowed Daisy to go first.

'Where can I get a pot of tea?' she asked the boy as the lift started down.

'In the lobby, m'lady.' He tipped his cap, the gesture of respect cheekily exaggerated. His native Irish was overlaid with nasal New York. 'Stanley – that's the bellhop, m'lady – 'll take your order to the dining room and a waiter'll deliver, m'lady.'

His cheek was good natured. Daisy laughed. 'I'm English,' she admitted, 'but not "my lady".'

'We can't all be bishops,' he commiserated. 'It's the real tay you want? You tell Stanley Kevin said to tell 'em make it good and strong, not the dishwater the yankees call tay.'

The man behind Daisy snorted. From the corner of her eye, she saw him take a flask from his pocket, uncap it, and swallow a hefty pull. She assumed it was neither tea nor dishwater he had swigged, as his face turned an unbecoming purple.

Not that she was looking. She wouldn't give him the satisfaction. 'I'll remember your advice,' she said to Kevin with a smile.

He winked. 'I can get you the other stuff, too,' he whispered. 'Not moonshine, gen-u-wine Irish whiskey straight from the Emerald Isle.'

'No, thank you.'

'It's safe enough. All the right people been paid off.'

'Paid off?' The man was suddenly sticking his long nose between Daisy and Kevin.

The lift boy gave him a wide-eyed, would-be innocent stare. 'Musta misheard, mister. I was tellin' the lady how me brother was laid off. Worked down on the waterfront, he did.'

It was obvious the man did not believe him. Daisy thought he might have pressed the issue if she had not been there. She did her best to look thoroughly respectable, and they reached the bottom with no further exchange. He strode off without a backward glance.

Stepping out, Daisy passed the untenanted reception desk and went on through to the lobby. The floor was patterned in white, grey, black, and dried-blood-coloured marble, and grey marble lined the walls to waist height. In every corner potted palms lurked unhappily, as de rigueur here as in London. In this unlikely oasis, a fire flickered beneath a dark, ornately carved mantlepiece. Against the wall on either side stood a stiff, uninviting bench of the same dark carved wood, with red and ivory striped upholstery.

The stripes reappeared on two armchairs and a small sofa arranged in front of the fireplace around a low glass-topped table. Matching stripes adorned the seats of the rather spindly wrought-iron chairs set out around several small, equally spindly tables. Two of these pushed together were surrounded by a group of earnest-looking women and rather long-haired men. Their clothes tended towards the flamboyant, the men with floppy, kaleidoscopic cravats in place of neckties, several of the women wearing corduroy trousers. Daisy felt positively staid in her powder-blue costume.

She had seen virtually identical gatherings in Chelsea – the London suburb, not the hotel – where she had lived before she married. They were discussing either the future course of serious literature or the malevolence of editors.

In Chelsea, such a group would have scorned afternoon tea as too bourgeois for words (their preferred drinks were beer or cheap sherry, depending on their pretensions), but here they all held teacups. In fact Daisy saw teapots on the tables, all occupied, on both sides of the lobby.

One young man sat on his own, on one of the stiff benches against the wall. His teapot was perched on a side table, at an awkward height and distance, his cup and saucer balanced equally awkwardly in one hand, as if he wasn't quite sure what to do with them. He was soberly dressed in a dark, businesslike suit, his fair hair cropped short above studious horn-rimmed spectacles. Three or four years younger than Daisy's twenty-six, he appeared to be deliber-ately avoiding her eye.

Of course she would not have joined him even if invited, but she did wish she had someone to sit with.

She was a modern independent woman, she reminded herself. For years now she had looked after herself, having concluded that absolutely anything was preferable to living with her mother in the Dower House, after her father died in the 1919 influenza pandemic. Just because she was married now, had been married for a *whole month*, and her darling Alec was hundreds of miles away, it didn't mean she could no longer take care of herself.

The only free place was the other bench, but as she resigned herself to it, a couple stood up to leave a table on the other side of the lobby, by the door to the little-used ladies' sitting room. Daisy was moving to take possession when a short, plump woman with untidy grey hair bustled up to her.

'Oh dear,' she said, 'I do hope you don't mind?' She looked up appealingly at Daisy over half-spectacles.

'Mind?' Daisy asked, bewildered.

The little lady waved the knitting she was carrying, a beautifully patterned baby's jacket in pale yellow and white. The yellow and white yarn trailed behind her, Daisy noticed, back to the low table by the fire, on the far side of the lobby, where she had left her knitting bag.

'It's my sister,' she confided. 'Oh dear, so *awkward*, but she does like to know.'

'Know what?' Daisy asked cautiously.

'Oh dear, I'm muddling it as usual. My sister, Genevieve, insists on meeting everyone who comes to stay at the hotel. Do say you will?'

She looked a little reproachful when Daisy laughed, but brightened when Daisy said, 'I'd be glad to. May I know your name?'

'Oh dear, I ought to have introduced myself first thing! I am Miss Cabot, Ernestine Cabot Boston, you know – only a *very* junior branch.'

Why this obscure announcement should make Daisy think of fish she had no leisure to contemplate. Miss Cabot turned about, tangling her feet in her own yarn. She would have come to grief had not Kevin, playing truant from his lift, dashed over to prop her up.

'Happens reg'lar, once a week, like clockwork,' he murmured to Daisy.

Though no one else seemed to notice the minor imbroglio, the solitary young man must have been watching, for he also hurried to help. He stooped to unwind the wool, but Miss Cabot turned skittish.

'Oh dear . . . no, please . . . so kind, Mr er – hm . . .'

'Lambert.'

'Mr . . . I'm afraid . . . rather *indelicate* . . .'

Daisy gathered that female assistance would be appreciated. She disentangled the black lisle stocking-clad ankles while Miss Cabot twittered a series of *oh dears* above her.

Mr Lambert offered a hand to help Daisy up, with an oddly assessing look as though he were comparing her face with some inner ideal. Wondering whether she passed muster, Daisy thanked him with a nod and a smile.

'You're welcome, ma'am.' The words arrived with a whiff of Irish whiskey. Kevin's business was apparently a going concern, and not all teapots contained tea.

Daisy collected the yarn where it hung down from Miss Cabot's needles, intending to gather up the excess as she accompanied the old lady to meet her sister. The length of yarn rose a foot or two from the floor just as the impatient man from the lift strode past in his purposeful way. It caught him across the shins.

He barged on, oblivious. The knitting flew from Miss Cabot's grasp and the knitting bag attached to the far end of the yarn flopped to the floor.

Lambert caught the man's sleeve. 'Say, look here, wait a minute!'

'You know something about it?' He turned eagerly. Daisy could have sworn his long nose twitched. 'You're willing to talk?'

His face bemused, Lambert blinked. 'Talk? I can't see there's anything to talk about, buddy, except you might watch where you're going.'

'Watch ... ?' It was his turn to look blank; then he followed Lambert's gesture to the yellow and white strands adorning his legs. Turning to Miss Cabot, he said sarcastically, 'Ah, Madame Defarge strikes again.' His glance moved on to Daisy. 'Another victim for Madame Guillotine, I see.'

His French pronunciation was rotten, Daisy noted, even as she wondered if the hackneyed reference to Dickens had any significance beyond its evident malice.

Miss Cabot bridled. 'I'm sure I don't know what you can mean.'

'I don't suppose you do.' In an effort to disembarrass himself of the yarn, he stepped backwards. The wool clung to his tweeds. He bent down and snapped both strands. 'Beware of entanglements with women, sonny,' he advised Lambert. 'The only way out is a clean break.' And he strode on.

Lambert picked up the knitting, which had miraculously stayed on the needles. 'Sorry, ma'am,' he said sheepishly, handing it to Miss Cabot. 'Gee whiz, I guess there's not much you can do about a guy like that.'

'Oh dear, I'm afraid manners are not what they were,' agreed Miss Cabot.

Stooping again, Lambert retrieved the two loose ends of yarn. Since he obviously had not the least notion what to do with them, Daisy relieved him of them and proceeded at Miss Cabot's side, winding up the wool as they went.

Lambert moved ahead to pick up the knitting bag and replace it on the table. Any disposition to linger was firmly quashed by Miss Genevieve Cabot.

'Thank you, young man,' she said with a nod of unmistakable dismissal, and as he turned away, a trifle disconsolate, she added, '*Not* an interesting person.'

Mr Lambert's ears reddened.

'Guillotined,' thought Daisy, hoping she was not to meet the same fate.

CHAPTER 2

The armchair occupied by Miss Genevieve Cabot commanded a view of both the main entrance and the inner lobby leading to the lifts. *Commanded* was the appropriate word. Stout where Miss Cabot was softly plump, Miss Genevieve had a decisive air utterly at odds with her elder sister's dithers. At Daisy's approach, she remained seated, but she bowed and indicated the cane leaning against her chair as her excuse for not rising. Reason, perhaps, rather than excuse: she didn't look as if she was accustomed to make her excuses to anyone. Though her face had an invalidish pallor, there was nothing invalidish about her tone.

'Well, sister?'

'Oh dear, sister, I'm afraid I quite forgot to ask the young lady's name!'

'Mrs Fletcher,' said Daisy, taking a seat on the sofa without waiting to be invited. She had been summoned, after all. 'How do you do.'

'British,' observed Miss Genevieve, not with unalloyed approval.

Before Daisy could respond, a small boy in hotel livery scurried up to them – Stanley, the bellhop, familiarly known in England as a 'buttons'. Miss Genevieve ordered fresh tea, and more sandwiches, cookies and cake. Whatever her opinion of the British, she did not let it abate her enthusiasm for a proper afternoon tea, Daisy was happy to see.

While Stanley took Miss Genevieve's order, Daisy studied her hostesses. They both wore knit frocks with tatted collars and cuffs, beautifully made (by Miss Cabot?) but unflattering to their portly figures. Miss Cabot's dress was rose pink, Miss Genevieve's navy blue. Miss Cabot's hair, drawn back into a bun, escaped vigorously in all directions from its pins and nets. Miss Genevieve's, equally grey, was trimmed in a short, severe bob.

Daisy wondered whether they were chance residents or had some connection with literature or the arts. Then she caught sight of a ruled notebook in Miss Genevieve's ample lap, with a pencil tucked into the spiral binding. The top page was half filled with what appeared to be shorthand.

'You are a writer, Miss Genevieve?' Daisy enquired.

'Why, yes!' The old lady's surprise, and evident displeasure, suggested that she was more accustomed to interrogating than to being interrogated.

Daisy pressed her advantage. 'May one ask what you write?'

Miss Genevieve frowned, but Miss Cabot put in eagerly, 'Such nice knitting columns. For the women's magazines, you know. I expect you have them in England, too? I invent new patterns and Genevieve writes them down. Then she adds a bit of friendly chat, you know the sort of thing, I'm sure, so clever, I could never do it.'

'Tripe!' said Miss Genevieve.

'Oh dear! The patterns are really quite nice, sister. We do

get such a lot of letters, such nice letters, from all over the country. But I'm afraid Genevieve doesn't consider it real writing,' she confided to Daisy. 'Even the gossip columns are preferable.'

'Gossip columns?' Daisy could not quite see the sisters mingling with the sort of high society which provides grist for the gossip columnist's mill.

'Literary gossip,' Miss Genevieve growled grudgingly. 'For *Writers' World*,' explained Miss Cabot.

'This is the perfect place to collect information,' Daisy said.

'Many writers visiting New York do stay at the Hotel Chelsea. I manage to speak to most. I find most writers are eager to talk about themselves, even that obnoxious specimen who marched through Ernestine's knitting.'

'Oh dear, no serious damage, no stitches dropped, and I can sew the ends in so that they won't show, sister.'

'I dare say.'

'Who is he?' asked Daisy, who considered 'obnoxious specimen' an excellent description.

'His name is Otis Carmody and he is a muckraking reporter. A necessary breed, no doubt, with a necessary brashness, but I'd have thought a more conciliating manner might serve him better.'

'I dare say he moderates his manner when necessary.'

'Possibly. I do write about more literary figures, too.' Miss Genevieve sounded defensive. 'I drop in at the Algonquin when I can, but I don't get about much these days and anyhow, Franklin Adams writes about the Round Table crowd in the *World*. Besides, Dorothy Parker and Benchley and friends are poseurs, witty, perhaps, but not half as clever as they like to think. Not one of them could tackle the job I used to do.'

Daisy judged that a question about the Algonquin and the Round Table crowd would not be well received. 'What job was that?' she asked.

'I was a crime reporter.' Miss Genevieve warmed to Daisy's interest – or succumbed to what Alec persisted in describing as her 'guileless blue eyes'. 'The first woman crime reporter in New York, and the only one yet, as far as I know. Eugene Cannon was my byline. Of course, in those days there was no question of using my own name. They wouldn't even let me use a female name, as Lizzie Seaman did a bit later.'

'Lizzie Seaman?'

'Nellie Bly, she called herself. Now, there was a girl with a talent for self-advertisement. Around the world in eighty days, my foot! Not that I wanted the limelight, mind you. All I asked was the opportunity to do a good job of work.'

Miss Cabot sighed, her needles continuing to click busily. 'At least you succeeded in escaping from home, sister.'

'Yes,' said Miss Genevieve, her tone grim, 'but the life would not have suited you, sister.'

At that moment a waiter arrived. As he unloaded his tray and reloaded with the Cabots' empty teapot and becrumbed plates, Daisy glanced around and caught Mr Lambert watching her. He immediately averted his gaze. There was something odd about that young man, she decided.

The interruption gave Miss Genevieve the chance to turn the conversation from herself. 'And you, Mrs Fletcher,' she said as her sister poured tea, 'your husband is a writer?'

Surprised that 'Eugene Cannon' should regard her as a mere adjunct of her husband, Daisy said, 'No, a policeman.' She regretted the words as soon as uttered. A month had sufficed to teach her that almost as many people looked askance at a policeman's wife as at the policeman himself.

However, Miss Genevieve was all agog. 'An English policeman? I have never met one, but I've heard they are very different from our New York "bulls". He is here with you?'

'He's in Washington, advising a department of your government.'

'Aha, a man of importance, then. Not ... not by any chance Scotland Yard?'

'Yes, actually, he's a Detective Chief Inspector at the Yard.' Daisy decided it was her turn. 'I'm a writer.'

Miss Genevieve had the grace to look a little abashed. She picked up her notepad with a show of attentiveness. 'What do you write, Mrs Fletcher?'

'Magazine articles. I've written several for an American magazine called Abroad.'

'I always read Abroad,' said Miss Cabot eagerly. 'It is the next best thing to travelling. I should have liked to travel, but Papa ...'

'I do not recall a Fletcher among the contributors,' Miss Genevieve interrupted with a frown.

'I use my maiden name, Dalrymple.'

'Oh!' Miss Cabot dropped her knitting – fortunately she was not holding a teacup – to clasp her hands. 'Oh, my dear, not the Honourable Daisy Dalrymple?'

Less easily impressed by an honorary title, Miss Genevieve was nonetheless moderately flattering about

Daisy's articles on the museums of London, two of which had already appeared. She wanted to know what had brought Daisy to New York. Daisy explained that her editor had paid her fare to America so that she could write about the voyage.

Miss Genevieve took copious notes in her neat shorthand. 'What are your plans now that you are here?' she asked.

'Mr Thorwald wants my first impressions of America. We stayed with friends in Connecticut for a few days, and now I have a couple of days here.'

That led to a discussion of what she had seen in New York, what she planned to see, and what the Misses Cabot thought she ought to see.

'Will Detective Chief Inspector Fletcher join you here?' asked Miss Genevieve at last, almost shyly. 'I should greatly like to meet him.'

Daisy shook her head. 'No, I'm afraid not. I'm going to see Mr Thorwald tomorrow, and the next day I shall take the train to Washington.'

'Perhaps it is just as well,' sighed Miss Genevieve. 'I guess British cops don't like crime reporters any better than ours do. Sister, pass Mrs Fletcher the fruitcake.'

The leaden fruitcake was all that was left of the spread. Daisy declined a slice, hoping she had not been unheedingly responsible for the disappearance of too large a proportion of the rest. The no bosom, no bottom figure, emphasized by the hip-level 'waist', was as fashionable here as at home. Though it was not a look Daisy would ever attain, she did not want to find herself with the silhouette of a blimp.

'Thank you so much for my tea,' she said. 'I've enjoyed

talking to you. I think I'll go for a bit of a walk now, before it gets dark.'

'Yes, better get back before dark,' said Miss Genevieve. 'It's Halloween. There will be all sorts of mischief tonight.'

'I'll just go and look at the General Post Office and Pennsylvania Station, as you suggested.'

This she did. The station was modelled on the Baths of Caracalla, she had been told, though she had not been told precisely what the Baths of Caracalla were. They sounded vaguely Roman. The station was certainly impressive, more so than the post office building on the other side of Eighth Avenue, though both boasted vast numbers of classical pillars. Daisy made a dutiful circuit of the post office to read the motto carved on the architrave: *Neither snow, nor rain, nor heat, nor gloom of night stays these couriers from the swift completion of their appointed rounds.*

Then she strolled back by a roundabout route towards the hotel. On Twenty-eighth Street she came across a small park. Most of the trees were leafless, but it was still refreshing after the dusty streets. Children were playing there in the twilight, and she lingered to watch. Though the voices were American, the games seemed much the same as in England – hopscotch, marbles and tag.

The tag players swirled around her. As she turned to watch, she caught a glimpse of a man dodging behind a tree, as if he were trying not to be spotted.

He looked remarkably like young Mr Lambert, but she must be mistaken. Why on earth should Lambert follow her?

* * *

Next morning she set off for her appointment. The offices of *Abroad* magazine and several associated publications were in the Flatiron Building. On her first visit, Daisy had been too anxious to appreciate the merits of the unusual structure.

This morning she had a few minutes to spare. She strolled through Madison Square Park, noting the ashes of a Halloween bonfire and the corpses of firecrackers. Pausing on the corner of Twenty-third Street and Fifth Avenue, she gazed across at her destination. The Fuller Building, as it was originally named, had been designed to fit on an awkward triangular plot where Broadway crossed the other two streets. To Daisy, its shape made it look less like a flat iron than the prow of a great ship forging its way north across Manhattan.

The chilly wind whistling around it increased the resemblance. As she crossed the wide, busy intersection beneath the gaze of a harried policeman on point duty, Daisy, along with many another passer-by, held on to her hat.

Walking south towards the entrance, she gazed up at the ornate stone and terracotta details of the facade. And up and up. She had thought she was accustomed to New York's 'skyscrapers', but now she felt quite dizzy. The building seemed to sway, then to lean over her, threatening.

Quickly she returned her gaze to mundane street level, only to see a man step hurriedly backwards out of sight around the far corner of the building – a man who looked remarkably like young Lambert.

An illusion, of course, like the toppling building. She must have squished the blood vessels in the back of her neck, as revoltingly described by her friend Madge, a VAD nurse in the hospital where Daisy had volunteered in the office during the war. (Naturally anatomy had not been considered a suitable subject for the young ladies at Daisy's school.)

She blinked, and shook her head to clear it. As she stepped into the lobby, no further illusions met her eyes, just a brass-buttoned doorman.

He recognized her from the previous day's visit. 'The English lady, Mrs Fletcher, right?' he greeted her with a smile. 'For Thorwald, *Abroad*? Eighteenth floor, ma'am. You go ahead up. I'll phone through and tell Mr Thorwald you're on your way so's he can meet you at the elevator.'

'Thank you. You must have heard how I got lost yesterday trying to find his office.'

'Lots of folks do, you betcha. It's the shape of the building, confuses people, see. Elevators to your right, ma'am.'

Whether at the doorman's behest or off his own bat, Thorwald was waiting for Daisy when the elevator reached the eighteenth floor. He was a pear-shaped gentleman, with a Vandyke beard above which his clean-shaven upper lip looked oddly naked. So did his pale blue eyes when he took off his gold-rimmed pince-nez and gestured with it or rubbed his eyes, as he did frequently.

He led the way through an outer room to his tiny office, crammed with heaps of manuscripts and galley proofs. Dumping a pile of copies of *Abroad* from a chair to the floor, he invited Daisy to sit down and carefully inserted himself behind his desk.

'I trust your accommodations are proving satisfactory, Mrs Fletcher?' he said.

Rotund and orotund, Daisy thought, assuring him, 'Eminently so.' As usual when talking to Mr Thorwald, she found herself succumbing to his polysyllabicism, like an exotic disease. Fortunately it did not infect her articles, or no one would have read them.

'I've made the acquaintance of a number of uncommonly intriguing people,' she went on. She told him about Miss Genevieve Cabot, and the various hotel guests Miss Genevieve had introduced to her the previous evening. 'Incidentally,' she said, 'are you able to elucidate the curious connection my mind persists in forming between the name Cabot and fish?'

'Ah yes.' Mr Thorwald tittered. 'I believe the piscatorial association must be in reference to

"good old Boston,
The home of the bean and the cod,
Where the Lowells talk to the Cabots,
And the Cabots talk only to God."

A feeble versification at best, but since it was, I understand, pronounced as a toast after, one must presume, considerable pre-Volstead jollification, not utterly without merit.'

Volstead had something to do with Prohibition, Daisy thought. 'I must have heard the rhyme somewhere,' she said. 'Mention was made of Boston, I recollect. Ought I to see Boston for the second article?'

'While I hesitate to declare Boston unworthy of a visit, such a peregrination is unnecessary, my dear Mrs Fletcher. There is so much to be admired in this magnificent nation that you cannot conceivably encompass its entirety. Your sojourns in Connecticut, New York and Washington will suffice. It is not universality I desire but freshness of vision. And now, as our own visionary Benjamin Franklin observed, "Remember that time is money." Permit me to peruse the fruits of your exertions.'

While he read the completed article and the beginnings of the next, Daisy gazed out through the narrow window. What she saw was not the treetops of Madison Square, far below, not the visible sliver of the great city and the East River, but the greater continent beyond. South to the Caribbean and Mexico, north to Canada, three thousand miles to the Pacific Ocean – she sighed, envying the shipboard friends who had plans to see as much as was humanly possible.

'Excellent.' Mr Thorwald approved Daisy's work. He made a few suggestions about the rest of the unfinished article; then they discussed her ideas for articles to be written when she returned to England. 'And now, dear lady,' he said, taking out his watch, 'it is long past noon, I perceive. Will you permit me to take you to lunch at the Algonquin?'

As well as being curious to see the Algonquin, Daisy was more than ready for lunch, having missed elevenses. Everyone else appeared to have preceded them. The publisher's offices were all but deserted as they passed through.

As they approached the elevators, Daisy immediately recognized the man waiting there, if waiting was the right word.

She knew him as much by his actions as his looks – Otis Carmody had opened one of the gates and was peering impatiently down the elevator shaft.

Presumably he had long since worked out how to tell by the esoteric movements of cables which elevator was on its way. Though the Flatiron's lifts were twenty years younger than the Hotel Chelsea's, the machinery proceeded with almost as much creaking, groaning, clanking and rattling.

Daisy assumed the loud report was just part of the general cacophony until it was followed by an unmistakably human sound, a yelp of pain. A firecracker? She had heard plenty last night. Perhaps an office boy had unwisely kept one in his pocket.

But not ten paces ahead, Carmody teetered on the brink for a moment, then toppled over.

CHAPTER 3

'Jumping jiminy!' cried Mr Thorwald.

'He didn't jump,' Daisy said grimly. A pace ahead of the editor, she saw a man dart across the passage beyond the elevators, heading for the stairs. 'Stop!' she shouted.

He turned a white, wild-eyed face to her, then ducked his head and dashed on. His boot nails rang on the marble steps as he started down. Daisy ran after him.

'Hey, stop!' yelled someone behind her.

'Stop!' Mr Thorwald squawked.

Hesitating, Daisy looked back. To her astonishment, she saw Lambert chasing her, brandishing a gun. She hadn't time to be afraid before Mr Thorwald launched himself at Lambert's ankles in a very creditable rugby tackle and brought the young man down. Lambert's gun flew towards Daisy, while his horn-rims and Thorwald's pince-nez slithered across the floor.

To Daisy's even greater astonishment, she caught the gun. So the dreaded cricket practice at school hadn't been wasted, after all!

But what on earth was going on? Had *Lambert* shot Carmody? And if so, was he aiming at *Daisy*?

She had assumed the fugitive to be the villain. Was he a

conspirator or, more likely, just a terrified witness? In any case, while she dithered he was making his escape, and even if he was only a witness, he ought to be stopped and made to return to give evidence.

Daisy sped on, holding Lambert's revolver by the barrel so that she could not possibly fire it by accident. She hoped.

'Come back!' shouted Lambert.

'Ugh!' uttered Thorwald breathlessly.

From the head of the stairs, peering over the rail, Daisy saw the fugitive leaping downwards like a chamois, already two floors below.

'Come back!' she called, trotting down the first flight.

'Stop!' Lambert, dishevelled and looking younger than ever without his glasses, appeared at the top. 'I'll get him, Mrs Fletcher. You stay out of this. *Please!*'

Daisy froze as he bounded down the stairs towards her. At the last moment she remembered the gun in her hand. She swung it behind her to prevent his grabbing it. It slipped from her fingers and between two of the barley-sugar-twist banisters. A moment later a distant clang arrived from the bottom of the stairwell.

By then Lambert had passed Daisy and she, deciding discretion was definitely the better part of valour, had scurried back to the top of the stairs.

Mr Thorwald was tottering to his feet, bleating plaintively, 'My pince-nez, my pince-nez! Would someone be so kind as to find my pince-nez?'

Two persons of clerkly appearance and a probable typist had emerged from surrounding offices to gather about him, clucking and tutting in no very helpful fashion. Daisy spotted the pince-nez and returned it to him. As he clipped it to his nose, the top of the lift cage reached their floor at last.

Sprawled across its flat roof lay Otis Carmody, his neck all too obviously broken.

At Daisy's gasp, the others all swung round to gape. The typist shrieked and fell into the arms of one of the clerks. Meanwhile, Carmody continued to rise at a stately pace until he disappeared from sight. The elevator stopped.

'Hey, wha'z goin' on here?' the aged lift man demanded querulously, peering with suspicion through the inner gate, making no move to open it. 'See here, one of you lot throw something down the shaft? Against reggerlations, that is.'

Everyone, even Mr Thorwald, turned to Daisy.

'A man fell down the shaft,' she said.

'Izzat so? Against reg . . . Huh? Wha'zat you said?'

'There is a dead body on the roof of your lift.'

'Lift? Wha'z . . . ?'

'Elevator. A man fell down the shaft and landed on your elevator.'

'Wuz a almighty whump,' the old man admitted, at last opening the gate. 'Didn't sound like no garbage hitting. Lessee.'

'You can't see anything as long as the lift . . .' Daisy stopped as feet pounded towards them from the direction of the stairs.

'What's going on?' panted Lambert. 'I lost him. He just kept going down. I couldn't keep up, let alone catch up.'

'You saw him running on down?' Daisy asked, surprised. She recalled clearly the time she had gone up the Monument in Fish Street Hill. Built to commemorate the Great Fire of London, it had 311 steps. Going up was bad enough, but going down, her knees had been wobbling uncontrollably long before she reached the bottom. Only a mountain goat could have run down.

'I heard him. Never caught sight of him, actually. I can't see much without my glasses. Where are they?' He peered around myopically. 'And where's my automatic?'

'Automatic?' The two clerks looked at each other and backed away. The typist, who had recovered enough to listen to Daisy's exchange with the lift man, squealed again and hid behind them.

Knowing the gun was safely out of reach for the moment, Daisy looked around for the horn-rimmed specs. They were dangling by one earpiece through the gate of the next lift. Gingerly she retrieved them and, holding them, turned to Lambert. He blinked at her. At the moment he didn't look very dangerous.

'What were you doing, waving a gun around?' she asked severely.

'Waving a gun around?' squeaked the typist.

'I can explain. But not here,' Lambert added, waving at the spectators, three of whom melted away while the fourth, the lift man, was spectating his lift in a puzzled way. 'What's going on? Gee whiz, please give me my glasses,' Lambert pleaded. 'Where's my automatic?'

Daisy handed over the glasses. 'Eighteen storeys down, at the bottom of the stairwell.'

This news perked Mr Thorwald up no end. 'Who are you?' he demanded belligerently. 'What were you doing pursuing Mrs Fletcher with an automatic pistol? Did you shoot that unfortunate person?'

'I don't see no body,' interrupted the lift man.

'You'll have to take the lift – elevator – down a bit,' said Daisy.

'There really is a body?' Lambert asked. 'A man was shot? And fell down the shaft?'

Daisy exchanged a look with Thorwald. They both nodded solemnly. 'Yes,' she said, 'and if you didn't shoot him, that other man did, and he's getting away! We must telephone the police at once.'

Lambert started towards the nearest office suite. 'I'll find a phone.'

Thorwald grabbed his arm. 'Oh no you don't, my fine fellow. I shall not allow you also to elude the authorities! We'll go to my office.'

'I'm a federal agent,' Lambert snapped, reaching for his inside breast pocket, 'and you, sir, had better stop interfering with me in the course of my duty! I must call Washington.'

Daisy and Thorwald gaped at him in shared disbelief. Whether he was going to pull an identification card or a second gun from his pocket remained to be seen, for the double clang of two lift gates made them all swing round.

The lift started down.

A moment later, Carmody hove once more into view. He still looked very dead. When he reached floor level, the lift stopped.

'Gawd!' gulped the federal agent.

Daisy was not much happier with the sight. Nor, apparently, was Thorwald. As one they all three turned away, only to turn back as the lift again clanked into motion.

It rose until the upper half of the inner gate was visible, then came to a halt. The inner gate opened.

'Hey,' said the lift man irritably, 'don' jist stand there starin'. Open up and help me outta here. Gotta see me that stiff.'

Daisy had prevailed – ringing up the New York police had taken precedence over calling Washington, and in fact Lambert seemed to have lost his enthusiasm for reporting to his superiors. The local beat patrolman was standing guard over the elevator and the body. Detectives were on their way, and the DA had been notified.

'DA?' queried Daisy, as Mr Thorwald abstracted a bottle, soda water siphon, and two glasses from a desk drawer.

'District Attorney,' Lambert explained. 'He's in charge of prosecution, so his office oversees the collection of evidence in major cases, such as homicide.'

Mr Thorwald pushed two glasses of gently fizzling pale amber liquid across the desk. Then he upended the bottle and swigged directly from the neck. Recent events seemed to have deprived him of both speech and his usual courtly manners.

Mindful of a recent occasion when imbibing spirits on an empty stomach had knocked her for six, Daisy sipped cautiously. She had never much liked whisky, but this was a step below any Scotch she had ever tasted. Setting the glass down, she turned back to Lambert.

'So you're a federal agent, you say! I suppose it must be true as the bobby accepted your credentials and gave you back your gun. But what exactly does that mean?'

'It ... er ...' Lambert hastily put down his already

half-emptied glass as far away on the desktop as he could reach. 'It means I'm an agent of the Investigation Bureau of the US Department of Justice. We're ... er ... responsible for enforcing federal law.'

'Such as Prohibition?' Daisy enquired with a touch of malice. 'You don't seem mad keen on enforcing that one.'

'That's the Treasury Department does that,' he said defensively. 'I'm Justice.'

'Well, I haven't, to my knowledge, broken any other laws. So why have you been following me?'

'F-following you?' stammered Lambert, blushing.

Daisy gave him an old-fashioned look. It proved as effective in American as in English.

'I ... er.' He swallowed. 'That is, my boss, Mr Hoover, sent me to keep an eye on you.'

'Indeed!' said Daisy, hearing echoes of her mother in her tone. 'And does Mr Hoover – am I correct in assuming you refer to J. Edgar Hoover, whom my husband is at present advising, in Washington?'

'Yes, ma'am.'

'Does Mr Hoover make a practice of spying on his colleagues' wives?'

'I don't think you could exactly say that Mr Hoover makes a practice of anything,' Lambert said dubiously. 'He's not actually officially in charge yet. He's assistant director. Only we don't have a director at present.'

'Well, if he suffers from persecution mania, or delusions of grandeur, or whatever ails him, I don't expect he'll remain in charge very long,' Daisy predicted with asperity. 'Kindly tell him I strongly object to being treated as a prospective criminal.'

'Gee whiz, it's not that. The surveillance is to stop you getting into . . . er . . . for your own safety, Mrs Fletcher.'

'Then tell him I'm no babe in arms and I can take care of myself.'

'I can't do that!' Lambert looked horrified at the thought. 'This is my first assignment, see. If I fail, I'm out on my ear. But I guess I've already failed,' he concluded miserably. 'You've gotten mixed up in this horrible business. I suppose I better call Washington now and confess . . . report. Is there a telephone somewhere I can use privately, sir?'

Mr Thorwald started. 'Eh? Tephelone?' He waved his bottle – nearly empty – at the apparatus on his desk. 'Be my guesht.'

Daisy stood up. 'Mr Lambert wants to talk privately,' she said. 'I think it would be a good idea if we went to find something to eat, Mr Thorwald.'

'Lunch,' he agreed, and followed her docilely from his office.

The outer office was long and narrow, lined with shelves of magazines, interrupted by several doors. Against one wall stood a table piled with manuscripts and unopened manila envelopes, with chairs around it. In one corner of the room was a round table and more chairs. As Daisy entered, the murmur of which she had been distantly aware resolved itself into the voices of five or six men and a smart, rigidly marcelled and carefully made-up woman. They looked round as the door of Thorwald's office clicked shut. Silence fell.

'Howdy, ma'am.' One of the men pushed forward. His sack suit looked as if it might once have actually held potatoes, and his tie was that bilious green potatoes turn when exposed to light. He looked, in fact, like a well-dressed tramp, except for the eye shade and ink-blotched cuff protectors. Daisy guessed he was an editor. 'Hey, Thorwald,' he continued, 'is it true Otis Carmody's dead?'

'Shtiff,' Thorwald said succinctly, and sat down rather suddenly on a nearby chair.

'Not actually stiff,' said Daisy. Everyone turned to her. 'He hasn't been dead long enough for rigor mortis to set in. And I'm not absolutely certain it was Otis Carmody.' She had not seen his face, having avoided a close examination of the corpse. 'Though if you know him, and he was here this morning, I'm about ninety-nine per cent sure.'

'He was here, all right,' said the man in the sack. 'He brought me an article. Pascoli, editor of *Town Talk*.'

He stuck out his hand, so Daisy shook it. 'How do you do. I'm Mrs Fletcher.'

'Pleased to meetcha, Mrs Fletcher. *Town Talk's* a weekly news magazine, anti-administration.'

'Anti-administration?'

'The New York administration, that is. We got nothing against Coolidge – yet – but our publisher would sure like to get the goods on Tammany. Carmody looked like the guy who was going to do it. He brought me an article, hot stuff, but it wanted a few loose ends tying up. I left him to finish up when I went to lunch.'

'Lunsh!' said Mr Thorwald loudly, and hiccuped.

'Oh, you poor things!' said the marcelled woman. 'Haven't you had lunch yet? I'll send out to the corner drugstore. Thorwald usually has bratwurst on rye. Will that do for you, Mrs Fletcher?'

'Uh, yes, thank you.' Daisy wondered just what she was

saying yes to, but she decided she was so hungry she could eat practically anything. 'It's very kind of you, Miss . . . ?'

'Louella Shurkowski, Mrs, *Ladies' Gazette*, and you're welcome.'

'Lunsh,' repeated Mr Thorwald, plaintively this time.

'Better order in plenty of coffee,' suggested one of the other men. 'I never saw Thorwald pie-eyed before. He's had the same bottle of rye in his desk for months. He's really a Scotch man, but honest-to-goodness Scotch is rare as an honest politician these days. He doesn't even like rye. Must be real shook up.'

'So Carmody's dead?' mused Pascoli. 'What happened, Mrs Fletcher?'

Daisy thought about what had happened. She had had too little time and too many questions before to take it in properly. Now the horror struck.

'Hey, this little lady's real shook up, too,' said someone, and hands guided her to a chair by the round table.

Trying to avoid a vision of the grotesque figure sprawled puppetlike on top of the lift, with his head at a crazy angle, Daisy thought instead of what Alec was going to say. He was bound to be furious that she had got herself involved in yet another murder, even though she was thousands of miles from home. Could she keep it from him? He was hundreds of miles away, after all.

But Lambert was telling J. Edgar Hoover, and Hoover would doubtless report Daisy's misdeeds to Alec.

And she was going to have to report to the New York detectives at any moment. 'I don't think I'd better talk about it till the police come,' she said. 'I'll just tell you that Mr Thorwald was magnificent, a hero. He believed I was in danger – I did too – and he went right ahead and tackled the man he thought was after me, a man with a gun.'

'It wazh nothing,' said Mr Thorwald. This modest disclaimer was followed by a huge yawn, whereupon he fell asleep and started to slide gently off his seat.

His colleagues rushed to rescue the hero. While they gathered him up and laid him flat on top of the manuscripts on the long table, for want of anywhere better, Daisy had a few moments of peace.

Then the police arrived.

The first detective to enter was a stringy, dried-up man with a horrid little toothbrush moustache and an unlit cigar protruding from the corner of his mouth. As he came in, he looked back to say something in a high-pitched voice to the plain clothes man behind him, a blond giant who gaped past him and squawked, 'Geez, Sergeant, another stiff!'

The sergeant turned back and stared. 'O'Rourke,' he barked from the cigarless corner of his mouth, 'run and catch the doc before he leaves, and tell the guys there's two for the wagon.'

The second man behind him pounded off in the startled hush before several people simultaneously began to explain.

'He's not . . .'

'He is . . .'

'He's just . . .'

'Overcome by *horror*,' Pascoli overrode them, thus saving Thorwald from divulgence of his overindulgence in forbidden alcohol.

'Witness, izzy?'

'Yes, Sigurd Thorwald.'

'Name?'

'Yes, that's his name.'

'Your name, wise guy.'

'Oh, James Pascoli. And yours?'

The little man flipped his lapel, momentarily revealing a badge. 'Gilligan, Detective Sergeant, Homicide Bureau. Witness?'

'Me? Not exactly . . .'

'Didja,' said Sergeant Gilligan with exaggerated patience, 'or didja not see anything pertaining to the demise of the deceased?'

'No,' Pascoli admitted, 'but . . .'

'Who here's the witnesses, then, besides the guy on the desk?'

'I am,' said Daisy. 'My name is Dalrym . . . Fletcher, that is. Daisy Fletcher. Mrs Alec Fletcher.'

'That's a lot of aliases, lady.'

'I was married quite recently. I still get muddled sometimes.'

'British, are you?'

'Yes.'

Gilligan rolled his eyes. He looked as if he didn't have much trust in her as a witness, if any. 'Anyone else see what happened?' he asked hopefully.

'Just Mr Lambert,' said Daisy. 'He's an agent of the Department of Justice.'

'Don't that beat the Dutch!' Gilligan groaned. 'A reliable, trained witness, every 'tec's dream, but he'll want to make a federal case of it, you betcha sweet life, and the election's next week. So where's this Lambert?'

Daisy pointed. 'In there, telephoning Washington.'

'Rats!'

'If I might be permitted to speak,' said Pascoli with a touch of sarcasm, 'there's a federal angle to this business anyway. The victim . . .'

'Right, where is he?' The man who bustled in was small, like Gilligan, but otherwise the detective's antithesis, being chubby with a round, pink, cheerful face.

'Where's who?' asked Pascoli.

'Smart-ass,' Gilligan muttered, swinging round as the newcomer replied, 'The victim, the second victim.'

'Hi, doc,' said Gilligan a trifle sheepishly. 'Sorry, looks like there's only one been croaked. But maybe you oughta take a look at this guy anyway. He's a witness, passed out cold from the shock, they say.'

The doctor went across to Thorwald, bent over him, and straightened immediately with a grin. 'First time I've heard it called "the shock",' but there's a new euphemism coined every day. Let him sleep it off. Oh, there you are, Rosenblatt. I thought you'd be along, with the election coming up.'

'What do you have for me, doctor?' asked the fair, dapper man standing in the doorway, surveying the scene.

'Gunshot to the upper left thigh, superficial wound. It's the broken neck that killed him. I'll try to do the post-mortem for you this afternoon, but I make no promises.'

'Good enough. Thank you.' Rosenblatt stood aside to let the doctor depart. 'OK, Sergeant, what's going on?'

'Dangfino, sir,' sighed Gilligan.

CHAPTER 4

So far, Daisy was not impressed with the American police. If Rosenblatt and Gilligan were typical, no wonder J. Edgar was prepared to listen to advice from Scotland Yard on reforming his department.

Daisy wondered whether Rosenblatt, whom she assumed to be the district attorney, was more competent. Failing that, she could only hope that they would somehow muddle through to a solution without involving her more than absolutely necessary. Since she had once more – by absolutely no fault of her own – landed in the middle of a murder investigation, she wished Alec were in charge. However angry, he would at least start with a presumption of her innocence.

On the other hand, this was her chance to prove to him that she was quite capable of coping without him. Maybe she could even work out who was the murderer and help the local police collar him. What a coup that would be! Alec would never again be able to claim she impeded his investigations.

Rosenblatt and Gilligan, conferring, kept glancing at her. Of course, she was the only witness both present and compos mentis, as long as she didn't faint from starvation.

Mrs Shurkowski had returned long since from her errand, but so far the promised 'bratwurst on rye' had not materialized.

Right now, Daisy would be happy to devour any old brat, best or worst, on barley, or millet, or any other grain available. She had to assume the 'rye' in the order was not yet more whisky.

The editors had remained in an uneasy, whispering huddle around the recumbent Thorwald. Daisy saw several of them nod, as if they had come to an agreement. High heels clicking, Mrs Shurkowski moved towards her while the rest drifted unobtrusively away.

Rosenblatt looked round. 'Mr Pascoli?' he queried; and when the *Town Talk* editor stopped, 'Stick around, if you wouldn't mind, sir.'

'I have work to do,' Pascoli complained, 'and Sergeant Gilligan didn't seem too interested in what I had to say.'

'But I am. I'll be with you in just a moment.'

Pascoli pulled a face and came to join Daisy as Mrs Shurkowski said to her, 'Honey, us girls have to stick together. You want me to stay and hold your hand?'

'Thank you, it's very kind of you, but I wouldn't want to keep you from your work. I'm sure I shall be all right.'

'Don't you just love the way she talks?' Mrs Shurkowski said to Pascoli. 'Now, you mind what you say to them, honey, and call a lawyer pronto if they try anything on you. Your sandwiches'll be here any minute.'

'Thank you so much,' Daisy said sincerely.

Mrs Shurkowski went off to edit the *Ladies' Gazette*. Pascoli sat down in a chair beside Daisy. 'Cigarette?' He offered a gunmetal case.

'No, thanks.'

'Whoops, pardon me, don't English gals smoke?'

'Some do. Not awfully many.'

'OK if I light up?'

'I don't mind,' Daisy lied. She disliked cigarette smoke almost as much as cigar smoke, but she felt guilty about her continued presence here and the disruption of work, as though her propensity for falling over bodies was actually responsible for the latest crime. What she longed for was the comforting smell of Alec's pipe. 'Is there really a federal dimension to the case besides Mr Lambert's being a witness'?' she asked.

'Sure thing!' Pascoli became earnest. 'Carmody spent the last several years in Washington, DC, digging up the dirt on the Harding administration, and he didn't have to dig far, trust me.'

Daisy recalled a comment about Augean stables. 'So I've heard.'

'His articles tweaked a whole lotta noses. President Coolidge is already cleaning house and lotsa people are getting the can because of what Otis Carmody wrote. It wouldn't surprise me one little bit if one of them came to town looking for revenge.'

'It does seem possible.'

'It's a dead cert.'

'What about the article he wrote for you?' Daisy suggested. 'Wouldn't that upset people?'

Pascoli grinned. 'Sure would. He's written three so far, every one calculated to get up someone's nose. But none of 'em has been published yet.'

'Still, he must have talked to lots of people to get his information. It couldn't be kept secret. Perhaps someone wanted to stop him before he dug any deeper.'

'Or scare me into not publishing,' Pascoli said soberly. 'You got a point there, ma'am.' He cast a nervous glance over his shoulder at Gilligan and Rosenblatt.

'The articles are about Tammany? Who *is* Tammany?'

Pascoli lowered his voice. 'It's a what, not a who. Leastways, Tammany was an Indian chief way back, but he hasn't anything to do with today's politics. Tammany Hall's the building that's come to stand for the Democratic machine that runs this burg. Crooked as anything President Harding's Republican pals were mixed up in, but much harder to oust. Heck, half the population owes their jobs to them, including Rosenblatt over there, looking like butter wouldn't melt in his mouth.'

'He is the District Attorney, is he?'

'Deputy DA.'

'That's a political appointment?'

'Got it in one. So are garbage collectors, and a whole lotta folks in between.'

'Garbage collectors? Dustbin men? Heavens, it sounds to me as if it will be just as well if the federal investigators take an interest in the case.'

'You've said a mouthful, sister! Where's this guy Lambert? No kidding, I wanna stand behind him.'

Daisy rather doubted Lambert would be much protection, but she didn't have time to say so as Rosenblatt and Gilligan came over to them. Gilligan, chewing on his dead cigar, looked truculent, Rosenblatt worried.

'Mrs Fletcher? Rosenblatt, Deputy District Attorney. Say, who's this guy Lambert? What's his connection with this business?'

'You'll have to ask him, Mr Rosenblatt.' Daisy wasn't

going to let herself be drawn into any complications. 'I only know that he told Mr Thorwald and me that he is a federal agent. All I can tell you is what I saw.'

'Yes, we'll get to that in a minute, ma'am. Mr Pascoli, you know something about the federal connection, sir?'

'Not exactly,' Pascoli hedged. 'Nothing to do with the Justice Department specifically, more of a general Washington connection. Otis Carmody ruffled plenty of feathers in the capital. He was an investigative journalist, see, and a good one.'

'A muckraker,' said Rosenblatt, depressed. 'Probably had half of the last administration out for his blood.'

'Got what was coming to him,' Gilligan grunted.

'Maybe,' Rosenblatt snapped, 'but we still have to pin it on someone. What was he doing in New York?'

'He, uh, wanted to write for the magazine I edit,' Pascoli said evasively.

'Which magazine is that?'

'*Town Talk*,' admitted Pascoli with obvious reluctance.

Rosenblatt gave him a hard stare. 'I know *Town Talk*. That's an opposition paper.'

Pascoli shrugged. 'Hey, I don't set policy. You don't like it, you talk to my publisher.'

'Had Carmody written anything for you yet? Leopards don't change their spots. What's he been writing?'

'Ever heard of the First Amendment, buddy?'

'Say, listen,' interpolated Sergeant Gilligan, 'maybe we don't wanna know—'

'Samwidges!' A boy in a cloth cap and a jacket several sizes too large ducked under the arm of the plain clothes man on duty at the doorway to the hall. He bore a white cardboard box in his hands. 'Samwidges and coffee for Thorwald.'

'At last,' sighed Daisy, reaching for her bag.

'I'll get it,' said Pascoli. 'It'll come out of petty cash, don't worry.' He went over to the boy.

'Say, listen,' Gilligan repeated, 'maybe we don't wanna know who the stiff was digging up the dirt on here in Noo York.'

'We gotta find out,' Rosenblatt said gloomily. 'The Feds are sure to. And we gotta clean this up quick, with the election next week, or the Hearst papers will wipe the floor with us again.'

'You think that's what this guy Lambert's after, sir? Maybe he ain't got nuttin to do with what Carmody was up to in Washington. Maybe he's here to make trouble for us.'

'No doubt we'll soon know,' said the DA as the door of Thorwald's office opened and Lambert came out.

He and the sandwiches reached the round table at the same moment. 'Food!' he exclaimed, sniffing the air. 'And coffee. Gee whiz, I could kill for a cup of coffee.'

Pascoli glanced at Thorwald, now whuffling gently in his sleep. With a sigh, he pushed one of the sandwiches and a large mug of coffee across the table towards Lambert.

Meanwhile, Sergeant Gilligan was staring suspiciously at Lambert. 'Kill?' he growled, his right hand sliding inside his jacket. 'You talk mighty easy about killing. Is that maybe what you was sent from Washington for? To croak the guy that blew the gaff on your boss?'

Lambert's mouth, open to take a bite of sandwich, stayed open though the sandwich came to a halt in midair. After a horrified moment, he squeaked, 'Who, me?'

Daisy recalled that Lambert had been given back his automatic, and she knew all New York police were armed. Was it time to dive under the table before a gun battle erupted? She hastily swallowed the bite of sandwich in her mouth, just in case (rye had turned out to be a darkish, sourish bread and bratwurst a sort of German sausage, the consumption of which made her feel vaguely unpatriotic).

'Yes, you, mister.' Gilligan drew his gun from his shoulder bolster.

Lambert dropped his sandwich and put his hands up. 'I didn't! Mrs Fletcher, tell him I didn't.'

'I can't,' Daisy said regretfully. She did not honestly think the inept agent had shot Carmody, but he had, after all, rushed on stage brandishing a pistol immediately after the murder.

'Lemme pinch him, sir?' begged Gilligan.

'Holy mackerel!' Rosenblatt exclaimed. 'You can't go arresting a federal agent without evidence, Sergeant, just like he was anyone. Not without landing us all in deep . . . er,' – he glanced at Daisy and amended whatever he had been going to say – 'in big trouble. It's no go.'

'Rats! But how do we know he's really a Fed?'

'My papers are in my pocket,' said Lambert eagerly. He lowered one hand, but it shot up again when the Sergeant waved his gun.

'I'll get 'em,' Rosenblatt offered.

'OK, but don't get between me and him.'

The DA retrieved the papers and studied them. 'US Department of Justice, Bureau of Investigation. All in order,' he sighed.

Lambert's sigh was considerably more heartfelt. 'Can I put my hands down, please?'

Reluctantly Gilligan nodded, but he did not put away his gun. 'Who's to say he wasn't hired on as an agent just to croak Carmody?' he demanded.

'Mr Hoover, my boss, isn't one of the people Carmody had an interest in. He's working to get things running on the level again, after the mess Burns made of the Bureau.'

'Oh yeah?'

'Yes,' Lambert assured him. 'See, Burns used federal agents to run his own detective agency. I wasn't one of them, I've only just joined.'

'Just outta college and still wet behind the ears,' Gilligan muttered, returning his gun to its holster at last. Then he noticed that Pascoli, all ears, was scribbling in a notebook. 'Hey, you!'

'Me?' Pascoli said innocently.

'Yeah, you. Whaddaya think you're doing? You're not a reporter.'

'No,' said Rosenblatt, 'but he's editor of a news weekly, which isn't that different. I guess it's useless to ask you to hand over your notes.'

'Damn right!'

'But we have no more questions for you at present, Mr Pascoli, and I'm certain you're anxious to get back to your work.'

Pascoli grinned. 'If you say so.' He waved his notebook in a jaunty farewell, which made Gilligan bite through his dead cigar to grit his teeth audibly.

Rosenblatt turned back to Lambert. 'All the same,' he said, 'I get notified whenever a new federal agent is stationed here, as a courtesy and to prevent mix-ups, and you're not on the list. If you weren't after Carmody, what brought you to the "Big Apple", and to the Flatiron Building just when he was killed?'

Lambert threw an apologetic look at Daisy. 'I was tailing Mrs Fletcher here.'

Rosenblatt and Gilligan swung round to stare at her. The sergeant's hand hovered over his chest as if he wasn't sure whether to draw again. 'Her?' he asked, incredulous. 'The dame's "wanted"? Geez, she looks like butter wouldn't melt in her mouth.'

'No, no,' Lambert sputtered, 'just to protect her. Mr Hoover was told by an English cop, a Superintendent Stork, that Mrs Fletcher has a habit of landing herself in trouble.'

'Superintendent Crane,' corrected Daisy. 'The rotter! How beastly of him!'

'You know this superintendent bird, ma'am?' said Rosenblatt dryly.

'He's my husband's superior in the Metropolitan Police,' Daisy admitted, hoping they would not have heard of the Met.

'Metropolitan . . . Isn't that Scotland Yard?' The Deputy DA blinked. 'Your husband's a Scotland Yard man?'

'Yes, actually. He's a Detective Chief Inspector.'

'Geez, Chief Inspector? Whassat in our ranks?' demanded Sergeant Gilligan.

'I'm afraid I don't know. I'm sure the system is quite different, and in any case he has no official standing here,' Daisy said tactfully.

'Chief Inspector Fletcher is in Washington in his official capacity,' Lambert contradicted her with a certain relish. 'He is advising our government.'

'Aw, rats!' said Gilligan.

'In Washington,' Rosenblatt pointed out. 'Not here. Mrs Fletcher, ma'am, I'd be grateful if you could see your way to giving us your evidence now, so that we need not keep you any longer.'

Daisy decided to exploit her newfound advantage. 'Would you mind awfully if I finish my sandwich first, Mr Rosenblatt? I really am frightfully hungry.'

Gilligan turned an interesting shade of purple, and Rosenblatt looked as if he was biting his tongue. Fortunately, a large, stolid uniformed policeman – patrolman? – came in to report, so Daisy didn't discover the limits of her power. She listened as she munched.

'Whole building's been combed, sir, roof to basement. Ain't nobody that don't have a good reason to be here.'

'Whassa doorman say?' asked Gilligan.

'Doormen, Sergeant. There's two main entrances, on the Avenue and Broadway. They say nobody's been let to leave since the first patrolman got here after the homicide was phoned in. But gen'rally they don't make a note of everyone that comes in and don't take no notice of them going out, 'specially at lunchtime. It's a commercial building, see, not like one of them fancy apartment buildings that no stranger gets in without they buzz the residents.'

'I know it's a commercial building,' Gilligan snapped.

'And then there's the doors from the lobby to the shops on the street level. They got outside doors, too. We talked to all the shop clerks, but there's people going in and out alla time, specially in the lunch hour. They don't notice 'em 'less they looks like they're gonna buy sumpin or pinch sumpin.'

The sergeant groaned. 'What about the elevator attend-
ants? Someone gotta of seen sumpin!'

'Seems three of 'em goes unofficially off duty between the
lunch rush out and the lunch rush in. Poker in the basement,
I reckon. They ain't none of 'em noticed nuttin outta the
way, 'cepting the old buzzard what the stiff fell on toppa his
elevator.'

'And what did he see?' asked Rosenblatt.

'The stiff on toppa his elevator, sir.'

The DA's mouth twitched, whether in amusement or
irritation Daisy couldn't tell. 'The stairs start at the
second-floor level,' he said. 'So our fugitive must've taken
the elevator down to the ground, so one of the men must've
seen him.'

'There's service and emergency stairs from first to second,
sir. I guess he musta took 'em. The doors ain't locked.'

'They wouldn't be,' Rosenblatt sighed. 'You took the
name and address of everyone in the building that doesn't
work here? And where they claim to have been when
Carmody was shot?'

'Yessir. Detective O'Rourke's got the dope.'

'OK, we'll try to get a decent description of the guy that
was seen running off, then we'll need – lessee – make it four
men to go round again. The rest of you can go for now.'

'Figure we'll need more'n four, sir,' grunted Gilligan. 'Or
it'll take all day.'

It was the first unmistakable sign Daisy had seen that the
detective was not happy to have the District Attorney's
Office supervising his investigation. She wondered just
what Rosenblatt's duties were in such a case. There was no
equivalent in England to his position.

Rosenblatt conceded. 'OK, OK, Sergeant, however many you need. Now, Mrs Fletcher, if you've quite finished your sandwich, let's hear what you have to tell us about Carmody's death.'

Daisy swallowed the last bite and followed it with a draught of strong black, lukewarm coffee. Other than Alec's presence, the one thing in the world she wanted was a hot cup of tea to fortify her for the interrogation.

CHAPTER 5

Whenever Alec was forced by circumstances beyond his control to take evidence from Daisy, he always started by insisting that she give him only facts, not her speculations. He always ended up taking her comments and theories into account, if not counting on them, but Daisy suspected pure conjecture would not go down well with Rosenblatt and Gilligan.

'Where would you like me to begin?' she asked.

Gilligan sighed heavily.

'At the beginning?' suggested Rosenblatt, not without irony.

'But is the beginning when Mr Thorwald and I approached the lifts – elevators – and saw Carmody . . .'

'Fine!' said Gilligan.

'. . . or when I heard him yesterday,' Daisy persisted, 'arguing in the room next door?'

'Next door?'

'At the hotel where I'm staying.'

The sergeant was incredulous. 'Carmody was in the next room?!'

'I guess we could go back to that later,' Rosenblatt said hastily. 'For now, let's stick with today. Just the facts, ma'am.'

'Right-oh. It was after most people had left for lunch. That's usually twelve noon here, isn't it? Mr Thorwald said it was long past noon and invited me to lunch at the Algonquin.'

'The Algonquin?' said Gilligan. 'That's quite a joint for an editor to treat a reporter at.'

'Oh dear, is it a speakeasy?' Surely not, or Miss Genevieve would not visit it – or would she? 'I can't believe it, Mr Thorwald is fearfully respectable.'

Gilligan and Rosenblatt guffawed. Well, at least she had cheered them up, Daisy thought.

'Speakeasy! No, ma'am,' said the DA, 'the Algonquin is one of the smart hotels, though it's true it's frequented by literary types. What sort of money spinners were you writing for Thorwald?'

'I'm a journalist really, not a reporter. I write travel articles for *Abroad* magazine.'

'That's wunna them glossies. Still, geez, the Algonquin!'

'I expect,' put in Lambert, 'Mr Thorwald considered it suitable because Mrs Fletcher is a titled lady.'

'Titled?' yelped Rosenblatt. 'Whaddaya mean, she's Lady Sumpin or sumpin?'

With a silent groan – what else had Crane told about her? – Daisy said quickly, 'No, not Lady anything, and it's just a courtesy title, not a proper one. Mr Thorwald and I went out to the elevators. Mr Carmody was already there. I recognized him at once, though I couldn't see his face, because—'

'Hang on! You recognized him?' asked Rosenblatt. 'You had met him, not just heard him talking? Here or at your hotel?'

'I hadn't *met* him. We hadn't been introduced. I'd seen him and been told who he was. As I was about to say, I recognized him at once because I'd seen him doing exactly the same thing at the hotel. He's . . . he was an impatient sort of chap. If an elevator didn't appear right away when he rang for it, he'd open the gate and look down the shaft, I suppose to see how far down it was, how long he'd have to wait.'

'Say, there's five elevators out there,' Gilligan objected, 'not counting the freight elevator. Howd'e know which one to look down?'

'They make a frightful racket, and you can see the cables moving.'

'Oh, sure.'

'That's what he was doing when you saw him,' said Rosenblatt, with exaggerated patience, 'peering down the shaft?'

'Yes. He was holding the handle of the gate – you know, the bit you grab to open it – and leaning forward to look down. The shock of being shot must have made him let go. Once he'd done that, he hadn't a hope.'

'Could you tell which direction the shot came from?'

Daisy shook her head in negation. 'I thought the sound was just part of the noise of the machinery until I saw him fall. It could have come from anywhere.'

The sergeant shook his head in disgust. 'Coulda come from anywheres, huh? In backaya, in frontaya, anywheres at all.'

'I guess it reverberated,' said Rosenblatt soothingly.

'At the time, I assumed it had come from ahead of me, because I saw a man run across the passage and down the stairs.'

Rosenblatt and Gilligan both leaned towards her. 'Yeah,' breathed Gilligan, his pencil poised over his notebook, 'the man at headquarters that took the report on the phone said the killer was seen escaping. This guy, whaddy look like?'

Daisy tried to picture the man. 'He was very pale,' she said, 'and he looked absolutely horrified. I had an impression of something vaguely familiar about him. But I didn't get a really good look. I thought I ought to keep him in sight, so I started chasing him . . .'

'Geez!' said Gilligan, shaking his head again, whether in admiration at her courage or disbelief at her folly Daisy did not enquire.

'But then,' she continued, 'someone yelled at me to stop and I glanced back and saw Mr Lambert running after me waving a gun, and . . .'

'Waving your gun, were you?' Rosenblatt said reprovingly.

'To protect her,' Lambert protested. 'I didn't know what was going on.'

'Nor did I,' said Daisy. 'I guessed that you must be the murderer, but before I could work out what to do, Mr Thorwald brought you down.'

'That was some tackle,' Lambert admitted grudgingly. 'I lost my glasses and my gun.'

'Which I caught. So I stopped worrying about what you were up to and went on chasing the man who was running away, who had to be either an accomplice or a frightened witness. In any case, he ought to be stopped if possible.'

'Whaddy *look* like?' demanded Gilligan.

'Well . . .' Daisy considered, then shrugged. 'Just ordinary. I only had a glimpse before he started down the stairs.'

'No distinctive characteristics?' said Rosenblatt gloomily.

'I don't think so. Once he was going down I couldn't see much but his hat, and that was a sort of bowler, rather shabby.'

'Bowler?'

'I think you'd call it a derby.'

'Dahby – oh, durrby. A derby hat doesn't tell us much.'

'I'm afraid not.'

Gilligan snorted. 'You don't see many of 'em around these days. It's all soft felts, homburgs and trilbies and fedoras. But you can't arrest a bird for wearing a derby,' he said severely.

'I can't describe him any better, but I have a feeling I'd recognize him if I saw him again.' She frowned. 'I'm pretty sure I haven't seen him before, so it's odd that he seemed familiar. If only I could think why!'

'Yeah, well,' said Gilligan, 'you think why, you let us know. Guess you better have a go at the mug book.'

Not for the first time, Daisy wished she spoke American. 'What's a mug book?' she asked cautiously.

'Scotland Yard don't have 'em yet?' Gilligan snickered, with mingled scorn and pride. 'When we pinch – arrest – someone, see, we make 'em mug for the camera. We take a photo shot of their mugs, so we got a record.'

'Oh, of course. I think Scotland Yard calls it their rogues' gallery.'

Gilligan looked chagrined at not being a step ahead of the Yard. 'Yeah, well, we call it that, too.'

'What next, ma'am?' asked Rosenblatt. 'You were chasing the man down the stairs.'

'He was far ahead of me by then. It was obvious I'd never catch him.'

'You didn't shout to him to stop?'

'I did call, "Come back", but not very loudly. I mean, I was always taught that ladies simply don't shout in public. And to tell the truth, I wasn't absolutely sure I wanted to catch up with him. After all, I didn't know whether he was just a witness, or a murderer, or Lambert's accomplice.'

'You had a gun,' Rosenblatt pointed out. 'You said you caught Mr Lambert's.'

Daisy stared at him. 'Gosh, but . . . but I couldn't *shoot* it!'

The DA sighed. 'No, I guess a lady that can't shout out in public isn't gonna know how to fire a gun. Heck,' he went on generously, 'there aren't too many women in America could do it, not in the East, anyhow. It's not like we live in the Wild West, with rustlers and bandits and rattlesnakes all over. So you gave up the chase, ma'am?'

'Not just like that. Mr Lambert came running down the stairs after me. He said he'd get him and I must stay out of it. I hadn't the foggiest what was going on, but it seemed wisest to go back up to Mr Thorwald.'

'You betcha!' Gilligan exclaimed. 'A dame that can't fire a gat's got no business chasing crooks that can. So you went after him, Lambert?'

'One thing at a time,' said Rosenblatt. 'We'll take Mr Lambert's evidence when we've finished with Mrs Fletcher's.'

Storm clouds gathered on the sergeant's brow, but they gradually dissipated as Daisy described the arrival of Carmody's corpse, riding on top of the elevator. Tears came to his eyes when – mindful of Alec's frequent injunction to omit no detail, however apparently insignificant – she told of the elevator attendant's efforts to view the 'stiff'. She didn't think Gilligan's tears were tears of sorrow. It *had* been funny in a macabre way.

She reported Lambert's return, and his admission that he couldn't see much without his glasses. That was a detail whose significance Gilligan did not miss.

'Rats!' he said. 'What's the use of chasing a guy without you can see him?'

'I could see a running figure,' Lambert protested. 'If I'd caught up with him—'

'Later!' Rosenblatt snapped. 'Go on, Mrs Fletcher.'

There was not much more to tell. She had urged ringing up the police. Lambert had wanted to call his superiors in Washington, but Daisy had insisted on Mr Thorwald notifying the local police first.

For the first time, Rosenblatt and Gilligan eyed her with something amounting almost to approval. It did not last long.

'I feel I ought to warn you,' she said, 'that as Mr Lambert has reported to Mr Hoover, and my husband is working with Mr Hoover, it is not beyond the bounds of possibility that he – my husband – will shortly turn up in New York.'

'Rats!' groaned Gilligan.

'I'm sure we'll be glad of any tips Scotland Yard has to offer,' Rosenblatt said sourly. 'Now, what's all this about you overhearing Carmody at your hotel? Where are you staying?'

'The Hotel Chelsea. It's—'

'Full of bohemians.' The sergeant did not appear thrilled by the prospect of having to interview the Chelsea's residents.

Daisy told them of the sounds of altercation she had heard through the walls. 'The first time it was just one other man, I'm pretty sure. The second time there was a woman and another man.'

Gilligan brightened. 'So there's a dame involved! That's the answer, you betcha.'

'But you didn't hear what they were saying?' Rosenblatt asked.

'Not most of it. Then I went out on to the balcony for a breath of air. Carmody's window was open.'

Once again Rosencrantz and Guildenstern – blast! Daisy had been trying so hard not to think of them like that. If she wasn't careful she would address them as Hamlet's friends. They might not recognize the reference, but it would not raise their low opinion of her wits – *Rosenblatt* and *Gilligan* leaned towards her.

'I heard the woman call him by a rude name, and she said she would not return to him if he had a million dollars. And he said that if he made a million dollars, she still wouldn't squeeze one . . .' Daisy hesitated. 'I think she said "red cent".'

'That just means a penny,' Lambert explained.

'He said she wouldn't squeeze one out of him.'

'Blackmail!' cried Gilligan. 'Say, listen, this is how I figure it. This dame is Carmody's frail, and she's gotten the goods on him. She knows sumpin he done that if she told the right people, they could put pressure on him to stop writing about them, and then kablooey goes his career. And they break up, see, and she finds this other guy and tells him, and they put on the screws.'

Rosenblatt frowned. 'Could be, but a blackmailer doesn't usually kill his victim. It's the other way around.'

Gilligan was only momentarily taken aback. 'OK, so maybe it *is* the other way around.' He turned to Daisy. 'You sure it was Carmody said that? About not a red cent?'

'Pretty sure. I heard him speak later, in the elevator and then down in the lobby. But there was some traffic noise, a tram – streetcar – going past.'

'So it coulda been the other guy. Carmody finds out sumpin about him. That's his business, after all, digging up the dirt. Whatever it is, he figures it's worth more to keep quiet than to sell it to the noospapers, so he puts the screws on this guy. And the dame's this guy's wife and she finds out and she leaves him, so that's another count against Carmody!'

'But she left with the other man,' Daisy protested. 'I saw them going down in the elevator together.' Then she recalled that while she had assumed the pair she saw had been in the room next door, she had no proof. The lift had stopped at her floor, but perhaps the woman in it had come from a higher floor.

They had been standing much closer together than strangers would, though. Daisy was sure enough of her guess, and reluctant enough to admit that it was a guess, to let her statement stand.

'So the dame was talking to Carmody,' Gilligan reasoned. 'She just found out he was a dirty blackmailing skunk, and she left with this other guy he was blackmailing. It was him talking next, refusing to pay up. Now we just gotta find this dame, and she'll lead us to the guy, and there's our murderer.'

'Could be,' Rosenblatt said with more enthusiasm. 'In which case, there's no federal angle.'

'So sonny boy here can run along home,' said Gilligan with a triumphant glare at Lambert.

'I still have to keep an eye on Mrs Fletcher,' Lambert said stubbornly. 'Besides, Mr Hoover's sending another agent to deal with the case. He's afraid our men up here may have gotten too pally with Tammany Hall.'

Rosenblatt and Gilligan exchanged a foreboding look. Then Gilligan scowled.

'Say, if your job was just tailing the d . . . lady, how didja know this stiff had anything to do with Tammany?'

'Mr Thorwald told me. That is, when Mrs Fletcher recognized Carmody and told us his name, Thorwald recalled that Pascoli had talked about him and the articles he was writing. Naturally I informed Mr Hoover.'

'Naturally,' said Rosenblatt gloomily. 'Why the heck did this hafta happen the week before the election? Even if it all happened like you said, Sergeant, the Hearst and opposition papers will make hay. OK, Lambert, let's hear what you saw out there.'

Daisy was pretty sure Lambert had nothing to add to her evidence, so she only half listened. She pondered the scenario Sergeant Gilligan had built up.

It sounded reasonable, if one assumed Daisy had wrongly identified Carmody's voice. An expert at ferreting out secrets, he might have turned to blackmail. Though her impression of him was of an unrelenting honesty, it was based on nothing more than his ferocious forthrightness. She had scarcely exchanged a word with him.

But she *had* heard him speak, and she was almost convinced he was the one who made the remark about the 'red cent'. Almost.

CHAPTER 6

Daisy returned exhausted to the Hotel Chelsea, with instructions not to depart from New York.

After leaving Rosencrantz and Guildenstern trying to rouse the somnolent Thorwald to give his evidence, she and Lambert had descended to ground level to find a mob of reporters on the pavement. Sidewalk.

Held off by the friendly doorman and a patrolman, they were baying for blood, or at least for any scrap of information. They obviously knew, presumably through Pascoli, that one of their own had been foully done to death. Fortunately the *Town Talk* editor had apparently not described either Daisy or Lambert. The newsmen harassed them on general principles – they had actually been inside the building where murder had taken place! – but did not guess they were witnesses.

The young agent forged ahead through the crowd, forcing a path for Daisy. She kept her mouth shut. If they knew anything about her at all, the sound of her voice would give her away.

As they walked back along Twenty-third Street to the hotel, Lambert kept trying to apologize, for having been set on to follow her and for having failed to keep her out of trouble. Wearily, she cut him short, drawing his attention to an evening newspaper billboard with a notice about a 'special' on the murder.

Someone had nosed out that the victim was staying at the Hotel Chelsea. A lesser mob of reporters had gathered on the sidewalk, but they were less aggressive than their brethren at the Flatiron Building. Balfour, the black door-man, was managing single-handedly to keep them out of the lobby, with constant reiterations of 'A *private* hotel, ge'men. Residents and their visitors only'.

Daisy reflected that Alec would long since have sent a constable or two to take charge.

She and Lambert entered without too much difficulty. 'It won't be so easy,' said Lambert gloomily, 'once this lot of newshounds puts their heads together with the others and they figure out we're connected with both the hotel and the Flatiron Building.'

'I expect there's a back door they'll let us use,' Daisy consoled him.

'Yeah, sure! I'll go speak to the manager right away.'

He forged ahead towards the registration desk, while Daisy paused in the lobby. It was teatime, and the Misses Cabot were lying in wait.

Miss Genevieve raised an imperious hand. Daisy considered pretending she had not seen, but she wanted her tea, not to mention information which Miss Genevieve was more likely than anyone else to provide. She went over to the pair.

The younger Miss Cabot's pale cheeks were flushed, her eyes bright. 'My dear Mrs Fletcher, I guess you have heard that one of our residents has met an untimely end?'

'Otis Carmody,' Daisy confirmed.

'I wondered – Mr Carmody is reported to have died in the Flatiron Building, and I know the offices of *Abroad* are located there – did you happen to hear any details of events when you were visiting with your editor?'

'I know a fair bit about it,' admitted Daisy, 'and I'll tell you what I can, but I'm rather tired and grubby. I hope you'll excuse me while I go up and take off my hat first.'

'Of course! In fact, would you care to come and take tea in our suite rather than down here?'

'So much more comfortable,' twittered Miss Cabot.

'And private,' added Miss Genevieve.

Daisy agreed, and they gave her their suite number, on the third floor. Heading for the lifts, she glanced back to see Miss Genevieve struggling from her seat with the aid of her sister, her stick, and the bellhop.

How painful it must be, Daisy reflected, for a woman who had led the active, independent life of a crime reporter to be so dependent – very likely worse than the actual physical pain of her crippling disease. Miss Genevieve might well have become a morose hermit. That she had instead retained her spirit and her lively interest in the world was admirable. The old lady deserved to have her curiosity satisfied.

Besides, if Daisy told her what had happened at the Flatiron Building, she was bound to reciprocate with all she knew about the late Otis Carmody.

Young Kevin took Daisy up in the lift. He was bubbling with excitement. 'Gee, ma'am, I took Mr Carmody down in this same very elevator just this mornin'. Jist think o'that! And now he's bin croaked. I wish it was my elevator he broke his neck in,' he said wistfully. 'D'ya think the 'tecs'll want to talk to me anyways?'

'Do you know anything which might be of interest to them?'

'Do I! D'ya know what our Bridey told me?'

'No, but I can tell you that the police will want to hear it from your sister, not from you.' *As do I*, Daisy added silently.

'Leastways,' Kevin sighed, 'I can tell 'em she's got sumpin to tell 'em. Seventh floor, ma'am. Going up!' he called to the empty passage. 'Going down! Going anywheres you wanna go.'

Daisy laughed. 'I'll be going down again in a few minutes, so if no one rings for you, you might as well wait.'

'OK, ma'am.'

'Is Bridey – Bridget – still on duty?'

'Yes'm, till eight.'

'Kevin, the detectives may not want to talk to you, but the press will, and they'll hound Bridget unmercifully if you mention that she knows something.'

'Mercy!' cried the boy, sounding very Irish. 'I'll spin 'em a yarn'll keep 'em happy without never breathing a word about our Bridey.'

'Do that,' said Daisy, 'and better not tell anyone else, either. Thank you, Kevin.'

Going to her room, she tossed her gloves on the dressing table, took off her hat and coat, then rang the bell to summon the chambermaid. She had washed the grime of New York from her face and hands and was tidying her honey-brown shingled hair when the tap came at the door.

'Come in.'

''Tis sorry I am to've kept you waiting, ma'am,' the girl apologized. 'I was ironing an evening gown for another lady. What can I do for you?'

'Nothing just now, thank you, Bridget. I just wanted to warn you. Your brother told me you know something about Mr Carmody that may interest the police. Until you have spoken to them, you would do well not to talk to the press, nor to mention the matter to anyone else. If the murderer were to find out . . .'

'Oh, ma'am, 'tis not a soul I'll be telling!' gasped the maid. Her freckles stood out like a rash in her white face, Daisy saw in the looking-glass – she was now wielding a powder puff in the perpetual effort to conceal her own few freckles. 'Oh, ma'am, d'ye think he'll come after me wi' a gun?'

'Not if you're sensible and keep quiet. I didn't mean to frighten you. Have you already told anyone?'

'Oh no, ma'am, savin' me brother. You're the only guest has been friendly at all, at all, and I wouldn't gossip about the guests wi' the other maids. Father Macnamara says gossiping is a sin,' she added virtuously.

'Very true,' said Daisy, hoping the stricture did not apply to reporting on one guest to another, particularly a friendly other. 'I must go now, but I shall see you later, Bridget.'

'Yes, ma'am. Thank you, ma'am. Will I press a frock for you for dinner?'

'Yes, would you, please? I expect you're less busy now than you will be later.' Daisy went to the wardrobe and took out the black georgette she had bought for the transatlantic voyage. 'I'll wear this one.'

Suitable for mourning, she thought as she returned to the lifts. Not that she exactly felt like mourning Otis Carmody, but all the same, she would dress up the plain frock with one of her more subdued scarves this evening.

Kevin was awaiting her, kneeling on the passage floor, playing at dibs with an astonishing agility. He grinned at Daisy, tossed all five jacks and caught them on the back of his hand. A last toss and catch, and he shoved them into his pocket. Standing up, he brushed off the knees of his livery trousers.

'Gotta do sumpin to keep from going nuts,' he observed. 'Third floor?'

'Yes, please. How did you guess?'

'I keeps me eyes and ears open,' said Kevin with a knowing look.

'You went back down to pick up the Misses Cabot,' Daisy accused him, 'and heard them talking on the way up.'

'I keeps me eyes and ears open,' Kevin repeated with his infectious grin. 'Going down!'

The Misses Cabot's residence comprised a small foyer, a large sitting room, two bedrooms, a bathroom, and a small kitchen at the rear of the hotel. The sitting room had a splendid fireplace, faced with green tiles and topped with a carved rosewood mantelpiece, where a small, cheery fire glowed, adding its might to the already oppressive heat.

There were built-in rosewood bookcases, but most of the furniture was the Cabots' own, heavy mahogany uphol-stered in faded crimson plush. Whatnots crammed with bibelots and photographs in silver frames were surely the elder Miss Cabot's. One corner of the room was dedicated to Miss Genevieve's business, with a spartan kneehole desk, a cabinet for files and reference books, and a typewriter which matched the one in Daisy's room.

On the walls, whose white paint somewhat relieved the Victorian gloom, hung watercolours of little girls with kittens and little boys with puppies, alternating with framed newspaper cuttings. Daisy would have liked to examine the latter, but the Misses Cabot awaited her, and tea was laid out on a small, lace-draped table by a lace-draped window.

'Tea!' she exclaimed. 'You cannot imagine how I long for a cup.'

'Oh dear!' clucked Miss Cabot. 'You must drink as much as you like, Mrs Fletcher. I can easily make more.'

'Do tell me what happened at the Flatiron Building,' Miss Genevieve requested eagerly.

In the course of drinking the pot dry, Daisy described the events she had witnessed. She was careful not to pass on any speculation. The police would have a right to be unhappy if she revealed their ideas on the identity of the murderer, though they had had no business to discuss it in front of her.

But, in finishing, she did say, 'I gather Mr Carmody had written articles which earned him the enmity of people in high places in Washington. And that he was well on the way to doing the same in New York.'

'I have read his Washington articles,' said Miss Genevieve, eyes sparkling. 'They were hard-hitting, all right. They have led to at least one official hearing, into Colonel Forbes, Director of the Veterans' Bureau, who was selling surplus government material for his own profit. I wonder if Forbes hired a hoodlum to rub Carmody out.'

'The man I saw running away didn't look like—' Daisy started to protest, but Miss Genevieve wasn't listening.

'No, more likely the Tammany bosses sent one of their local thugs to stop his investigation before they got hurt.

And since both the police and the District Attorney's Office are firmly under Tammany's thumb, they'll get away with it.'

Miss Cabot continued the running refrain which had punctuated Daisy's story: 'Oh dear!'

'Not necessarily,' said Daisy. 'I understand a federal agent will be involved.'

'The Feds stationed in New York are all in Tammany's pockets,' declared Miss Genevieve cynically.

'A man is coming from Washington.'

'Indeed! Now how did that come about, I wonder?' Her penetrating gaze fixed Daisy, who was immediately certain she looked guilty. She had no intention of revealing that J. Edgar Hoover had sent an agent to take care of her.

However, Miss Genevieve forbore to probe. 'That will put a cat among the pigeons, and no mistake!' she went on. 'So close to the election, they can't afford to be caught hiding evidence. It would be worse than letting Carmody publish, and almost as bad as being proved to have hired an assassin!'

'Oh dear!'

'You don't think there might have been a more personal motive for the attack on Carmody?' Daisy ventured. 'I don't know anything about his private life.'

'He was married,' revealed Miss Genevieve consideringly. 'His wife came with him from Washington.'

'Oh dear, the poor woman!'

'But she left him, as you know very well, sister?'

'Only think how guilty she will feel, sister, to have left him in his hour of need!'

'She can hardly have foreseen that he was to be murdered, sister. Unless,' Miss Genevieve mused, 'she was responsible for his death.'

'Oh dear!'

Married? Then the woman Daisy had heard must have been Mrs Carmody. Did the fact reinforce or destroy Sergeant Gilligan's pet theory?

'There was also the man he quarrelled with in the lobby the other day,' continued Miss Genevieve. 'A Mr Pitt, a fellow resident and fellow writer. He has written a novel, poor man. I had noticed them together previously.'

'What did they quarrel about?' Daisy asked.

'That I cannot tell you, alas. Mr Pitt spoke quite quietly, and they were at some distance from us, in that area between the lobby and the registration desk. Mr Carmody's voice was not lowered, however. He repeated several times, in different ways, that he could do nothing for him. In the end, Mr Pitt raised his voice and called him a—'

'Sister!'

'A rude name. Several, in fact. He continued the abuse as Carmody pushed past him, heading for the street.'

'What did Mr Pitt do then?' Daisy wanted to know.

'The manager came out and – I presume – desired him to moderate his language as there were ladies present, where-upon he departed, I assume by way of the stairs.'

'The stairs? Not the elevators?'

'He turned to the right, and I happened to have noticed young Kevin sneaking out about his nefarious business a few minutes earlier,' said Miss Genevieve dryly.

Daisy laughed. 'Pitt went up by the stairs, then. Heavens, look at the time. My husband will be back at his hotel by now. I must phone him and tell him I shan't be taking the train tomorrow. Excuse me for running off, and thank you so much for the tea.'

Returning to her room, Daisy saw that a uniformed policeman had been stationed at the next door along the passage, the door to Carmody's room. She wondered whether it had been searched already. Perhaps Gilligan was still busy with Thorwald and other possible witnesses at the Flatiron Building, such as the doormen. The sergeant might well want to search the victim's room himself, for fear of turning up evidence incriminating his bosses at Tammany Hall.

While she waited for her telephone call to be put through, Daisy paced her room. She hardly dared think what Alec was going to say, but she simply could not fix her mind on anything else, even the burning question of who had killed Carmody.

It was twenty minutes before the switchboard rang back to say she was connected. Then Alec's voice came through, crackling and scratchy but unmistakably Alec.

'Great Scott, Daisy, tell me it's not true?'

'Darling, I couldn't *help* it!'

His sigh whistled down the wire. 'I know, love. You'd better not talk about it. There's no knowing who might be listening in. Just tell me, are you all right? You're not too upset? The police didn't threaten you with what they call the "third degree"? If they did, by God I'll have their livers and lights!'

'No, no, darling, they were fairly polite. But this isn't the moment to remind me of American police methods! Surely they wouldn't use violent methods on a respectable married lady who has been utterly cooperative? Besides, my watchdog was by my side most of the time. I'm going to have your super's liver and lights when we get home!'

A laugh entered Alec's voice. 'So you've discovered Crane's meddling, have you?'

'Alec, he didn't tell you he was going to . . .'

'Great Scott, no, love. The gentleman I'm working with here told me, to reassure me that you wouldn't run amok without me. Little did he know . . .'

'Don't be beastly, darling. I do miss you. I wish you were here.'

'Oh, I shall be. I'm taking a train to New York tomorrow afternoon. Should be there by teatime. Hoover has exacted a promise from me to protect the New York police from you.'

'Horrid beast! But I'm glad you're coming. I'll meet you at the station. What time?'

The rest of their conversation was taken up with practical details followed by sweet nothings. After she had hung up the earpiece, Daisy sat for several minutes revelling in the glow left by the latter.

Then curiosity, her besetting sin, reasserted itself. She reached out determinedly for the bell to ring for the chambermaid. It was time to find out what Bridget had to tell about the late Otis Carmody.

CHAPTER 7

'Come in, Bridget.' Daisy noted the girl's weary stance. It was a busy time for her, and towards the end of a long work day. 'Can you spare me a few minutes?'

'O' course, ma'am. What can I do for you?'

'Come and sit down. I would like to talk to you.'

'Oh, ma'am, I didn't ought, but faith, I'll be glad to get the weight off of me feet.' With a little sigh, Bridget sank into the easy chair Daisy indicated. She sat bolt upright, though, with her red, chapped hands folded neatly in her lap. 'Is it Kevin you wanted to talk about, ma'am?' she asked anxiously. 'He hasn't been fresh, has he?'

'Fresh?'

'Saucy, ma'am. Cheeky. 'Tis how they say it here.'

'Oh yes, he's been "fresh", all right,' Daisy said, laughing, 'but in such a friendly way I couldn't possibly take offence. I like Kevin. Actually, I wondered whether you had spoken to the police yet.'

'Only to pass the time of day wi' the bluecoat guarding Mr Carmody's door. Kevin says there was a detective went to the manager's office and wrote down the name and address of all the staff and residents. I wish they'd hurry up and get it over with. Sure and I might forget what I heard.'

Daisy knew an opportunity when she saw one. 'Would it help to tell me, now?' she suggested. 'Then it will be fresh in your mind. Fresh in the English sense.'

Bridget was eager to oblige. She never listened at doors, she was quick to explain, but she had been putting clean towels in Mr Carmody's bathroom. He knew she was there, but he hadn't told her to leave, and she had not dared to creep out in the middle of the Donnybrook.

'Irish that is, ma'am, that word, not American. A fight, sure enough, though being a lady and gentlemen they used hard words, not shillelaghs.'

The chambermaid had the Irish gift for storytelling. While she talked, Daisy could imagine herself cowering in the bathroom, listening involuntarily to the harsh voices.

First had come the peremptory rap on the outer door. Brisk footsteps crossed the room to answer it.

'What the heck do you want now, Elva?' That was Carmody, bored, irritated.

'We can't talk in the hallway, Otis.' A female voice, high-pitched, with a hint of a whine – Mrs Carmody. She was a pretty woman, with an air of fragility, Bridget said.

A long-suffering sigh next reached the maid's ears. 'OK, come in then if you insist. Yes, you too, Bender. I don't know what more you think there is to say.'

'Not my idea,' spluttered the unknown Bender. 'Leave it to the lawyers.'

'Honey, the lawyers can't help if Otis won't cooperate.' Mrs Carmody now spoke in tones of sweet patience. 'He's not one of your tenants to be evicted. I don't see why you won't give me a divorce, Otis.'

'I'm quite ready to divorce you, sweets.' Carmody's voice

conveyed a sardonic grin. 'For desertion, or adultery, whichever you choose.'

'You know that'd damn me in the eyes of the best New York society. Why can't you be a gentleman and give me grounds to divorce *you* for adultery?'

'Because I'm too much the gentleman ever to be unfaithful.'

'Oh, don't give me that hooey!'

'Now, now, Elva, don't be vulgar,' chided Carmody. 'The best New York society won't stand for vulgarity.'

'Damn you! I'm sick of your sarcasm. I'm sick of never knowing when you're gonna get paid. I'm sick of playing second fiddle to your damn career, running around at all hours digging up dirt that makes important people hate your guts. I'm never coming back to you, so why won't you just go and have a fling with some little chorus girl?'

'So you can set your private dick on my tail, peering through keyholes and jumping out of closets with his Kodak to catch me in flagrante?' Carmody was angry now. 'Sordid, Elva, sordid! No, I'm not putting myself in the wrong for your sake, so Bender's goddamn blood-sucking lawyers can strip me of what little I possess!'

'Hold it there, buddy!' bleated Bender. 'I don't need your two bits to keep the little woman in furs and diamonds.'

'Maybe not, but I'm not taking the risk. And it's no good saying you'll sign a paper. I know what a smart lawyer can do with a piece of paper, and I know all the judges in this burg got elected on the Tammany ticket, and I know you're in cahoots with Tammany. So forget it, buster. You're not gonna wring a nickel out of me, let alone two bits. Why don't you take her to Reno?'

'It takes six weeks to get a Reno divorce,' snapped Elva Carmody. 'Barton can't leave his business that long. You can't expect me to go through an ordeal like that without his support.'

'Afraid you'll lose him?' sneered Carmody. 'Out of sight, out of mind.'

'Bastard! Of course not. I trust Barton absolutely.' Her voice changed to a coo. 'We're in love, aren't we, honey?'

'Sure thing, honey baby. Come on, let's go. It's like talking to a brick wall.'

The door to the hall had not quite slammed. Bridget heard the scrape of a match, then Carmody had drawled, 'It's safe now, girl. You can come out.'

He was seated at his desk, smoking, apparently unruffled, when the chambermaid scuttled past him with her armful of dirty towels. She had not dared to face him since, making sure he was absent when she had to enter his room to perform her duties.

So much for Sergeant Gilligan's theory, Daisy thought. But that did not mean Mrs Carmody's lover had no motive for shooting her husband, especially if he truly loved her. Surely, though, it would have been much simpler to manage somehow to take her to Reno, wherever that was.

Except that Tammany Hall had once again reared its ugly head. A Reno divorce would not solve that side of the equation.

Or maybe something had been said on the return visit, of which Daisy had heard the end, which made Carmody's death imperative. She wished she had seen more of Barton Bender than the balding top of his head. Could he have been the man who escaped down the Flatiron Building's stairs?

'Did you see Mr Bender?' Daisy asked Bridget. 'Then or at any other time?'

'No, ma'am. 'Twas when Mr and Mrs Carmody first came to the hotel I saw her, before she up and left. I never seen Mr Bender.'

'Never mind. You can tell the police his name and they'll find him. And however slow they are, I don't think there's much fear of your forgetting what they all said. You had every word down pat, and they won't expect such accuracy.'

'Yes'm. I was listening hard 'cause I was scared, so it stuck in my mind zackly what they said. But the other time I heard Mr Carmody quarrelling, I only heard a little bit and I don't remember so well.'

'There was another time?' Daisy said hopefully.

'I was going to make up his bed,' explained the chambermaid. 'The door hadn't been closed all the way. I stopped to knock, and I heard him talking to someone he called Willie. He said he couldn't help him. Well, this Willie, he gets excited and says he could if he would. He says he has no loyalty to his family and he always was a bully. I remember that. "You always was a bully," he said.'

'That's William speaking?'

'Yes. This Willie called Mr Carmody a bully. Then Mr Carmody, he said, "And you were always a little tick. A real pest you were, when we were kids, and you still are. Just like a burr under a saddle. I can't do anything for you. Go away, do."'

'You've remembered that very well,' Daisy commended her.

'Well, when I thinks back on it, it all kinda comes back to me. Anyways, when Mr Carmody told him to go away I thought as he'd be coming out, this Willie, so I went and did the bed in the next room, not this one, the other side. But he didn't leave right away, 'cause I heard him shouting, only I couldn't make out the words. Did I oughta tell the police about this Willie, ma'am?'

'Certainly. I suppose you didn't see him, either?'

'No, but I reckon he must be a relative, don't you, ma'am? Talking about family loyalty and all?'

'It certainly sounds like it,' Daisy agreed. 'I expect the police will track him down. You'll want to get back to work now, won't you?'

'Yes, ma'am, and thank you, ma'am. Telling you, I've got it all straight in my head for when the police come.'

Bridget left, and Daisy contemplated what she had learnt.

A relative, she thought, now that was more in her line. An amateur sleuth hadn't much hope of solving a political assassination. Not that she was an amateur sleuth! It wasn't her fault she kept getting mixed up in murders, whatever Alec said.

When it happened at home, Alec always ended up in charge of the investigation. The Met's Assistant Commissioner for Crime considered him the only person capable of reining in Daisy once she had the bit between her teeth, not that he had much evidence for that comfortable conclusion. In fact, Alec's involvement tended to lead to Daisy's further involvement.

Here in New York, however, he would be a bystander, and when he arrived he'd make sure she played her role as a witness and nothing more.

That was not likely to be much of a role, since she was a witness whom the police did not hold in high regard. Daisy sighed. She would have liked to prove her mettle to them. Perhaps she could at least find out who William was.

If he was a resident of the hotel, Kevin probably knew all about him. So, of course, did the manager, who had already yielded his lists to the police. If he was not a resident, Daisy hadn't the slightest idea where to start looking. Blast! That was a dead end.

What about Mrs Carmody and her presumed lover? Was there anything she might discover or deduce about them?

Her ruminations were interrupted by the ring of the telephone bell.

It was the hotel doorman. 'Mrs Fletcher, ma'am, ge'man to see you. A Mr Thorwald.'

'Please tell him I'll come down at once.'

So poor Mr Thorwald had escaped from Sergeant Gilligan's clutches. Daisy hoped he had fully recovered from his encounter with the bottle of rye whisky. As she powdered her nose, she wondered what, if anything, he had told the police. Had he observed something he had not mentioned to her? He couldn't have seen much after he tackled Lambert and lost his pince-nez, besides which the alcohol might well have achieved its intended function of blotting out unpleasant memories.

For a moment, the memory of Carmody's body was unpleasantly clear in Daisy's mind. Dismissing it with a shiver, she patted her curls into place and went to the door.

Out in the passage, a disconsolate Lambert awaited her. 'Gee whiz, I was hunting for you for ages,' he said. 'Where did you go?'

'When you went off to enquire about a back exit? Really, Mr Lambert, you may have a duty to follow me, but I have absolutely no obligation to keep you informed of my movements,' Daisy pointed out a trifle tartly, continuing towards the lifts.

The young agent kept pace, his lips pursed in a sulky near pout. 'It's for your safety,' he reminded her. 'And now you're a vital witness to homicide, anything could happen.'

'How reassuring! The police don't seem to think I'm a vital witness. I couldn't give them a good description of the man who ran away.'

'No, but *he* doesn't know that.' Lambert pressed the button to call an elevator. 'And you said you would recognize him if you saw him again.'

'I think so.' Again Daisy wondered whether 'this Willie', Carmody's presumed relative, was a hotel guest. If she had seen him about, it would explain why she had thought the fugitive vaguely familiar – if he was the fugitive.

If, if, if. The 'if' phase of a murder investigation was always a lengthy and frustrating one, in Daisy's experience.

If you can keep your head when all about you
Are losing theirs, and blaming it on you . . .

Kipling, 'If'. One of those tags and snippets from her schooldays which tended to flit through her mind, called up by frequently inapposite associations. Perhaps not totally inapposite this time: Rosencrantz and Guildenstern blamed her for losing her head and not getting a precise and detailed description of the murderer for them; and they were in danger of losing *their* heads over the possible Tammany connection.

The lift arrived. Had Kevin come with it, Daisy might, in

spite of Lambert's presence, have asked the boy what he knew of William. But Kevin's shift was over. The attendant was a stout, lugubrious man who wheezed as if he had personally pushed the elevator all the way from ground level. He didn't so much as glance at Daisy and Lambert as he asked them which floor they wanted.

'Lobby, please,' said Daisy.

'You're going out?' Lambert asked.

'No. Not that it's any of your business. As a matter of fact, Mr Thorwald is here to see me.'

Lambert's eyes narrowed behind his horn-rims. 'Say, you don't think Thorwald did it? He was behind you, wasn't he? He could have pulled a gun without you seeing it. And he had his back to me, and I didn't have much of a view where I was standing.'

'He was only just behind, practically beside me. I might not have seen, but if the shot was so close, it would have sounded much louder than it did, and surely I would have smelt the smoke?'

'Probably,' Lambert conceded reluctantly.

'Anyway, I'm sure Mr Thorwald had nothing to do with it. He's just not that sort of person.'

'You can't tell by just looking at someone,' the fledgling agent argued. 'That's one of the first things they taught us.'

'I didn't "just look" at Mr Thorwald,' Daisy retorted. 'I first met him months ago, in England. We have correspond-ed regularly. And I have had two long talks with him since I arrived in New York. Here we are,' she said as the elevator came to a halt. 'Now, if you insist on hovering over me, do try a little harder to make yourself inconspicuous!'

'I'll try,' said Lambert, abashed.

For all her indignant denial, as Daisy crossed the lobby to greet Thorwald she could not help wondering whether he might have shot Carmody. Suspicion faded at the sight of him. He came to meet her with a hangdog air.

'My dear Miss Dal ... Mrs Fletcher, I cannot apologize sufficiently for my disgraceful behaviour. I am unaccustomed to intemperate bibulation and I fear I was overcome.'

'Perfectly understandable,' Daisy assured him. 'It was a natural reaction to such a beastly business. And when you saved me from Lambert' – who, in an unconvincing manner, was studying a Cubist painting hanging nearby which Daisy guessed had been given to the hotel in lieu of rent by a particularly unsuccessful artist; she glared at the agent's oblivious back and turned back to Thorwald – 'you were simply splendid.'

Her editor blushed but lamented, 'That such an atrocious incident should have occurred upon the occasion of your appointment with me!' He took off his pince-nez and attempted to rub his eyes, only to discover his hat and gloves in his other hand. It was a topper, and he had on a dinner jacket – a tuxedo – under his overcoat.

'Please, don't worry about it. I cannot possibly hold you responsible. But you look as if you are going out to dinner, Mr Thorwald. Don't let me delay you.'

'My dear young lady, as a matter of fact I was permitting myself to hope ... That is, I telephoned Mrs Thorwald ... My wife is at present sojourning with her mother in Jersey. I telephoned to describe to her the disastrous course of the day, and she insisted that the only way to make amends ... In short, Mrs Fletcher, since I was unhappily prevented from taking you out to lunch, will you do me the honour, that is, give me the pleasure, of dining with me?'

'I shall be delighted,' said Daisy, who had sampled once too often the dinners the hotel restaurant served to those whose minds must be presumed to be occupied by higher things. 'Will you excuse me while I go and change? I shan't be long.'

'Of course.' Mr Thorwald beamed. 'No need to hurry.'

Lambert caught up with her on the way to the lifts. Glancing back, he said suspiciously, 'He's taken a seat. Is he waiting for you to come back?'

'Yes,' said Daisy. 'He's taking me out to dinner. If you must follow, for pity's sake dress properly. And buck up. We won't wait for you.'

'Gee whiz! Where are you going?'

'I don't know. He didn't say.'

'You mustn't go without me, darn it,' Lambert said anxiously. 'The old codger's probably planning to slip knockout drops in your soup!'

CHAPTER 8

Daisy was not one to dilly-dally when there was a good meal in the offing. Yet Lambert changed his clothes with such speed that he was waiting for her when she stepped out of the elevator in the lobby. He had buttoned his stiff shirt wrong, and his tie was lopsided. Otherwise his evening dress was perfectly adequate. Daisy supposed it was one of the disguises essential to his job.

She gave him a distant nod and walked on. Mr Thorwald stood up as she approached, but he was looking over her shoulder with a puzzled expression. Daisy turned to find Lambert lurking unhappily so close behind that Thorwald couldn't help but recognize him.

Almost recognize him: the bottle of whisky had done its work to the extent that he said hesitantly, 'Don't I know that young fellow?'

'That's Mr Lambert, whom you so bravely tackled.'

'The fellow with the automatic pistol? Yes, I recollect him. Don't tell me he continues to pursue you! I'll eject him.'

'He's staying here. And he's a federal agent, remember? Charged with my safety.'

'So he would have us believe,' muttered Thorwald. 'He appears to have escaped police surveillance, but I consider it unwise to leave him to his machinations unobserved. Aha, I have it. Hi, you there, Lambert or whatever you call yourself!'

'Me, sir?' Lambert said cautiously.

'Well, is your name Lambert or isn't it?'

'Yes, sir, it is.'

'Then presumably it is you I'm addressing.'

'I guess so,' Lambert admitted.

'Do you care to join Mrs Fletcher and me for dinner?' Thorwald invited him.

'Who, me?'

'No!' roared Thorwald. 'Some other young idiot called Lambert who's been following Mrs Fletcher around all day!'

'Gee whiz, sir, yes, thank you, I'd be honoured to join you. But let's get outta here quick. Here comes Sergeant Gilligan. This way!'

As Gilligan entered by the front door, turning to bellow at a reporter who dared to pursue him with questions, Daisy and Thorwald hastened after Lambert. He led them past the reception desk and down a narrow, badly lit and indifferently cleaned corridor, down stairs and up again, past kitchens, storerooms, and laundry rooms. Thorwald showed a disposition to baulk at this undignified proceeding, but Daisy hustled him onward. For once she was in complete agreement with Lambert: she had no desire whatsoever to come face-to-face with either the sergeant or the press.

She was explaining this to Thorwald as they emerged into a dark alley and turned towards the bright lights of Seventh Avenue. Coming towards them, silhouetted against the lights, was a man in a bowler hat.

'It's him!' she cried. 'Stop him!'

'Who?' Mr Thorwald asked reasonably. He had been absent in spirit(s) when she described the fugitive to the police. 'The man in the bowler hat.'

Lambert's face turned to her palely. 'Bowler ... ? Oh, derby!' And he started running.

By then the man in the bowler hat was fleeing. When Daisy, hampered by a long skirt and high heels, caught up with Lambert at the alley's exit, their quarry had mingled with the passers-by and disappeared. The street was busy. Among the silk hats, soft felts and caps were several derbys. They could not accost them all.

Thorwald puffed up. 'Who?' he repeated. 'No, don't reply now. Taxi!' He waved.

A chequered cab swooped down to pick them up.

Lambert would not let them discuss 'sensitive material' where the driver could overhear. When they reached the restaurant, Thorwald demanded their concentrated attention on the menu until they had ordered. So it was while they waited for the soup that he reiterated his question: 'Who? Who is the man in the derby?'

'Didn't you see him?' Daisy asked.

'Only silhouetted against the illumination, which was insufficient to permit recognition.'

'I meant, at the Flatiron Building. He's the man I chased down the stairs.'

'No, I did not observe the object of your pursuit. I was otherwise occupied, in arresting the progress of your pursuer.' He turned a still suspicious gaze upon Lambert.

'A mighty fine tackle, I'll allow,' Lambert said, glowering, 'but I could bear to know just why you got in my way when I was aiming to protect Mrs Fletcher.'

'Please, gentlemen! Cease hostilities!'

Daisy's plea was aided by the arrival of their soup. A truce was observed until the waiter departed.

'Mr Thorwald,' Daisy said quickly, 'Mr Lambert knows far too much about my husband's doings to be an imposter. And Mr Lambert, Mr Thorwald is an altogether respectable and knowledgeable editor who has never been anything but extremely helpful to me. Please, let's concentrate on catching the murderer. It was an unbelievable stroke of luck to see him tonight, though it's a pity we weren't a couple of minutes later, when he'd already entered the hotel.'

'But what persuades you to suppose—?' began Thorwald.

'Gee whiz, Mrs Fletcher,' Lambert overrode him, 'we don't have any reason to believe it was the same guy.'

'Then why did you run after him?'

Lambert looked sheepish. 'I guess when you yelled "stop him" I just reacted without thinking. The chances of his being the guy we're after are, oh, about one in however many men in New York wear derbys.'

'Bosh! What was he doing sneaking down a back alley behind the very hotel where his victim had been staying? And why did he run away?'

'If I was taking a short cut down a dark alley and someone yelled, "It's him, stop him," I guess I'd run.'

Mr Thorwald stopped spooning in soup for long enough to nod agreement.

'It's too much of a coincidence,' Daisy argued. 'I'm sure it was William.'

Two pairs of bewildered eyes blinked at her from behind their glass shields.

'William?' Lambert queried uncertainly.

'I'll tell you about William in a minute. Let me eat my soup before it's stone cold.'

After her late lunch, Daisy had eaten nothing at tea. She was hungry, and the cream of mushroom soup quickly disappeared. Then, careful to conceal her source, she told them what little she had learnt about the quarrel between Otis Carmody and the man he addressed as Willie.

'Since he talked about family loyalty,' she pointed out, 'he's obviously a relative.'

'A reasonable deduction,' Lambert conceded.

'And they were children together. I think they were cousins. If they had been brothers, William would have the same surname as Otis, in which case the hotel people would have noticed and told the police.'

'How do you know they didn't?' Lambert asked sceptically.

'I can't be certain, of course. I'm betting, though, that at least one of my sources of information would have found out and told me. About the surnames being the same, I mean, if not whether the police have been notified.'

'My dear young lady,' Thorwald interjected, 'your rationale presupposes that the person in question is a resident of the Hotel Chelsea.'

'If he isn't,' said Daisy, 'then what was he doing skulking around in the alley by the service entrance?'

The men pondered this question while the waiter served the fish course.

'Circular reasoning!' said Lambert, triumphant.

Daisy looked back on her chain of deductions and was forced to admit he had a point. She must be tired. 'Well, maybe. But don't you think it's all rather fishy?'

'Mmmm,' said Thorwald happily, and delved into his halibut.

Giving up for the present, Daisy turned her attention to her *sole bonne femme*. It was excellent.

While she ate, she considered her two companions. Thorwald, she suspected, had much rather not think about the murder at all. Even the memory of his heroic gesture was not enough to make the 'atrocious incident' a desirable subject for contemplation. Lambert, on the other hand, was quite willing to discuss the case. Unfortunately, his only contributions so far had been to shoot down her theories. He had yet to make any useful suggestions of his own.

She resolved to drop the topic for this evening. Tomorrow morning she'd see what further information Kevin could give her, and then she would take all she knew to Miss Genevieve, who would certainly have her own ideas to add to the seething pot.

When Daisy went down in search of breakfast, Kevin was on duty, and more or less at leisure. The majority of the hotel's guests did not put in an appearance so early, he explained. *La vie bohémienne* allowed, indeed demanded, that they rise at noon or later. 'Time is money' was not a phrase which dominated them as it did the world of American business.

When Daisy said she'd like to ask Kevin one or two questions, he was delighted. He stopped the lift between the sixth and fifth floors so that they could talk in peace.

'I don't mind telling you stuff,' he said. 'Them bulls, now, I wouldn't give 'em the time o' day. Not after they come round our place last night and scared me mam and bullied Bridey. Bulls!' he exclaimed in disgust. 'I told 'em I got better things to think about than listening to the flap-doodle people talk in the elevator, and up and down all day, I got no time for hotel gossip. Ha!' He grinned.

'Whereas I know,' said Daisy with a smile, 'that you listen to every word and spend as little time as possible in your elevator. Do you know anything about the man Bridget heard addressed as Willie? Do you know his last name, for a start?'

'Pitt,' said Kevin promptly. 'Wilbur Pitt, tenth floor.'

'So he is a resident! Wilbur Pitt?' Daisy mused. 'I assumed he must be William. That name sounds familiar. Was he related to Carmody?'

'Dunno 'bout that, ma'am. I guess maybe. I saw 'em together a few times and they didn't look like they liked each other, so they wasn't friends, anyways. Yeah, maybe they *was* related. You wouldn't notice seeing 'em apart, but when you saw 'em next to each other, there was something about their faces . . . Yeah, they wasn't twins or nothing like that, but they coulda been related.'

'Cousins, perhaps.'

'Could be. Mr Pitt's older'n Mr Carmody, and he don't look so well fed, 'fya know what I mean. Kinda tough and stringy. More like he worked hard outta doors, like my brother on the waterfront.'

'I know what you mean. Pitt! That's the chap Miss Genevieve saw quarrelling with Carmody in the lobby. I don't suppose you know what they were arguing about?'

'Not zackly,' Kevin admitted regretfully. 'I wasn't there, but what I heard is it was sumpin about interductions.

Seems like Mr Carmody wouldn't give Mr Pitt an interduction.'

One didn't kill one's cousin simply because he refused to provide an introduction, Daisy thought, disappointed. Now if they had been fighting over money, or a woman . . . But so much for Cousin Wilbur. A great pity, she had rather fancied him as the villain.

'What about Mrs Carmody and Mr Bender?' she asked.

'They was mighty lovey-dovey, them two. Spooning in the elevator,' said Kevin with scorn, 'like I wasn't there. Course, last time they came, it wasn't me took 'em down, but I heard she was blubbing and he promised he'd fix things so they can get married. He said he wasn't going to let any pen pusher push him around, no sirree!'

'That sounds promising,' said Daisy. 'But isn't that someone ringing for the lift again? You'd better take me down now.'

'Darn it, can't they leave a guy in peace for two minutes?' the boy complained. 'OK, here we go.'

Lambert was skulking in the lobby. He looked so relieved to see Daisy that she wondered whether he was afraid she had done a moonlight flit. With an inward sigh, she decided she could not decently avoid inviting him to join her for breakfast.

'Don't worry,' she said as they sat down, 'Alec arrives late this afternoon and you'll be relieved of your arduous duty.'

Lambert blushed. 'Not at all,' he stammered. 'It's been a pleasure. But I'll be helping Mr Whitaker, who's coming to figure out whether it was Tammany sent the thug that killed Carmody, or someone in Washington. That's real police work.'

Real police preconceived notions, Daisy thought, but she held her tongue. They gave their orders, which led to a discussion of the differences between American and English food and language. Daisy was still bewildered by an offer of eggs 'over easy' or 'sunny-side up', but she approved of waffles and simply adored maple syrup. She hadn't quite accustomed herself to getting syrup on her sausages or bacon, though.

After breakfast, Lambert expressed his willingness to escort her to visit any of the sights of New York she wished to see.

'No, thanks,' said Daisy. His face fell. 'It's all right, you don't have to tail me,' she reassured him. 'I expect you're tired of lurking round corners and behind trees.'

'I have to go wherever you go,' he said stubbornly.

'I'm not going anywhere. Unless Sergeant Gilligan has absolutely written me off as a useful witness, he's bound to get around sometime to wanting me to look at his "mug book", don't you think? I'd better stay where he can find me.'

'I guess so. But you shouldn't see him alone.'

'Why on earth not?'

'Gee whiz!' Lambert ran his finger round inside his collar. 'Uh, well, after all, you were there when Carmody was killed, and you admitted to having held my gun, so your fingerprints would have been on it – not that they checked and I've polished it since, of course, but they might wonder if you just made the admission to explain the fingerprints, and if I'm protecting you by saying it's mine and I had it when Carmody was killed, not forgetting that all they know about you is what I've told them, though it hasn't been fired of course, so even if it's the same calibre bullet, but who knows if the New York cops can figure out what kind of gun it's been fired from . . .'

Daisy rescued him from his entangled clauses. 'In short, you think they regard me as a suspect?'

'They might.'

'But I didn't do it,' she reminded him, 'and I haven't done anything else nefarious which I need to conceal, unless you count taking a sip of Mr Thorwald's revolting rye whisky. So I have nothing to worry about.'

'Maybe you wouldn't in England, but these are American cops, remember. With the election coming up, the DA needs to solve the case quick, and without involving Tammany.'

'With the election coming up, the DA would be an absolute ass to try any funny business on the wife of a Scotland Yard detective in America on official business. Not to mention a writer whose publisher also puts out an opposition news weekly. I can imagine what our papers at home would make of that. I don't suppose yours would exactly ignore it.'

'Gee whiz, I hadn't thought of it like that. I guess you're right.'

'So I shall cooperate with Rosencrantz and Guilden-stern . . .'

'Who?'

'Blast, I knew I was going to come out with that sooner or later! Oh well, better to you than to them.'

'To who?' Lambert asked blankly.

'Whom. Hamlet,' Daisy explained, further bewildering him. 'Oh, never mind! I'll cooperate fully with the police and the district attorney when they get around to asking for my help. In the meantime, I'm going to see the Misses Cabot. I'll be perfectly safe with them, so there's absolutely no need for you to try to barge in.'

Lambert shuddered. 'You won't catch me trying,' he affirmed.

CHAPTER 9

During Daisy's stay, she had never seen the Misses Cabot early in the morning. She had assumed they were among the late risers. However, Kevin, that inexhaustible fount of information, told her they retired early and rose early, but breakfasted in their apartment suite. When she knocked on their door, Miss Genevieve's strong voice bade her enter.

'Good morning, I hope I'm not disturbing you.'

'Good morning,' Miss Cabot greeted her, 'not at all, Mrs Fletcher, always happy . . .'

Miss Genevieve dispensed with such superfluities. Dropping the newspaper she was reading on top of a pile of others on the table, she said, 'Ah, Mrs Fletcher, perhaps you can tell me what's going on? I quite expected to have received a visit from the police by now.'

'I haven't seen any about this morning,' said Daisy, 'except the man posted outside Carmody's room. I know they interviewed some of the staff last night. I gather they rather upset the chambermaid who attended Carmody?'

'Oh dear, poor girl! Won't you sit down, Mrs Fletcher?'

'I suppose they will question all the staff first,' said Miss Genevieve, discontented. 'If they can bully sufficient information out of them, they won't have to tackle the residents, who are better able to take care of themselves.'

'They're bound to want to speak to you,' Daisy soothed her. 'Someone is sure to tell them you are acquainted with most, if not all, of the hotel's guests?'

'Tactfully put! You mean I'm a nosy old woman who makes a point of delving into everyone's business.'

'That's what a gossip columnist is supposed to do. I'll mention it to them, if you like. I've been wondering what you know about Wilbur Pitt. You told me you saw him quarrelling with Carmody, and that he had written a novel. I'm inclined to believe he might have been Otis Carmody's cousin.'

'Ha! Very likely. Their tiff had more the appearance of a family squabble than a fight between acquaintances. Mr Pitt told me he comes from somewhere out west. Do you recall where he mentioned, sister?'

'Ohio, I think, sister,' said Miss Cabot, her forehead wrinkling in a doubtful frown. 'Or was it Omaha? Or Oregon? I'm sure it began with an O. Oh dear, or was it Idaho? That ends with an O, you know.'

'Somewhere in the West,' Miss Genevieve said impatiently. 'Pitt was the son of a farmer. He'd worked on the farm—'

'Colorado!' cried Miss Cabot. 'Or was it?'

'. . . and also as a logger and miner. He has written a novel based on his experiences, and he brought the manuscript to New York to find a publisher.'

'San Francisco?'

'He'll be lucky to get an editor even to look at it,' Miss Genevieve continued. 'A person of small education, as one might expect from his background. He need only open his mouth to be rejected.'

'Poor chap.' Daisy sympathized. She wanted to write a novel some day, but it was a dauntingly mammoth undertaking. 'I dare say he was trying to persuade his cousin to recommend him to an editor.'

'I suppose,' said Miss Cabot, 'it could have been Oklahoma?'

'That's it!' cried Miss Genevieve.

'I knew I should remember in the end, sister.'

'Oh, no, not Oklahoma, sister. Mrs Fletcher's surmise as to Pitt's business with Carmody.'

'New Mexico?' Miss Cabot proposed sadly and unhopefully.

'But Carmody wouldn't have been acquainted with the right kind of editor,' Daisy went on, 'only Pitt didn't believe him and thought he was just being obnoxious when he refused to help. It hardly seems an adequate motive for murder, does it?'

'There's plenty of passion goes into the writing of a novel,' Miss Genevieve observed. 'Still, in my opinion, Carmody's demise is far more likely to have something to do with his wife. A pretty enough creature, of the fluttery butterfly sort which seems to appeal to many men and generally causes trouble of some kind.'

'Oh dear!'

'You mentioned that she had left him,' Daisy prompted.

'Yes, since they arrived in New York. She went off with another man.'

'Oh dear!'

'The grass was greener, if you ask me. I did not speak to

him, but he looked like a prosperous businessman of the more vulgar variety. Freelance writing is an uncertain profession, as you are aware, my dear Mrs Fletcher, and rarely as remunerative as one might wish.'

'Alas,' said Miss Cabot for a change.

'If money was Mrs Carmody's reason for leaving her husband,' said Daisy, 'what do you suppose was Mr Bender's reason for taking up with her? Did he genuinely fall in love with her?'

'I should call it infatuation, rather,' Miss Genevieve said tartly, 'though, to be fair, I may be mistaken. I have not, after all, spoken to him.'

'Genevieve is *never* mistaken as to character once she has spoken to a person,' put in Miss Cabot.

'However, infatuation may be as powerful a motive force as true love.'

'Then if Bender wanted to marry Mrs Carmody,' Daisy suggested, 'and her husband stood in the way . . .'

'I dare say he might hire someone to put him out of the way. I doubt he would perform the dreadful deed himself.'

Daisy remembered the horrified face of the man who had run off down the Flatiron stairs. She simply could not believe that a hired assassin would be so distraught at the result of carrying out his assignment. 'Would Bender be so inefficient as to hire a man who couldn't shoot straight?' she wondered. 'The bullet didn't kill Carmody, just wounded him in the leg.'

'True,' Miss Genevieve mused. 'The papers say it was the fall that killed him, and the gunman could not have guaranteed that he would fall down the elevator shaft rather than backwards on to the floor.'

'He might not have fallen at all. He was holding on to the gate when he was shot. If he had just kept his hold he would have been all right.'

'Oh dear!'

'Maybe the shot wasn't intended to kill,' Daisy speculated. 'Couldn't it have been intended just to frighten him? As a threat of what might happen if he didn't cooperate in obtaining a divorce?'

Miss Genevieve frowned. 'Possibly. Otis Carmody did not strike me as a man easily frightened.'

'On the contrary, but Bender might not have realized that. Not everyone has your gift for understanding character, Miss Genevieve.'

'No gift, but an interest in people coupled with long experience of every variety of human being, down to the lowest dregs of society.'

'Oh dear!'

'The life would *not* have suited you, sister. To resume, Mrs Carmody, however self-centred, must certainly have known her husband was not to be cowed. His work positively invited threats of retaliation. People are understandably averse to having their dirty linen washed in the headlines, and he offended powerful men.'

'In some ways, he was an admirable man, wasn't he?' Daisy acknowledged. 'Without courageous reporters like him dragging corruption into the daylight, it would self-perpetuate forever.'

'A necessary breed, as I said, which doesn't make Carmody any more likable.'

Daisy sighed. 'No, but it does make me think I'm on altogether the wrong track. Rather than a personal motive, it seems far more likely that one of the people he was investigating here in New York meant to warn him off, and it went wrong. He wasn't supposed to be killed at all.'

'Tammany won't be happy,' said Miss Genevieve with glee. 'Didn't I say they were mixed up in it? A homicide is much harder to sweep under the carpet than mere assault. But no doubt the police will manage it, unless someone keeps on their tail. I'm going downstairs.' Both hands on the table, she levered herself to her feet and reached for her cane.

'Oh, sister,' wailed Miss Cabot, '*you* can't fight City Hall single-handed!'

'Maybe not, but City Hall and Tammany Hall are not quite synonymous, and there's an election coming up. What's more, I haven't completely lost touch with everyone I used to know. Come along, Ernestine.'

'Oh dear, oh dear!'

'Miss Genevieve, you needn't worry about Tammany Hall having things all their own way,' Daisy intervened. 'Remember, I told you the Justice Department is sending an agent.'

'My dear Mrs Fletcher, you can only have learned that from the police. A few of them are cunning enough to talk as if it were a done deed in order to mislead anyone who might think of calling in the feds. I shall not take it as fact until I see the agent with my own eyes.'

'Detective Chief Inspector Fletcher, sister,' murmured Miss Cabot, 'of *Scotland Yard*!'

'Of course, how clever of you, sister.'

Miss Cabot blushed, beaming. 'I just wondered, sister, whether perhaps . . .'

'Mr Fletcher must have told Mrs Fletcher an agent was being sent from Washington.'

'Dare we hope, Mrs Fletcher,' said Miss Cabot hopefully, 'that Mr Fletcher will rush to your side? I should so like to meet a Scotland Yard detective.'

'Yes, as a matter of fact, he's taking a train this afternoon. I'll be happy to introduce him to you.'

'Oh, sister!'

'We shall naturally be delighted to receive Mr Fletcher,' said Miss Genevieve, 'but at this moment, I'm going down to the lobby to be sure of catching the New York detectives.'

'I'll come with you,' said Daisy.

Lambert was seated in the lobby. Anyone but Daisy would have assumed he was reading the *New York Times*, but she knew he was just hiding behind it to keep an anxious eye on the exit in case she tried to evade him. He visibly relaxed when she appeared.

As Miss Genevieve stumped past him on her way to her favourite seat, she observed loudly, 'Has that young man no business to attend to?'

Blushing, the federal agent shrank behind his newspaper.

Miss Cabot had brought her knitting, one of a pair of mittens, and while they awaited events she explained to Daisy how she created the snowflake pattern. Daisy hoped she looked as if she were listening. Actually, she was recalling the reasons Lambert had given why the police might suspect her of shooting Carmody. Now that her second meeting with Sergeant Gilligan was surely immin-ent, her nerves were twitching. She was quite glad to have the redoubtable Miss Genevieve at her side.

They did not have long to wait. Gilligan arrived, followed through the swinging doors by his retinue, Detective O'Rourke and the large plain clothes man, whose name Daisy thought was Larssen.

Gilligan marched straight towards the reception desk, but O'Rourke scanned the lobby, saw Daisy, and tapped the sergeant on the shoulder. 'There's the dame we want, Sergeant,' Daisy heard him say.

'The *lady*, O'Rourke, the lady!' Gilligan snapped. 'Let's remember the lady's husband is one of the higher-ups "over there".' He advanced on Daisy with a would-be ingratiating smile. Someone must have given him an exaggerated idea of Alec's importance. 'Good morning, ma'am.'

Before Daisy could respond, Miss Genevieve put her oar in: 'So you made sergeant at last, Gilligan!'

Gilligan swung towards her, his expression changing to one of dismay amounting almost to alarm. 'Miss Cabot? Rats!' he muttered.

'Miss Genevieve, if you please. My sister is Miss Cabot.' She waved regally.

'Delighted, I'm sure,' twittered Miss Cabot.

'Don't tell me they've put *you* in charge of the investigation into Otis Carmody's death?'

The sergeant bridled but sounded resigned. 'Yes, ma'am. At least, the DA's Office is on the case, too.'

'And the Justice Department, I hear.'

'That isn't in the papers!' Gilligan scowled at Daisy.

'Not yet,' said Miss Genevieve pointedly, 'but I'm still in the business, you know. I keep my ear to the ground. I hear things.'

'Rats!'

Miss Genevieve's smile made Daisy think of a Cheshire cat with stolen cream on its whiskers. 'I'm not on the crime beat any longer, to be sure. I have no *obligation* to turn over what I find out to an editor.'

'I guess not, ma'am.'

'At present I'm inclined to keep my knowledge to myself, for the sake of my young friend, Mrs Fletcher. Of course, I may change my mind.'

Daisy did not rate Gilligan high on the evolutionary ladder, but a hint so broad was not beyond his comprehension.

'There's sure no need to change your mind, Miss Genevieve, no reason at all. I just wanna go over what Mrs Fletcher saw again, case maybe she's remembered sumpin else, and then we'll go downtown so she can check out the mug book.'

'Oh no!' said Miss Genevieve sharply. 'Police headquarters is no place for a gently bred young lady.'

'Sure ain't!' Larssen agreed.

The sergeant glared at him. 'OK, Larssen, you can go get the book, pronto. And make it snappy.'

As the blond giant hurried off, looking martyred, Gilligan glanced around the lobby. It wasn't exactly busy, but a few people were coming and going, and Kevin was leaning against the wall at the corner near his elevator, keeping a watchful eye on proceedings.

'This is too public,' Gilligan grunted. 'We'll go up to your room, Mrs Fletcher.'

'Oh no!' Miss Genevieve objected again. A glint in her eye, she went on with a primness quite foreign to her, 'Most improper, Sergeant. Mrs Fletcher may be a married woman, but she is young and pretty.'

'Spare my blushes!' Daisy uttered, trying not to laugh.

She wasn't at all surprised when Miss Genevieve next suggested, in a tone as martyred as Larssen's face had been, 'You'd better all come up to our suite, I guess, so that Ernestine and I can play chaperone.'

'Geez, save me from nosy old maids!' Gilligan muttered, obviously no more deceived than Daisy. Thoroughly disgruntled, he gave in. 'OK, your place, then, if that's the way you wannit. Course, I'll hafta bring my other witness along. Hey, you, Lambert! I wanna word with you.'

'Oh dear,' said Miss Cabot, at last breaking her appalled silence.

Miss Genevieve was momentarily disconcerted. However, by the time Gilligan gave her a sly glance to see how she reacted to his adding Lambert to her invitation to her suite, she looked intrigued.

Disappointed, he turned back to Lambert, who stammered, 'Who, me?' – apparently his standard response when addressed unexpectedly.

'You gotta twin brother?' Gilligan asked nastily.

As Lambert jumped up and came over, Miss Genevieve said to Daisy, 'That young nonentity was a witness, too? What a coincidence! I suppose he was also visiting an editor, though he failed to mention to me any ambition in the writing line.' She bent a severe frown upon him.

'Excuse me, ma'am,' he apologized. 'I don't want to intrude—'

'Come on, come on,' Gilligan interrupted. 'Let's get this show on the road.'

At Miss Genevieve's halting pace, which slowed

deliberately when Gilligan started to chivvy, they went across to the elevators. Kevin jumped to attention.

'Going up?' he asked eagerly, no doubt hoping to glean a few grains of information.

O'Rourke opened his mouth for the first time. 'This here's the young shaver whose sister was chambermaid to Carmody, Sergeant.'

'That right? Gave you some trouble, din't he?'

'He didn't have to put the screws on, Sarge! Bridey tole him everything right off.'

'Doncha get fresh with *me*,' Gilligan snarled, reaching out to cuff the boy.

Daisy put her hand on his arm. 'I'm sure he's only telling the truth, Sergeant. Bridget was eager to put her knowledge at the service of the police.'

'Oh yeah?' He stared at her. 'Whadda *you* know about it?'

'She's my chambermaid, too.'

'That don't mean—'

'Come on, come on, Sergeant!' said Miss Genevieve, who with her sister had entered the lift by now. 'Let's get this show on the road.'

'Aw, the heck with it!' Gilligan surrendered, to Daisy's relief. She didn't want him delving into just how much Bridget had told her.

'Third floor, please, Kevin,' she said, joining the Misses Cabot.

'Going up!' he said in his usual jaunty manner and winked at her. The men crowded in after her and Kevin shut the gates with a double clang.

'Geez, I'm glad Larssen ain't in here, too,' said O'Rourke as the laden lift creaked upward.

'The other detective?' ventured Lambert, squeezed into a corner. 'Where did he go?'

'To get the mug book,' Daisy informed him, 'so that you and I can try to identify the fugitive.'

'I never saw him! I swear, Sergeant, I never saw his face!'

'Then you won't reckernize any of the shots, will you?' Gilligan grunted.

'Third floor,' Kevin announced.

The Misses Cabot's sitting room was large enough to accommodate everyone easily, but by no means large enough to afford Gilligan any privacy he might have hoped for. Miss Genevieve, installed by the fireplace, listened avidly to every word as he took Daisy through her evidence again. This time he started with the overheard argument.

'Word for word, near as you can remember, including the rude word the dame used.'

'Cover your ears, sister,' advised Miss Genevieve, making no move to cover her own.

'"You bastard,"' said Daisy, '"I wouldn't come back to you if you made a million dollars." Then Carmody said, "If I made a million dollars, you still wouldn't squeeze one red cent out of me." More or less.'

'He said, "More or less"?'

'No, Sergeant, *I* say that's more or less what *they* said.'

'More or less!' said Gilligan in disgust. 'It can'ta been Carmody, though, it was this guy Bender he was blackmailing said that.'

'I still think it was Carmody,' Daisy persisted.

'Sure, more or less!' the sergeant jeered.

Daisy wanted to point out that, considering what Bridget had overheard, it made perfect sense for Carmody to have been the speaker. But she didn't want to get the chambermaid into hot water. Besides, Gilligan had probably bullied the poor girl into changing her story to fit his preconceived notions.

Miss Genevieve put her oar in. 'You believe Carmody was blackmailing Mr Bender?' she asked.

'Sure thing!' said Gilligan. 'There's enough stuff in Carmody's papers up in his room to worry Barton Bender plenty.'

'Such as?'

In the face of Miss Genevieve's scepticism, the sergeant was too eager to prove his point to remember discretion. 'He owns a whole lotta tenements, slum property, that he's been paying off the city inspectors not to see they're falling down. Not that that's any big deal,' he added hastily.

The inspectors must be Tammany appointees, like Gilligan, Daisy guessed.

'His tenants don't like it, they can go somewhere else.' Miss Genevieve's sarcasm was obvious.

'Yeah, and he ain't above encouraging 'em. Gotta gang of hoodlums he sends round to evict troublemakers, and he don't care who gets hurt. Well, troublemakers, I got no beef with that, but them that's a bit behind with the rent . . . The public don't like reading about widders and orphans getting roughed up. That gets in the papers, the Police Department's gonna sit up and take notice.'

'I should hope so!' Daisy exclaimed.

Gilligan shrugged. 'It's a free country.'

'Sister, may I remove my hands from my ears now?' Miss Cabot asked plaintively.

With an impatient nod to her sister, Miss Genevieve said,

'Unpleasant, but I can't see Bender killing to save his reputation. Isn't he wealthy enough to hire the best lawyers, and to pay his toughs to take the rap without splitting on him? Murder is a whole different ball game. It would raise the stakes too high for his liking.'

'You been talking to the guy?' Gilligan demanded.

'No, but that sort of person generally runs true to type. You've talked to him, what did you think of him?' She paused. 'You *have* talked to him, haven't you, Sergeant?'

'No,' Gilligan admitted sourly. 'I didn't get to Carmody's room till last night. Bender was out – some nightclub his housekeeper said, she didn't know where. I left a man to watch, but he didn't come home. I guess he musta gone on to Mrs Carmody's hotel room, and we ain't got a line on that yet. I got men out going round the hotels. But messing with his tenants ain't all Carmody had on him.'

'No?'

'There's some funny business with mortgage loans on his properties. I turned it over to our fraud people. If it's what it looks like to me, he'll go down for a stretch anyways, even we can't pin the murder on him though I ain't giving up on that, not by a long shot!'

'You'd do better to stick to what Carmody was digging out about Tammany's business,' Miss Genevieve declared. 'What did you find in his papers on that subject?'

Gilligan turned sullen. 'You know I can't discuss evidence. Give a dame an inch and she wants all hell. I didn't oughta've told you nuttin and I ain't gonna tell no more.'

Miss Genevieve had already induced the detective to reveal far more than Daisy would have dared hope for. 'Eugene Cannon' must have been a first-rate crime reporter.

Daisy hadn't had to lift a finger to obtain masses of information about Carmody's wife and her lover. She wished she could meet them. One learnt so much by actually talking to a person, but at least she had plenty of food for thought.

Leisure for thought she had not.

'OK, let's get on with your story, Mrs Fletcher,' Gilligan growled. 'Maybe you'll remember sumpin useful this time around.'

CHAPTER 10

When Daisy reached the point in her story where Lambert erupted on to the scene of the crime brandishing a pistol, Miss Genevieve glanced at the young man with a new interest. Possibly, her look said, he might be worthy of further acquaintance. His subsequent downing at the hands of Mr Thorwald brought a snort of disbelief.

'Sigurd Thorwald tackled him? I remember him as a copy-boy, and he was a pedantic old fusspot even then. He brought down that great lummox? There's more to the old geezer than I thought, and even less to the young one.'

'I didn't expect him to jump me,' Lambert said sulkily. 'Besides, I lost my glasses.'

'*And* your gun,' said Daisy, 'which I caught, by a miracle.' She was about to continue when someone knocked at the door.

'Oh dear,' said Miss Cabot, dropping her knitting, 'who can that be? Were we expecting visitors this morning, sister?'

'Whatever our expectations, sister, we seem to have collected quite a crowd,' observed Miss Genevieve, as Detective O'Rourke, who had remained standing in the archway to the foyer, turned to open the door. 'The more, the merrier. Who is it?' she called. 'Come in, come in!'

'Sorry to disturb you, ma'am. The elevator boy told me Detective Sergeant Gilligan is here.'

'Who . . . ? Oh, young Rosenblatt! You followed in your father's footsteps, didn't you? I'll never forget the time he brought you into court – eleven or twelve, you were—'

'*Please*, ma'am!'

Miss Genevieve grinned maliciously. 'Oho, we mustn't upset your dignity. You're on the Carmody case, I take it, looking out for Tammany's interests.'

'Looking out for a murderer,' Rosenblatt corrected her. 'We have to clear this up before the election. It would be almost as bad to have the press saying we're incompetent as to have Tammany involved. Which they aren't,' he hastened to add.

'Well, then, you'd better get on with it. Don't mind me.'

Rosenblatt nervously smoothed his sleek, fair hair, thinning a little on top. 'Good morning, Miss Cabot, Mrs Fletcher,' he said, with a curt nod for Lambert. 'Sergeant? What's going on?'

'I was gonna take another look at Carmody's room, sir, and then escort Mrs Fletcher downtown personal, her being a foreigner. But Miss Genevieve said—'

'OK, OK!'

'Detective Larssen went to get the mug book, and I was just going over Mrs Fletcher's story with her, see if she come up with sumpin new.'

'Go ahead.'

Daisy went ahead. The only detail she was able to add to her previous description of the fugitive was that she rather thought he had been wearing an overcoat.

'Colour?' asked Gilligan.

'Not black,' said Daisy, 'and not that new shade of blue that's so fashionable at the moment. I suppose it must have been brown or grey. Or navy, possibly. No, not navy.'

'Not navy! That's a great help,' Rosenblatt said sarcastically.

'So we gotta look out for a man in a derby and a brown or grey overcoat. How many d'ya figure there are in Noo York, Mr Rosenblatt?'

'It might have been a disguise,' proposed Lambert. Rosencrantz and Guildenstern looked at him in silent disgust.

'Yeah, sure. You come up with any new ideas about where the shot came from, Mrs Fletcher? It coulda come from behind you?'

'Yes, but not from Mr Thorwald. He was quite close to me. I'm sure I'd have known if he had fired.'

'Even if his gun had a silencer?'

'Yes,' said Daisy, with somewhat less certainty.

'Thorwald!' Miss Genevieve exclaimed scornfully. 'Talk about clutching at straws. That man wouldn't have the guts to . . . though he *did* tackle Lambert,' she reminded herself. 'Still, what possible motive could Thorwald have?'

'He was with me for at least an hour beforehand,' Daisy pointed out. 'He had no reason to know Carmody would be there. Carmody worked for Pascoli, not Mr Thorwald.'

'No interest in politics,' Miss Genevieve confirmed. 'Words were always his passion, "Words, words, words", no matter what the matter.'

Gilligan gazed at her blankly. 'A word's a word. You mean Thorwald had words with Carmody?'

'No, Sergeant, I mean nothing of the sort.'

'Sergeant Gilligan,' Rosenblatt broke in, 'you better check with Pascoli whether Thorwald had anything to do with Carmody or expressed any interest, but I'd say you're barking up the wrong tree. Mr Lambert's another matter.' He turned to Lambert, who shrank.

'It wasn't me!'

'Maybe it wasn't, but there's this Washington connection we have to follow up. I've put in a telephone call to Washington to check your credentials.'

Lambert looked relieved. 'Oh, that's OK then.'

'I'm afraid not, not the way things have been in DC. One of the Harding crowd Carmody blew the whistle on could have hired you to put him away and used his own or his pals' influence to get you taken on as an agent, for cover.'

'I can't help feeling,' Daisy murmured, 'that they would have chosen someone with decent eyesight and a better aim.'

'It wasn't like that at all,' Lambert protested. 'My dad's in insurance, see, and I didn't want to go into insurance. I always wanted to be a federal agent, ever since I was a kid. My dad knows Mr Hoover, so he—'

'Pulled strings. Yeah, maybe, but it'll all have to be checked out, which could take a while. I'll have to ask you not to leave New York, Mr Lambert, and to notify me or Sergeant Gilligan if you move from this hotel.'

'Oh, I don't mind doing that. I can't leave before Mr Fletcher gets here, anyway.'

'What?' demanded Miss Genevieve. 'Why not?'

Daisy hastened to explain before anyone else could get their version in. 'I've been involved in one or two – well, maybe three or four – of my husband's cases. Apparently his superiors at the Yard saw fit to advise Mr Hoover to set a watchdog on to me to make sure I didn't get mixed up in anything over here.'

'In vain!' Miss Genevieve clapped her hands. 'My dear Mrs Fletcher, I just knew we were kindred souls. One of these days, you must tell me all about everything. But right now, I have to say the role of watchdog seems to me far more appropriate for Mr Lambert than that of hired assassin.'

Everyone stared at Lambert. His ears turned red and he looked like an overgrown schoolboy.

'Yeah, sure,' said Gilligan in disgust. 'OK, let's have what you saw and heard over again. Maybe if you think real hard, you'll remember noticing sumpin Mrs Fletcher didn't. Or even think of some other guy that coulda croaked Carmody.'

'Orlando,' interrupted Miss Cabot. 'Orlando, sister?'

'Who's this bird Orlando?' asked the sergeant suspiciously. 'Sounds like an Eyetie, like that Pascoli. I figured he was in it someplace. You know sumpin we don't, ma'am?'

'Orlando,' Miss Genevieve announced, 'is a city in Florida. Which is south of New York, not in the West.'

Gilligan was indignant. 'I know where Florida is!'

'I dare say.' Miss Genevieve sounded not altogether convinced. 'However, the latter part of my remark was addressed to my sister. She has been trying to recall where Mr Pitt told us he comes from.'

'The guy that had an argument with Carmody in the lobby? What he put in the register's Eugene City, Oregon. That's a hick town out west someplace, I guess.'

'Oregon is just south of Washington,' said Rosenblatt. 'That right, sir? Coulda swore it was out west someplace.'

'The state of Washington, not DC,' the Deputy DA explained impatiently. 'Miss Genevieve, may I ask why Wilbur Pitt should have told you where he came from?'

'The subject arose naturally in relation to his literary opus, which I understood to be a more or less fictionalized version of his life in the wilds of the West.'

'He was a cowboy?' asked Gilligan with sudden interest. 'That'd explain why he was packing heat.'

Daisy must have looked completely blank, because Lambert leaned over to whisper, 'Carrying a gun.'

'Was he?' Miss Genevieve wanted to know.

'Geez, ma'am, how could he of shot Carmody if he wasn't?'

'You have no reason to suppose he did shoot Carmody. As it happens he had been a farmer, logger and miner, leading, as far as I could gather, a life of considerable hardship and singular dullness.'

'Rats! What did he have to write a book about, then?'

'Not much. He described it as Proustian.'

'Huh?'

'Since he can hardly have meant that it concerns the doings of Parisian high society, I imagine he referred to Proust's custom of describing objects and sensations in obsessively minute detail.'

Daisy was impressed. She had once tackled Proust but given up after a very few pages.

'Geez, an intellectooal!' said Gilligan dismissively.

'So you don't believe Carmody's cousin was involved, Sergeant? I'm inclined to—'

'Wait a minute,' Rosenblatt interrupted. 'He told you he was Carmody's cousin?'

'Not exactly,' Miss Genevieve said cautiously, 'but I certainly have the impression they were related.'

'You didn't tell me that, Sergeant! What did Pitt have to say for himself?'

'I ain't grilled him yet, sir.' He cast an accusing glare at Miss Genevieve's bland face. '*I* didn't know they was cousins, so we ain't been looking for him pertickler. He's not the only guy had a beef with Carmody, not by a long shot.'

Daisy couldn't help thinking that if she could work out, from Bridget's report of the quarrel, that the men were related, the detective should have done likewise. It was his job, after all. Maybe he'd been sidetracked by assuming that Willie was William, not Wilbur, she thought charitably, but he ought at least to have been looking for a relative.

'How right you are, Sergeant,' said Miss Genevieve affably. 'Wilbur Pitt was by no means the only person to dislike Carmody, and many had far better reason to hate his guts.'

'Oh sister!'

'Don't be so mealy-mouthed, sister, or cover your ears again.'

'Oh dear!'

'If you want my opinion, young man,' Miss Genevieve continued in the serene certainty that Rosenblatt was going to listen, willy-nilly, 'this homicide has all the hallmarks of an attempt to warn Carmody off, which went wrong. Which of the Tammany bosses did he have his claws into?'

Daisy listened in admiration as the ex-crime reporter winkled the information she wanted out of the reluctant Deputy District Attorney. All Carmody's notes on his investigations had been found in his room, and Rosenblatt ended up telling Miss Genevieve exactly who was named in those papers. However, all the names were unfamiliar to Daisy, and she soon lost interest in the subsequent discussion of who was most likely to have sent a thug to scare Carmody off.

Sergeant Gilligan wasn't listening either. He had proceeded with his original intent to take Lambert through his story again. Unfortunately, Lambert had been thinking.

'And I think, just before Mr Thorwald knocked off my glasses, I noticed the man Mrs Fletcher was running after wasn't wearing an overcoat. He just had a short coat, a suit coat or sport coat, I guess.'

'I think he had on an overcoat,' said Daisy.

'But you ain't neither of you one hundred per cent sure,' Gilligan snarled, throwing down his hopefully poised pencil. 'Could this guy maybe have been wearing a short overcoat, like an automobile coat?'

'Maybe,' Daisy and Lambert chorused doubtfully.

'Aw, what the heck! It wouldn't help much anyways 'less you was both dead certain he was running around in scarlet pyjamas.'

Daisy had to stifle a giggle at a vision of a man strolling through the streets in scarlet pyjamas and a bowler hat.

'In that case,' said Lambert seriously, 'he would have changed before leaving the building, or he would definitely have been noticed.'

'You don't say! Wise guy!'

'Since he wasn't wearing scarlet pyjamas,' Daisy said soothingly, 'we don't need to worry about it. But do you know, now I come to think of it, I'm sure he was wearing boots, not shoes. He made too much noise on the stairs for ordinary shoes.'

'Whaddaya know?' marvelled Gilligan. 'What we gotta find is a guy in a derby and boots that prob'ly left Noo York City on the first train.'

'If he crossed state lines to escape prosecution for homicide,' Lambert pointed out with undeterred enthusiasm, 'it's a federal offence and you can call us in.'

'Just what I need, another bunch of gover'ment men muscling in on my case. You just ferget what I said about trains, bud. I'm gonna solve this business right here on home territory, and before the election next week. I'm not about to let the Hearst papers make any more cracks about the boys in blue. Where the heck is Larssen with that mug book?'

He went off to confer with Detective O'Rourke.

'What are the Hearst papers?' Daisy asked Lambert. 'Someone mentioned them before.'

'Geez, I don't know that much about it. I guess it's local politics.'

Miss Genevieve had caught Daisy's question and interrupted a vigorous argument with Rosenblatt to answer it. 'William Randolph Hearst is the proprietor of numerous major newspapers including some in New York, not to mention the International News Service, and a company producing "newsreels" for movie theatres.'

'Oh yes, I believe he owns several English magazines.'

'Very likely. He is also a Democratic politician, but he is bitterly opposed to the way Tammany Hall runs New York. Partly pique, of course. He stood for mayor of the city and governor of the state but lost the elections, and later failed even to win the Democratic nomination for governor. His papers regularly sensationalize anything they can find to the detriment of Tammany. He'd have been delighted with the course of Carmody's investigations.'

'I'm surprised Carmody took his information to Mr Pascoli, then,' Daisy said. '*Town Talk* doesn't belong to Mr Hearst, does it? I'm pretty sure he doesn't own *Abroad*.'

'No. I shouldn't be surprised if Hearst's political passions overcame his instinct for a scoop and he encouraged Carmody to disseminate his dirt as widely as possible. Besides, a weekly has a different readership from a daily, and goes into more depth, rather than concentrating on sensation.'

'Or maybe Carmody was double-crossing Hearst,' Rosenblatt suggested. 'Maybe he had promised Hearst an exclusive and went behind his back to Pascoli. Hearst wouldn't take kindly to that.'

'But I hardly think he'd resort to physical means to show Carmody the error of his ways,' Miss Genevieve retorted. 'All he had to do to retaliate was stop Carmody ever writing again for any of his publications. You can't get Tammany off the hook so easily.'

She and the Deputy DA resumed their argument about the likelihood of each of Carmody's targets having sent a thug to dissuade him from publishing his discoveries.

Meanwhile Gilligan had sent O'Rourke off on some errand. He returned to Daisy and Lambert. Whereas he would probably have responded to a question with a justifiable refusal to say where the detective had gone, he succumbed without a struggle to Daisy's enquiring look.

'Sent him to see if Pitt's in, and if not, to search his room. That's off the record.' Glowering at the oblivious

Rosenblatt, he complained, 'Geez, I'd never get nuttin done was I to follow every nitpicking rule. I can't do everything all at once. First you gotta figure out who the suspects are and then you gotta find 'em.'

'And it's less than twenty-four hours since Carmody died,' said Daisy sympathetically. 'Besides, you seem to have a huge cast of suspects.'

'Yeah. Me, I wouldn't put this bird Pitt among 'em. I mean, who's gonna start shooting over a bunch of bits of paper with words scribbled on 'em?'

Daisy rather thought words on paper had started more than one war, though she couldn't call to mind any precise instance. In any case, Pitt's reminiscences seemed unlikely to contain anything inflammatory, and if they did, Carmody would have shot him, not vice versa.

On the other hand . . . But her reflections were interrupted by a knock on the door and Miss Cabot's inevitable 'Oh dear!'

Gilligan jumped up. 'I'll get it, ma'am. That better be Larssen or . . . Hey, where you bin, Larssen?'

'Downtown to get the mug book, Sergeant. You sent me, remember?'

'Smart-ass! You wanna get busted back to patrolman? OK, Mrs Fletcher, Lambert, lessee can you pick out the guy you saw.'

'Me?' Lambert protested. 'I didn't see his face.'

'Maybe sumpin'll jog your memory.' Gilligan took the heavy tome over to Miss Genevieve's desk.

Daisy sat down at the desk, with Lambert leaning over her shoulder. They studied lean, mean faces and broad, brutal faces, coldly intelligent or piggishly stupid, some smooth-shaven, some with several days' growth of beard. Several were nondescript, but not in quite the same way the man on the stairs had been nondescript, Daisy was sure. She tried to picture each topped with a bowler hat.

Her concentration was not assisted by Lambert's mutinous mutter in her ear, over and over: 'But I *didn't* see his face.'

They were nearing the end of the book when again there came a knocking at the door, a peremptory rat-tat-tat.

'O'Rourke's found sumpin!' said Gilligan hopefully, striding towards the foyer as Larssen opened the door.

Daisy heard a babble of voices, one shrill and female and vaguely familiar. She and Lambert turned to watch the sergeant.

'Who . . . ? What . . . ?' he said in bewilderment.

'Patrolman Hicks, Sergeant. I nabbed 'em,' a proud voice announced. 'They was trying to sneak into Carmody's room!'

CHAPTER 11

Sergeant Gilligan backed into the Cabots' sitting room. After him swirled a petite woman in a scarlet coat trimmed with white fur, and a scarlet cloche with white feathers – definitely the hat Daisy had seen going down in the lift. Her scolding voice Daisy identified as belonging to the woman who had shouted at Carmody. Framed by the luxurious fur, her delicate features were twisted now in anger, but expertly made up and probably very pretty when good tempered, or in repose. She carried a large lizard-skin handbag, no doubt full of cosmetics.

Half a pace behind her came a man in a calf-length grey overcoat with an astrakhan collar. Of middle height, he had a plump, overfed face presently greasy with sweat. He was worried, even afraid. The hat he carried was a homburg, not a bowler, Daisy noted.

Behind the pair towered Patrolman Hicks, beaming. He was the uniformed policeman Daisy had last seen, looking bored, idly strolling along the passage outside her hotel room.

'This is an outrage!' screeched the woman.

Rosenblatt moved forward. 'What's going on? I'm Rosenblatt, Deputy District Attorney in charge of the Carmody case,' he explained when the couple and the patrolman all looked at him askance. 'What's up, ma'am?'

They all started talking at once.

'I was guarding Carmody's door, sir,' Hicks reported, saluting, 'like I was sent to, and—'

'I am Otis Carmody's wife,' Mrs Carmody affirmed icily. 'I just wanted to retrieve—'

'Don't say another word, honey baby,' bleated her gentleman friend, presumably Barton Bender. 'I'll telephone my—'

'Hold it, hold it!' said Rosenblatt. 'There's no need for lawyers, sir. I'm not planning anything but a friendly little chat here. Excuse me, ma'am, I better take the patrolman's report first so he can go back to his post.'

'I was guarding Carmody's room, sir,' Hicks repeated stolidly, 'like I was sent to, and these guys come along and the dame takes a key outta her purse and sticks it in the keyhole and starts to turn it. So I tells 'em the room's closed by police orders for investigation of a homicide and I gotta take 'em down to Centre Street. I says nice and polite they can come quiet or I can get out the cuffs, and they come all right but quiet ain't the word! Geez, that dame that looks like a wind'd blow her away ain't never stopped cussing me out since . . . OK, sir, I guess you don'wanna hear all that.'

'You can write it all down in your report. How did you end up here instead of headquarters?'

'The elevator boy tol' me Sergeant Gilligan's here, sir.'

'And what I want to know,' put in the sergeant, 'is how come the key was already in the lock when you stopped 'em if you was standing guard?'

'Geez, Sergeant,' said Hicks with an injured look, 'if I'd've stood right by the door alla time, there wouldn't no one have tried to get in. They'd've seen me and turned around right when they stepped out of the elevator and gone back down and we wouldn't never have knowed who they was. I went a ways along the corridor and waited where they couldn't see me but I could keep an eye on things, see.'

In the linen room – Daisy was prepared to bet – chatting with Bridget.

'OK,' Gilligan said grudgingly, 'you done good, I guess. You better get back up there pronto before someone else tries it on.'

'Did anyone else have a key to your husband's room that you know of, ma'am?' Rosenblatt asked.

'Not that I know of.' Mrs Carmody blinked hard and dabbed at her eyes with a corner of a lacy handkerchief, careful not to blot her eye-black. 'Oh, this is all so turrible! You must think I'm awful, telling off that poor policeman when he was only doing his dooty, but this has all been turribly hard on my nerves.'

'Won't you sit down and tell me about it, ma'am?'

Rosenblatt ushered Mrs Carmody to the far end of the room from the desk where Daisy sat, to her annoyance. The woman didn't seem to notice the presence of unofficial others, too busy wiping away tears, real or pretended.

Bender, however, glanced around the room and scowled. He opened his mouth as if to protest but thought better of it. Gem-laden gold rings flashed on his plump fingers as he took a large, purple-monogrammed handkerchief from his pocket and blotted his forehead. He hung his homburg on the hat rack in the foyer, then took off his overcoat, revealing a corpulent figure clad in a suit of grey-and-lavender check, and a purple bow tie with a flashy diamond pin.

Meekly, he followed his honey baby.

Gilligan went after them. As soon as all four had their backs turned, Daisy abandoned the mug book and Lambert, and tiptoed swiftly across to the Misses Cabot, who were much closer to the scene of the action. She sat down in the chair vacated by Rosenblatt.

Miss Cabot leaned towards her, about to speak. Miss Genevieve put her finger to her lips.

Miss Cabot mouthed a silent 'oh dear!' Her knitting needles clicked on.

'Such a turrible shock,' Mrs Carmody was saying, as she sank gracefully into the chair Rosenblatt held for her, 'finding out in the papers this morning Otis was dead.'

'We tried to notify you last night at your hotel, ma'am,' said Rosenblatt, 'and again this morning. You weren't there.'

'We went to a party, me and Mr Bender, that didn't break up till daylight. He persuaded me to take a drive out in the country and get breakfast.'

'Where was that, sir?'

'What does it matter?' Bender blustered. 'The papers said Carmody was shot at midday yesterday.'

'So what's the big deal?' Gilligan demanded. 'Whaddaya got against telling Mr Rosenblatt where you was this morning?'

'I don't know exactly. We went with a crowd, in a caravan. I just followed along.'

'Who else was there?' Rosenblatt asked.

'Uh . . .' A long pause, then Bender said cautiously, 'I couldn't exactly give you their names.'

Gilligan was instantly suspicious. 'Why not?'

'Who was there, honey baby?'

'Red and Billie, HJ, Mona, Jerry, I think, and wasn't that girl they called Midge with him? That's all the names I can think of.' Mrs Carmody waved a careless hand. 'I didn't know the others.'

'And you don't know their last names? Telephone numbers?' Rosenblatt suggested. Bender and Mrs Carmody both shook their heads. 'How do you keep in touch?'

'Oh, they weren't *friends*, just casual acquaintances. People we met at the party, weren't they, Bart?'

'Who gave the party?'

The pair gazed at each other blankly. They had steered themselves on to a reef, though Daisy couldn't quite see why Rosenblatt had bothered to chase them there.

Mrs Carmody abandoned the sinking ship. 'They were friends of Mr Bender's. I never caught their last name.'

Bender gave her a look at once wounded and forgiving. 'Uh . . . Not exactly friends. See, things are pretty casual in our crowd . . .'

'So you don't know their names.' Rosenblatt shook his head. 'But of course you know their address, since you took Mrs Carmody there. No? Look, why don't you just admit Mrs Carmody spent the night at your house?'

'The heck she did!' Gilligan exclaimed. 'I had a coupla men watching that place, and if they was there, they'da followed 'em here. What I figure is he's got an apartment that he takes his fancy women to, so his servants can't tell tales. I'da found it if I'da had another coupla days.'

'Fancy woman! Barton Bender, are you going to sit there and let a cop insult me?'

'No, no, honey baby. Don't you worry your pretty head. The truth is, Mr Rosenblatt, I did rent an apartment specially for Mrs Carmody when she left her husband. She didn't wanna let him know so she took a hotel room, too. It's not a crime to take a hotel room and not stay there.'

'Nor to spend the night with a lady friend.'

'I hadda try and pertect her good name, now, didn't I? You gotta unnerstand, Elva's real sensitive.'

'And you're ready to lie to the police to protect her feelings.'

'Sure, sure, no harm done.'

'Izzat so?' Gilligan broke in. 'I guess you'd be ready to do anything for the little lady, huh? Even croak her husband!'

'No!' cried Mrs Carmody. 'You didn't, Bart, did you?'

'No, of course I didn't, honey baby. Not that I wouldn't've if you'da been in danger from him, but he wasn't giving you any trouble a good lawyer couldn't straighten out.'

'He was giving you trouble, then, Mrs Carmody?' said Rosenblatt.

'Nothing serious,' she said quickly, 'like Barton says. We had a bit of a tiff, Otis and me, but we'd have patched things up. A girl can have her fling, same as a man. You know what it's like being married, all ups and downs but till death you part.'

'And death has you parted!' put in Gilligan. 'Mighty convenient, ain't it?'

Bender, who had gaped flabbergasted at Mrs Carmody's

last statement, found his voice. 'But honey baby, you're going to marry me!'

'So we understood,' said Rosenblatt. 'There was talk of divorce, not reconciliation.'

'Howdya know that?' shrilled Mrs Carmody. 'I wouldn't never have let Otis divorce me.'

'Maybe not. What were you looking for in your husband's room?'

'We didn't even get in,' she objected.

'Some stuff Elva left there,' said Bender at the same moment.

'No, it wasn't either. It was some of Otis's papers Bart said I'd need now he was dead. I dunno what, he was gonna look through everything and pick them out for me.'

'Gonna go through Carmody's papers, was you? Course, you wasn't looking for the stuff he got on you, no sirree. Where was you lunchtime yesterday?'

'Business meeting,' Bender said promptly. 'Started at eleven and we was still at it at twelve so we sent out for lunch. Didn't knock off till after two.'

'Who was there? Let's have names and addresses, and let's not try on any funny business about not knowing.'

Bender didn't try on any funny business. He gave the names and addresses of three men, one of which made Miss Genevieve raise her eyebrows.

Gilligan was impressed. 'Geez, Henry Morgan! The banker's son, huh?'

'Yeah, he just graduated Harvard and they got him starting at the bottom as a messenger, fifteen bucks a week. He wants to spread his wings a little, only nacheral. I got a bit of property he's interested in,' said Bender importantly.

'Waal, we'll check it out, but I guess if you was with him, you didn't shoot Carmody.'

'I'd have told you if he was the man I saw,' said Daisy indignantly.

Gilligan ignored her. 'Still, if you're swimming with the big fish, you don't want nuttin to spoil the deal, like maybe stories in the papers, like Carmody was writing. I figure you musta hired it done.'

'You're nuts!'

'Oh I am, am I?' Gilligan said nastily. Standing up, he loomed threateningly over Bender. 'Well, lemme tell you, *Mister* Bender, we know you got toughs on your payroll and we know who they are. I'm gonna pull 'em in and grill 'em and sooner or later one of 'em's gonna crack and spill the works to save himself some grief. And meantime, *Mister* Bender, I'm gonna take you downtown and try if we can improve your memory down at headquarters.' He signalled to Larssen, who lumbered over.

'But . . .' bleated Bender.

'You gonna come quietly? Don't wanna scare the ladies, do you?'

'I want to call my lawyer!'

'Now, now,' Gilligan reproved him, 'ain't no need for that. You ain't under arrest . . . not yet. I just wanna ask you a few questions where it's peaceful and quiet, that's all.'

'Elva!'

'I'll call him, Bart. What's his name?'

'Macpherson, James P. Macpherson.'

'See, your memory's improving already.' Gilligan put a heavy hand on Bender's shoulder.

'OK, I'm coming, I'm coming!'

'I'll telephone Mr Macpherson, Bart. Right away.' As the sergeant and his minion bore off the hapless man, Mrs Carmody jumped up, agitated. 'I never knew he did it, I swear.'

'I'm sure you didn't, ma'am,' Rosenblatt soothed her, adding with some asperity, 'that is, I dare say he didn't. Our good sergeant is inclined to jump the gun.'

But, Daisy noticed, he made no move to stop Gilligan.

'I must call his lawyer. Poor Bart. Will they use the "third degree"?'

'Of course not, Mrs Carmody. Not on a prominent citizen with a good lawyer. So there's no hurry for you to telephone. Just sit down, and maybe we can clear this all up here and now.'

Once more dabbing her eyes, Mrs Carmody sat. 'If he did it, I didn't know nothing about it,' she declared again.

'Did Mr Bender ever make threats against your husband?'

'Oh no, not seriously. Of course he's real sweet on me, so he was madder'n a hornets' nest when Otis wouldn't do the right thing by me. But he was talking mostly 'bout what his lawyer'd do to Otis, not his boys.'

'Mostly?' insinuated Rosenblatt.

'Well, he did say Otis'd change his mind in a hurry if he was to set the boys on him, but I said he mustn't and he promised he wouldn't. I still loved Otis, see.' Mrs Carmody sniffed delicately and dabbed again. 'I wouldn't've wanted anything bad to happen to him, however mean he was. I just didn't wanna fritter away my life playing second fiddle to his work. You unnerstand, don't you?' she asked Rosenblatt meltingly.

'Sure. You're only young once, right? A beautiful lady shouldn't waste her youth on—'

'Uh ...' Gilligan reappeared, rather pink in the face. 'Hey, you, Lambert!'

'Who, me?'

'Aw, geez, let's not get into this cross-talk deal again! You finished with that mug book?'

'Er ... I have, but I don't think Mrs Fletcher's gotten quite all the way through. I didn't recognize anyone.'

'I guess Mrs Fletcher better finish up. If you was to reckernize wunna Bender's toughs, ma'am, we'd have him cold.'

Daisy didn't want to return to those beastly faces when she could be listening to Rosenblatt and Mrs Carmody. 'I don't want to delay you,' she said. 'Suppose I give the book to Detective O'Rourke when he comes back, or is he going with you?'

Gilligan looked taken aback, as if he had forgotten O'Rourke's existence. Perhaps he had. 'That'll be fine, ma'am,' he said. 'O'Rourke can bring it back to Centre Street.'

'Shall I tell him that's where you've gone?'

The sergeant's face turned purple, but he reined himself in and merely snapped, 'You can leave that to me, ma'am.'

'Right-oh,' said Daisy, and Gilligan stalked out. Daisy stayed put.

'Who are these people?' Mrs Carmody asked plaintively. Daisy wondered whether she could possibly be so self-centred she actually had not noticed the other inhabitants of the room.

'The residents of this suite,' Rosenblatt explained, 'and a couple of witnesses. If they make you uncomfortable, we can go downtown to talk.'

'Oh no!'

'Not to police headquarters. The District Attorney's offices are in the Criminal Courts Building.'

'Criminal Courts! Oh no! No, let's stay here, but I don't think I got anything else to tell you.'

'Do you know if your husband had any enemies?'

'Enemies,' sneered Mrs Carmody. 'Better ask if he had any friends. That's what he did for a living, make enemies. I can't begin to list them.'

'Who were his friends?' Rosenblatt asked patiently.

'He didn't have any in New York, not that I knew anyway. If I hadn't've gone out and made friends for myself, I'd've never seen anyone.'

'In Washington?'

'There were a coupla guys, couples that we visited with, but I don't think he kept in touch. We'd've maybe exchanged Christmas greetings, you know, like we did with the folks in Chicago. That's where we met, Chicago.'

'Carmody wasn't from Chicago, though?'

'No, he worked there a few years, on the *Herald-American*. He came from some hick town out west, like I come from a hick town back in Iowa.' Mrs Carmody coyly smoothed the fur cuff at her wrist. 'You wouldn't guess it to look at me now, would you?'

'Not in a million years,' said Rosenblatt. 'The *Herald-American*, that's a Hearst paper, isn't it?'

'Huh? Oh, you mean Mr Randolph Hearst owns it? Yeah, could be. Now you come to mention it, Otis mighta mentioned that once. I don't remember for sure, though. Don't quote me!' she giggled.

'Did Carmody keep in touch with his family out west?'

'Just at Christmas. He may've wrote his mother sometimes, I dunno, or his sisters. His dad was a banker, a big
man in town. He went to college, you know, Otis. Not just
a farm college, either. They got a real university out there,
would you believe? I mean, it isn't no Yale or Harvard, but
he was real educated, my Otis.'

Mrs Carmody began to cry in earnest, the first real tears
Daisy had seen. Her tiny hankie proved inadequate. With
aplomb Rosenblatt handed over his own sizeable square,
reminding Daisy of Alec's injunction always to pack spare
handkerchiefs when he travelled on a case. She repressed an
urge to go over and comfort the woman, without great
difficulty as she simply couldn't care much about her.

'He's really gone, isn't he?' Mrs Carmody sniffed. 'I
didn't really realize before, not for real. We had good times,
him and me, back in Chicago. Only then he changed, and
he didn't seem to *want* to give me a good time anymore.'
She sounded bewildered. 'I thought it might be better in
New York, more like Chicago, but he was just like in
Washington. It wasn't me that changed.'

Daisy felt her sympathies rising, for both of the ill-
matched couple. Rosenblatt obviously did not. He went on
with his questioning.

'Did Carmody keep in touch with his cousins or other
relatives?'

'Nix! On his mother's side, they're just farmers and mill
hands and like that.'

'You didn't know one of his relatives is in New York?'

'Gosh darn, you don't say! No, he never told me. If you
want the truth, we didn't talk much the last few weeks.'

'A Mr Wilbur Pitt.'

'Never heard of him. Why would I? Otis didn't talk about his family. What's he doing in New York, this guy?'

'We haven't spoken to him yet,' Rosenblatt said guardedly. He glanced at his wristwatch. 'If he contacts you, will you let me know? Here's my card. I have to go now, I'm due in court. Don't leave town, will you? Either I or Sergeant Gilligan will probably need to ask you a few more questions.'

'Gee, not that sergeant. He gave me the willies. You're a gentleman, anyone can see.'

Flattery left the Deputy DA as unmoved as had tears. 'In any case we'll be in touch with you about your husband's possessions. If you're not using your hotel room, you better give me the address of your apartment.'

'Aw, gee, I dunno. Bart wouldn't like me giving out that address. It's kinda private, see.'

'I can take you down to police headquarters to ask Mr Bender's permission.'

'No, thanks! I guess they're gonna sweat it out of poor Bart anyhow, so I might as well tell.' She gave the address. 'I gotta powder my nose. Can I use Otis's room?'

'No, I'm afraid not. I'm sure Miss Cabot will oblige.'

'Oh dear! Oh yes, of course, do come this way, Mrs Carmody.'

As Miss Cabot ushered Mrs Carmody out, Rosenblatt came over to Daisy and Miss Genevieve. 'Satisfied, ladies?' he enquired sarcastically.

'Why did you stay here,' said Daisy, 'if you didn't want us to listen?'

'Strike while the iron's hot. Give 'em time to think and they realize they'd do better to clam up. I'm sure Sergeant

Gilligan will be most grateful, Mrs Fletcher, if you can find a moment to look through the rest of his precious mug book.'

'I expect I might find a moment.'

'And you will let us know if you plan to leave town, won't you? You're the only witness who actually saw the guy's face.' He cast a reproachful glance at Lambert, who reddened. 'Sigurd Thorwald swears he was looking at the elevator and then at Mr Lambert, not the guy you were chasing. Not that I'd give much for his evidence, the state he was in. Thank you for the use of your place, Miss Genevieve. I guess.'

'You're more than welcome,' said Miss Genevieve cordially. 'Any time?'

Rosenblatt departed.

'Sarky beast,' said Daisy. 'What do you make of all that?'

'You'd better finish up with the mug book first,' said Miss Genevieve. 'O'Rourke will be in for it any minute and we don't want him hanging around. Anyway, we can't talk freely till Elva Carmody's gone. Are you planning on staying the rest of the day?' she demanded of Lambert, still seated at her desk.

'Let him stay,' Daisy suggested, 'while I'm here, that is. Otherwise he'll just hang about in the passage outside your door, waiting to see where I go next. I hope you noted where I got to in that book, Mr Lambert. I don't want to have to go through all those beastly faces again.'

'Yes, I marked the place,' he said eagerly, pleased to have done something right for once.

Daisy returned to the desk and flipped through the last few photographs, without result. None of the beastly faces reminded her in the least of the man on the stairs.

CHAPTER 12

Mrs Carmody re-emerged into the sitting room with her face restored. She came over to the four by the fireplace, Lambert jumping to his feet at her approach.

'I guess you folks must be wondering about me and Otis,' she opened. 'I really am all broke up over him passing on, only you don't wanna be a killjoy, do you?'

'Oh dear, so very sorry!' said Miss Cabot. 'Of course you haven't had time yet to put on your blacks.'

'Blacks?' Mrs Carmody turned an astonished gaze on the old lady. 'Oh, you mean mourning clothes? That's kinda old fashioned, you know, and black doesn't suit me one bit.'

'Oh dear!'

''Sides, I figure now Otis is gone it won't worry him what I wear, and it's my duty now to cheer up poor Bart. He likes me in red. Heck, I gotta go telephone his lawyer.'

'You're welcome to use our telephone,' offered Miss Genevieve, as unwilling as Daisy to let her escape without coughing up a bit more information.

'Gee, can I? That's mighty kind of you. Say, d'you remember his name that Bart told me?'

'James P. Macpherson,' said Daisy.

'Have you a directory, ma'am?' Lambert asked. 'I'll look up his number for you, Mrs Carmody.'

Miss Cabot found the telephone directory in her sister's desk, Lambert found the number, and Mrs Carmody asked the hotel switchboard to connect her. Miss Genevieve made no pretence of not listening, even hushing Lambert and Miss Cabot when they would have spoken.

'Hello, Mr Macpherson? . . . This is Elva Carmody . . . No, nothing to do with that business. It's Bart – Mr Bender. The cops have taken him in . . . No, not Fraud, I guess it's the Homicide Bureau.'

A squawk came over the wire, loud enough for Daisy to hear, though not to make out the words.

'Heck no, not one of his goddamn tenants. My husband, Otis Carmody. You musta read about it . . . No, I don't believe he did and they haven't acksherly arrested him, but they're gonna grill him . . . Well, OK, if he did, it was for my sake, but it's sure landed us in a heapa trouble. You gotta get down to police headquarters right away.'

She listened for a moment, then said goodbye and hung up the earpiece on its hook.

'Everything all right?' asked Miss Genevieve.

'Mr Macpherson's going down there and make sure they don't violate Bart's rights. But if the cops got evidence,' Mrs Carmody went on disconsolately, 'he says he might not be able to get him out today. My husband dead, my friend in jail, what the heck am I s'posed to do?'

Miss Genevieve visibly withheld a pithy response. 'Won't you sit down for a moment,' she said, 'while you consider your options? Do you know the men who work for Mr Bender?'

'Nix. Bart didn't want me to trouble my head with business, not like Otis. Otis was always on at me to take an interest in his work. He used to get all excited and say nine-tenths of the people in the government was crooks, but like I told him, who cares? That's just the way things are, and worrying about it don't put diamonds around a girl's neck. Anyways, if Bart gets sent to the chair for having Otis croaked, his guys'll all be out of a job and no help to me.'

'True,' Miss Genevieve agreed. 'So we must try to figure out who else might have disposed of your husband. If you try real hard, maybe you'll remember which of the many public figures Mr Carmody antagonized made particularly virulent threats against him.'

'Who got maddest, that he wrote about? Gee, I dunno. Otis read me some real punk letters he got. Most weren't signed, but he often knew pretty much who they were from.'

'Did he tell you?'

'Yeah, but I don't remember.'

'What did he do with them? Did he keep them?'

'Nix. He just laughed and tore 'em up. Said they didn't none of them have the guts to do anything, specially after President Harding passed on and President Coolidge started cleaning house. You figure it was someone Otis wrote about in Washington had him shot?'

Miss Genevieve shook her head. 'I think it's far more likely that someone in New York wanted to prevent his publishing the results of his latest investigations.'

'You don't mean Bart, do you? I know Otis was digging up some dirt on Bart.'

'If it was Mr Bender, the police can be counted on to

prove it. They're going to bend over backwards to avoid pinning it on anyone more closely connected with Tammany, unless someone keeps an eye on them. I guess I'm the one. I've still got enough contacts in the right places to keep 'em on their toes if they don't want to find themselves pilloried in the opposition and Hearst press right before the election.'

'Aw, politics! But you mean you're gonna help Bart? Gee, I wish you would. Him and me get on real well together, and I don't wanna hafta go looking for someone else. I'm not as young as I look, see,' Mrs Carmody confessed with a moue. 'I wanna settle down with a man that thinks I'm worth giving a good time.'

'Most understandable,' said Miss Genevieve dryly. 'I'll certainly do what I can to make sure the police and the DA's office don't brush any Tammany connection under the carpet. Whether that will help Mr Bender remains to be seen.'

'Least he won't be railroaded for something he didn't do. I can't help wondering, did he . . .' She stopped as someone knocked on the door.

'Shall I get that, ma'am?' Lambert asked. At Miss Genevieve's nod, he went out into the foyer. 'Oh, it's you, Detective O'Rourke. Come in.'

Mrs Carmody jumped up. 'Say, you been real swell, but I guess I better get going now. Bye, folks.'

She hurried out, dodging past O'Rourke as if she was afraid he might without warning clap handcuffs on her. He swung round to stare after her.

'Who wuzzat?' he enquired suspiciously.

'A visitor,' Miss Genevieve informed him, accurate if misleading. 'What did you find in Wilbur Pitt's room?'

'Geez, ma'am, I didn't oughta tell you.'

'Mr Rosenblatt has already told me all about the case. I have considerable experience in criminal matters, you know. Did you find a gun?'

'No, ma'am.'

'No gun?' Miss Genevieve was disappointed.

'I thought men in the Wild West always had six-shooters,' ventured Miss Cabot.

Miss Genevieve looked self-conscious, as if she had also been momentarily prey to that misconception. 'Mr Pitt is presently in New York, not the Wild West, sister.'

'No cartridges,' Daisy asked, 'or whatever you put in a six-shooter?'

'No, ma'am.'

'What *did* you find, Detective?' said Miss Genevieve.

'Nuttin, ma'am.'

'He's skedaddled?'

'No, ma'am. Nuttin of int'rest, I shoulda said. Just a few clothes, coupla shirts, kinda old fashioned, nuttin fancy, no evening dress or nuttin, and a cardboard suitcase. There was a coupla packs of cigarette papers – no tobacco pouch, I guess he got it on him – and a big manila envelope with a stack of paper in it, writing paper, all written on.'

'Not typed?' Daisy said.

'No, ma'am, and the writing was dang near impossible to read, but it wasn't letters or nuttin useful.'

'His manuscript,' said Miss Genevieve. 'He won't leave without that.'

'Izzat so? The sergeant'll be pleased to hear that, ma'am. He'll still want to see Mr Pitt, I guess, but there wasn't nuttin useful anywheres, like I said.'

'Drat,' said Daisy. Wilbur Pitt was the only suspect she had much chance of investigating, but it seemed less and less likely that he had put a bullet into his cousin after a family squabble. She would still like to talk to him, though.

'You didn't reckernize none of the faces in the mug book, ma'am?' O'Rourke asked her.

Daisy shook her head. 'No, sorry. But I'm still sure I'd recognize him if I saw him. Pretty sure.'

'I'll tell Sergeant Gilligan, ma'am.' Detective O'Rourke departed with the mug book under his arm.

Turning to Miss Genevieve, Daisy asked, 'Well, what do you think?'

Miss Genevieve sighed. 'I expect Gilligan's right, and Barton Bender hired someone to kill Carmody. He did, after all, have a double motive.'

'Double?' said Lambert blankly.

'Fear of exposure of his unsavoury business methods, and to free Mrs Carmody,' Daisy explained, 'so that he could marry her.'

'Gee, I guess so.'

'Do you think Mrs Carmody knew what Bender planned, Miss Genevieve?'

'Hmm.' After a moment's thought, the old lady said reluctantly, 'Perhaps not. Though I wouldn't be surprised if she had asked him to put her husband out of the way and he told her it was too risky. And then he changed his mind when Carmody's investigations threatened him.'

'I doubt she knew,' said Daisy. 'She was a rotten liar.'

'Those crocodile tears!'

'Oh dear!'

'Don't be naive, sister.'

'She really was crying at one point,' Daisy argued. 'I believe she loved him once and his death hurt her when she let herself feel it. Actually, I'm rather sorry for both of them.'

'An ill-matched pair,' Miss Genevieve acknowledged. 'No doubt he fell for a pretty face, like most men, and didn't realize for some time that there was nothing behind it. He grew up. She didn't. Learn by his example, young man!' she admonished Lambert sternly.

'Gee whiz,' he said obediently, 'I'll sure try, ma'am.'

'She's trying to have it both ways, of course. She wants to keep Bender, yet she's afraid of being charged as an accomplice. It's not because I'm sorry for the dumb broad,' Miss Genevieve went on with one of her startling lapses into the vernacular, 'that I'll be keeping an eye on Rosenblatt and Gilligan. I'm not by any means convinced of Bender's guilt. I'll keep pushing them to make absolutely certain Tammany isn't involved.'

'Won't that guy Pascoli do that?' Lambert enquired. 'I mean, I bought a couple of newspapers this morning and they were full of the murder of a muckraker that was investigating Tammany Hall. I figure it must be Pascoli put them on to it.'

'Tell me about Pascoli,' Miss Genevieve requested. 'You were talking about him before, Mrs Fletcher, but I didn't catch exactly how he came into the business.'

Daisy explained that Pascoli was responsible for Carmody's presence in the Flatiron Building. 'And he pointed out to Mr Rosenblatt the possibility that the murder had some connection to Washington or New York politicians.'

'Which I reported to Mr Hoover, of course,' Lambert put

in eagerly. 'I mean, I had to report to him anyway because of Mrs Fletcher being in trouble, but he wouldn't have sent another agent just because of that. So between the newspapers and Agent Whitaker, I don't think you need to worry that the Tammany Hall side of things will be dropped without a thorough investigation, Miss Genevieve.'

'Possibly not,' said Miss Genevieve, displeased, 'but if you want something done well, you should do it yourself.'

'That's what Papa always said,' Miss Cabot ventured, 'though he applied it only to men. He never let me do anything except fine needlework. But I *have* learned to make good coffee, haven't I, sister?'

'Excellent, sister.'

'Would you care for a cup, Mrs Fletcher?'

'Yes, please. Heavens, it's past time for elevenses already. I had no idea it was so late.'

'Elevenses?' Miss Genevieve enquired.

'In England we lunch later than you seem to here, so a cup of tea or coffee and a biscuit is welcome at about eleven o'clock.'

'What a good idea. Ernestine and I usually take a cup of coffee a little earlier, but this has been such an interesting morning, I quite forgot.'

'*I* did not, sister,' said Miss Cabot reproachfully, 'but I was forever being hushed. Besides, we don't have enough cups for everyone who was here this morning, and they did keep popping in and out so. I think we have some macaroons in the cookie jar.'

Biscuit tin, Daisy translated. 'Perfect,' she said.

Miss Cabot trotted off to her tiny kitchen, to return a few minutes later with coffee pot, cups and saucers, and a plate of cookies. The macaroons were a disappointment to Daisy, since they turned out to be coconut biscuits, not her favourite almond meringue confections – something lost in translation. Her lack of enthusiasm went unnoticed as Lambert ate all but the last one, which he had manners enough to leave. The coffee was good, though. Daisy complimented Miss Cabot, who blushed and beamed.

'I do try to be useful to dear Genevieve,' she said with earnest modesty.

'Couldn't get on without you,' her sister said gruffly.

Her beam still brighter, Miss Cabot refilled cups and returned to her eternal knitting.

Daisy finished her coffee and said, 'I really must take myself and Mr Lambert off now and not take up any more of your time. It was most frightfully kind of you to insist on the sergeant coming up here instead of dragging me off to police headquarters, which sounds simply beastly.'

'It's a grim place,' Miss Genevieve said. 'But I promise you, you did me a favour by agreeing to come. You must have realized that curiosity is my besetting sin.'

'Mine too,' Daisy admitted with a chuckle.

'So you will understand, I feel sure, if I ask you to keep me current with what's going on in the investigation.'

'You shall know all that I know. But once Alec arrives, I'm not likely to get a chance to find out any more.'

'You're involved, though, as I cannot pretend to be. I could wish that Bender didn't know you're able to identify the killer.'

'Gosh, you don't think . . . But he's in the hands of the police.'

'Who can't stop him seeing his lawyer, and can't stop his

lawyer leaving their premises, and can't stop him passing information to anyone he chooses.'

'Gosh!' said Daisy, a cold frisson shuddering down her spine.

'Don't worry,' said Lambert manfully, 'I won't stir from your side till Mr Fletcher gets here.'

Miss Genevieve gave him a disparaging look and said, 'Pah!'

Which didn't make Daisy feel any safer.

CHAPTER 13

'Carmody was right about one thing,' observed Lambert as he and Daisy headed for the elevators.

'What's that?'

'When he called Miss Genevieve "Madame Guillotine". I bet she could sever heads with that look.'

'You haven't met my husband yet,' said Daisy. Alec's glance of icy displeasure was capable of freezing erring subordinates to the marrow or making criminals feel they might be better off at the North Pole. It even, occasionally, gave his wife pause.

'Gee whiz!' Lambert quailed. 'Mr Fletcher's not going to be too pleased with me.'

'Don't worry, he won't blame you. If he'd known in advance what Mr Hoover planned, he'd have told him not to bother to give me a watchdog. Even Alec's never been able to keep me from getting mixed up in things.' She pressed the elevator bell push. 'I'm going up to my room now, till lunchtime. If you don't want to lurk in the corridor, you could ask Patrolman Hicks to notify you if I try to sneak out.'

'I'll stay. Keeping you out of trouble is one thing, but after what Miss Genevieve said ... I'd never be able to face

Mr Fletcher if Bender's thugs came looking for you and I wasn't there.'

'Don't remind me. Though surely the lawyer can hardly have reached police headquarters yet, let alone learnt about me from Bender and passed word to someone else.'

'I'll stay,' Lambert repeated as the lift creaked to a halt in front of them.

'Right-oh, it's up to you. Hello, Kevin. Seventh, please.'

'OK, ma'am. Going up.' The boy seemed uncharacteristically subdued.

'Is anything wrong?' Daisy asked as the lift started off again.

'I din't wanna help the cops none,' said Kevin, 'not after how they treated Bridey. But I figured the DA'd put a crimp in Gilligan's style if he got to bullying you, so I tol' the dick where you was. And then after, I tol' that harness bull where to find the 'tecs 'cause I figured you and Miss Genevieve'd wanna know them two'd gotten theirselves nabbed.'

'How right you were,' Daisy said cordially. 'By the way, I don't suppose you've taken Mr Pitt up or down today, have you?'

'Nah, ain't seen him since yesterday, and it's no good asking the guys on the night shift 'cause they wouldn't neither of 'em notice if a hefalunt got inna their elevators.'

'Well, if he comes in, I'd appreciate it if you'd try to let me know.'

'OK, ma'am. Here we are, seventh floor.'

'Thanks, Kevin. And especial thanks for sending Mr Rosenblatt and the other policeman to the Cabots' suite.' Daisy felt in her purse for a tip.

Kevin put his freckled, grubby hand over hers. 'None o' that,' he said gruffly. 'I'da done the same for any pal.' He brightened. 'But I don't care if your minder wants to tip me.'

Lambert handed over a half-dollar with a sigh.

Daisy had scarcely shut the door of her room on him when the telephone bell rang.

'Mrs Fletcher?' said the hotel operator. 'There's a Mr Thorwald on the line. He's been trying to get ahold of you all morning.'

'Put him through, please,' said Daisy, instantly sure that he had reread her article and hated it.

The usual clicks and buzzes were succeeded by Thorwald's agitated voice. 'Mrs Fletcher, they think I did it!'

'I beg your pardon?' Daisy's mind was still on her article.

'The police!' Thorwald took an audible deep and calming breath. 'That is, the Deputy District Attorney requests my attendance at the Criminal Courts Building at three o'clock this afternoon, and Detective Sergeant Gilligan has dispatched a plain clothes man to escort me to police headquarters immediately.'

'Immediately?'

'I have contrived to delay the latter by means of a variety of stratagems, desiring to consult with you before placing myself irrevocably in their hands. My dear Mrs Fletcher, your husband is a senior detective officer, and you have given me to understand that you are not unfamiliar with police methods, in England if not in this country. Advise me!'

'Gosh,' said Daisy, thinking furiously. 'Right-oh, I'll do

my best. First, when did you get the summons from Mr Rosenblatt?'

'At approximately ten o'clock this morning. I telephoned you immediately, but the hotel operator was unable to discover your whereabouts.'

He couldn't have asked Kevin, Daisy thought. 'How much evidence were you, um, able to give them yesterday?' she asked.

'Er-hum, not a vast quantity,' Thorwald confessed sheepishly. 'I, hmm, found it extraordinarily difficult to concentrate upon their inquiries.'

'Then I should think Rosenblatt has simply given you time to, er, recover your equilibrium before asking you to repeat your account of what you observed and did. I shouldn't worry about him. As for Gilligan, how long have you been holding his minion at bay?'

'Approximately fifteen minutes. Seventeen, to be precise.'

'Well done!' said Daisy. 'Let's see, he must have sent for you after he took Barton Bender into custody, so . . .'

'The culprit has been arrested?' Hope rang down the wire.

'Not exactly. He's only classified as a suspect still, but sufficiently suspicious to be taken in for questioning. Grilling, as they say here. I expect Gilligan just wants you to take a look at him and see if you can identify him. The worthy sergeant has virtually no confidence in my competence as a witness.' *Nor I in his competence as a detective*, Daisy added to herself.

'Is that all?' said Thorwald with a sigh of relief. 'I can but reiterate that I did not observe the person whom you and young Lambert pursued down the staircase.'

'That's only my guess,' Daisy cautioned. 'With Rosencrantz and Guildenstern, anything's possible.'

An explosive snort of laughter reached her ear. 'Rosencrantz and . . . ? My dear Mrs Fletcher!'

'Blast, I've been trying not to say that. Mr Thorwald, have you got a solicitor? A lawyer? It wouldn't hurt to take him with you when you go to see those two.'

'A reasonable precaution,' Thorwald agreed, sobering. 'I shall telephone my legal adviser immediately and arrange for him to meet me there. However, I am persuaded that you have interpreted the situation correctly. I was foolishly apprehensive. Thank you, my dear Mrs Fletcher, for your inestimable reassurance.'

Daisy said goodbye, hung up, and started worrying. She found it hard to believe anyone could seriously suspect Mr Thorwald of shooting Carmody, or anyone else for that matter. On the other hand, she was the only person who could say with any certainty that her editor had not fired a gun from close behind her, and Rosenblatt and Gilligan were not inclined to credit her evidence.

As she had told Thorwald, with Rosenblatt and Gilligan anything seemed possible. They were at least as much concerned with politics as with the law, if not more so. If their case against Barton Bender fell through, Thorwald might be the next scapegoat.

Or Daisy might find herself filling that role.

Between Scylla and Charybdis, she thought uneasily. Bender's thugs on one side, the not particularly long but quite possibly crooked arm of the law on the other. Perhaps she ought to skedaddle, as Miss Genevieve put it.

She was sure of a welcome with Mr Arbuckle and the

Petries, in Connecticut, not too far away but in a different state. She could always leave a message for Rosenblatt, and another for Alec.

No, Alec would be here in a few hours. Though she hadn't much confidence in Lambert as a defender, she trusted Alec. His official status would protect her from the police and the DA, and with him beside her she wasn't afraid of Bender's bullyboys. And then there was Whitaker. The federal agent who was coming with Alec would surely force the New York authorities to stop looking for scapegoats and investigate Tammany's thugs.

Gosh, not another lot of thugs after her! Daisy groaned. She would be *very* happy to see Alec, even though it meant admitting, to herself if not to him, that she wasn't quite as independent as she'd like to think herself.

It was a pity, too, that she wasn't going to get a chance to work out for herself who was the murderer. Hired thugs were altogether beyond her purview.

In the meantime, while she had no intention of cowering in her room till Alec arrived, she was glad of an excuse to stay there for the moment. She had had the brilliant idea of writing up her experiences with the New York police to sell in England. To be published under a pseudonym, she supposed, so as not to upset Superintendent Crane and the Assistant Commissioner (Crime).

Turning to the typewriter, Daisy prepared to do battle.

When Daisy ventured forth from her room, urged onward by hunger pangs, she expected to find Lambert lurking in the passage near her door. His absence brought a frown.

Little though she felt able to rely on his abilities, his company would have been comforting.

Annoyance gave way to alarm. Had the thugs picked him off first, before tackling her? But before she could panic, she remembered Patrolman Hicks. A uniformed policeman would surely have given 'them' pause.

Not that Hicks was at his post, either. Daisy found them both by the elevators, where Kevin was teaching Lambert to play at jacks, while Hicks watched with avuncular interest. So much for the guardians of the law's majesty.

Lambert scrambled to his feet, his unfortunate blush mantling his ingenuous face. Daisy sympathized. 'Lunchtime,' she said brightly.

'Swell!'

'It's OK for some,' Hicks grumbled.

'You want I should fetch you a sandwich?' offered Kevin.

'Say, yeah, do that, willya? Here's a buck and you can keep the change. Anything 'cept toonafish. Me, I don't like toonafish.'

Kevin took Daisy and Lambert down. 'That guy's OK for a bull,' he said grudgingly. 'Some people, they expect you to fetch 'em summat out of your own pocket, and then when they pay you they want the change!'

'He must be grateful that you told him where to find Sergeant Gilligan,' Daisy suggested.

'He's OK. Say, where you gonna eat, ma'am? 'Cause if you're going out and you don't want nuttin fancy, there's a swell Eyetie place just round on Seventh Avenoo. Looigi's. Tell 'em I sent you and they'll give you the works.'

With a commission to the boy, no doubt, Daisy guessed, asking directions. She wondered just how many pies he had his fingers in. A sudden thought struck her. No one knew more than Kevin about what was going on in the hotel, at least during the day.

'Kevin,' she said impulsively, 'will you let me know, and Mr Lambert, too, if any rough-looking strangers ask about me?'

His blue eyes widened. 'Geeeez!' he breathed, impressed, 'are they after you, ma'am?'

'Probably not, but just to be on the safe side.'

'Sure! Don't you worry none, Mrs Fletcher, ma'am, I got my ways of finding out things. If any tough sticks his nose through them doors, you'll hear about it long afore he gets to asking questions.'

'That's a weight off my mind,' said Daisy as the lift reached the lobby. 'Thank you, Kevin.'

'You just stay here a minute, ma'am, while I go make sure the coast's clear.' Kevin dashed off, to return a moment later looking disappointed. 'All clear,' he reported. 'By the time you get back after lunch, I'll've gotten everything fixed up, so don't worry!'

'You've made his day,' said Lambert a trifle sourly. 'I can take care of you if there's any trouble, you know. I've got my automatic.'

'That *is* a relief,' said Daisy, hoping she sounded sincere. Judging by what had happened last time he drew his gun, she would on the whole have preferred him to be unarmed.

They had a delicious and uneventful meal, served by a befreckled cousin of Kevin's who was married to the Italian proprietor-chef. Lambert insisted on paying for Daisy's lunch, saying grandly, 'I'll put it on expenses.' He then proceeded to embarrass her thoroughly.

'Stay there a minute,' he ordered, as she picked up her handbag preparatory to leaving. To the bewilderment of the few other lunchers, he went to the window, stood to one side, and peered out. Returning to Daisy, he said from one side of his mouth, 'Looks OK. I don't see anyone suspicious.'

'What exactly are you looking for?'

'Gee, anyone that's not moving along. Not the newsboy, of course. Anyone hanging around with nothing special to do, I guess.'

'Lurking?' Daisy said unkindly, as he helped her on with her coat.

Telltale ears red but undeterred, Lambert preceded her to the door, which was set back in an alcove from the pavement (*sidewalk*, Daisy reminded herself). Again he told her to wait. After once more scrutinizing the far side of the street, through the glass door, he opened it just enough to slip out. His hat pulled down over his horn-rims, his hand in the breast of his coat, he tiptoed to the corner and stuck his head around just far enough to be able to gaze up and down the street.

Glancing back, he gave Daisy a significant nod, which she interpreted as permission to join him. Lambert's desire to be a federal agent, she decided, stemmed not from any burning ambition to uphold the law but simply from a love of cloak-and-dagger adventure. She couldn't take the possibility of danger seriously while he was play-acting.

'Can you pull your hat down further?' he asked in an urgent whisper.

'Not without crushing my hair,' she said tartly, in a normal voice. 'The villains can't possibly have much of a description of my face.'

'I guess not,' he admitted reluctantly. 'OK, let's go.'

'Would you mind very much taking your hand away from your gun? It makes me rather twitchy. People don't carry guns around in England, you see, not even the police. And I can't help feeling that wearing your hat so low may not only hamper your ability to see but draw unwanted attention.'

'Aw, gee, do you think so?' Crestfallen, he pushed it up.

'It's a frightfully good idea,' Daisy hastened to assure him. 'It conceals your features jolly well. But perhaps this isn't quite the right situation.'

Lambert nodded. 'I'm kind of new at this,' he acknowledged, 'so I guess no one knows my features yet anyhow.'

'Exactly! I'm sure they'll be famous one day.'

'I don't know about that,' he said dubiously. 'I figure agents are supposed to stay anonymous.' His hand moved towards his hat brim, but after a moment's uncertainty, he turned up his coat collar instead.

As the hotel, with its red-and-white-striped awning, was already in sight, Daisy held her tongue. After all, the breeze was quite chilly, if nowhere near biting enough to justify such a sartorial lapse. But if she had to go outdoors with him again, she would suggest a muffler to hide his ingenuous face in a more conventional manner.

The stout, black-faced doorman, instead of sheltering in the hotel's doorway, was standing out on the pavement gazing east with an anxious air. He brightened when he saw Daisy and Lambert.

'Glad you're back safe, ma'am,' he said. 'No problems?'

Daisy blinked, then realized he must be one of Kevin's cohort of spies. She smiled at him. 'No problems, thank you, Balfour.' It always struck her as odd to address a black man by the name of a British statesman. He ought to have had some exotic African name, but of course he was as American as Lambert.

'Anyone been asking for Mrs Fletcher?' asked Lambert officiously.

'Just one ge'man, suh.'

'Aha!' cried Lambert, swinging round to scan the street, his hand at his breast pocket, while Daisy, aghast, could only gape. She realized she had not for a moment credited that she was truly in danger.

CHAPTER 14

Balfour had not let the stranger enter the lobby, especially as he said he was a newspaperman and the manager had instructed that no reporters were to be admitted. Though he refused to give his name, the man also claimed to be a friend of Mrs Fletcher's.

'I don't know any reporters in New York,' said Daisy.

'An obvious ruse,' Lambert declared in a superior voice, as they crossed the lobby towards the registration desk.

'It's a pity Balfour couldn't give a better description of him than that he was a white man and rather shabby. It was clever to ask him to leave a note, though. Presumably he didn't sign it, but maybe the handwriting will tell the police something.'

'He'll have disguised his writing, you betcha.'

'Well, then, maybe he's left fingerprints. It's difficult to get them off paper, but not impossible.'

'I'll go ask Balfour if he took his gloves off.'

Lambert dashed off, and Daisy continued to the desk. As usual no one was there – for that very reason she had taken her room key with her when she went out but she could see two folded papers in the cubbyhole with her number. She was tempted to slip through the gate at the side to retrieve them, rather than ring the bell and have to explain why the notes must be handled with care. She doubted that the manager or the desk clerk, Kevin's bêtes noires, had been apprised of her situation.

While she hesitated, Kevin's lift came down. Her unorthodox protector saw her as soon as he stepped out into the passage to usher out his passengers. Abandoning them, he dashed to Daisy's side.

'Geez, ma'am, I'm mighty glad to see you. I been worrying. I shouldn'a let you go out to eat. You could've sent Stanley out to getcha sumpin, or I'da gone, for you.'

'Luigi gave us a very good meal.'

'Yeah, I tol' you. But a guy came round asking for you when you was gone.'

'So Balfour said.'

'He did pretty good, Balfour. Got him to write you a note, like I tol' him. I didn't read it,' said Kevin virtuously. 'There's another one, too, a message from Mr Fletcher, called in by Western Union. I'll get 'em for you.' He swung open the gate in the counter.

'Hold the note by the edge, Kevin, in case the police can get dabs off it.'

'Dabs?'

'Oh, that's English police slang for fingerprints.'

'Gotcha! Wish I'd've thought of that, though. I didn't think to warn Balfour and Stanley. Betcha it's got their fingerprints all over.'

'The guy kept his gloves on, anyway,' reported Lambert, joining Daisy, 'and he used a hotel pad that the doorman keeps in his pocket.'

'Blast!' Daisy took the two papers from Kevin without

bothering about how she held them. The first one she unfolded was the message from Alec. 'Oh, drat and double drat! An important meeting this afternoon – he's been delayed. He won't get here till nearly nine o'clock.'

'Aw, punk!' Kevin sympathized, leaning on the counter.

'What does the other one say?' Lambert asked eagerly.

Heart in mouth, Daisy opened it. Her eye went at once to the flamboyant signature, and she gave a half-hysterical giggle. 'James Pascoli! You remember, the *Town Talk* editor. He wants to make sure the police aren't giving me any trouble, and to see if I have any information I don't mind giving him. All that fuss and bother for nothing!'

'You know the guy?' Kevin was once more disappointed. 'Still, that don't prove nuttin. He still could've been paid to croak you.'

'I hardly think so. Anyway, I'll telephone him, and if he wants to meet, I won't go out. He can come here, and we'll talk in the lobby, and I'll ask Miss Genevieve to join us.'

'And me,' said Lambert, sounding hurt.

'Of course, I take that for granted,' Daisy soothed him.

'Oughta be safe enough,' Kevin agreed, frowning, 'but it still don't prove there ain't some other guy after you.'

He looked round at the sound of a door opening, and scurried through the gate and back to his elevator as the manager appeared.

The manager, a dour man, glared after him, then turned to Daisy. 'Can I help you, ma'am?'

'No, thank you.' Daisy waved the messages at him. 'Kevin kindly gave me these.'

'Not his job!'

'I dare say, but it was most helpful of him, and made it

unnecessary to disturb you.' With a nod of dismissal, she headed for Kevin's elevator, Lambert close at her heels.

Daisy had a little lamb, she thought with a sigh.

Having promised her persistent lamb not to leave the hotel without him, and to keep him apprised of her whereabouts inside, Daisy went to her room. She was fagged out after a morning of alarums and excursions and Rosencrantz and Guildenstern, topped by a large lunch. After a longing look at her bed, though, she went to the telephone and asked for Pascoli's number.

Not that she had any particular desire to provide him with information for his news magazine, but she appreciated his concern. More important, she wanted to ask him for news of Thorwald, and she hoped he might give her an unbiased opinion as to whether she was truly in danger. Kevin and Lambert and even Miss Genevieve were all too keen for a little excitement for their judgement to be trusted.

Pascoli was not in his office. Daisy left a message for him to ring her back.

She sat on at the desk, chin in hands, wishing Alec was there with her. However modern and independent one might be, it was comforting to have someone nearby who cared deeply what became of one. Even if he ballyragged her for getting involved – as he was bound to, although it was *not* her fault – he would support her and defend her.

Home was such a frightfully long way away.

The thought of home brought the thought of her ten-year-old stepdaughter, Belinda. The poor child had been left with her Victorianly unbending grandmother while her father and her new mother jaunted off to America. Daisy had kept her promise to write often, but letters took a week or longer. Bel must have felt quite deserted for the first few days, though she had expected to have to wait for the first letter. A gap now would make her feel even worse.

Writing a nice, cheerful letter would distract Daisy from her own woes, and Bel wouldn't mind if she typed it. She rolled a sheet of hotel notepaper into the protesting typewriter.

She was nearing the bottom of a second page when the telephone bell rang. 'Mrs Fletcher?' said the switchboard girl. 'I got a Mr Pascoli on the line. You wanna talk to him or shall I tell him you're out?'

One of Kevin's cohorts, no doubt. 'Put him through, please,' Daisy said.

'Mrs Fletcher, you OK?'

'Yes, thanks. It's kind of you to ask.'

'We've all been concerned. Tell the truth, I've got Louella Shurkowski hanging over my shoulder right this minute. You remember Louella?'

'Certainly. Please give her my thanks. I wanted to ask you about Mr Thorwald. He went to police headquarters?'

'Yeah. I guess he's still there, but his lawyer was going to meet him there, so we're not too worried. Not *too* worried. Say, listen, I'd like to have a word with you about the situation, only not on the phone. Too many ears, get me? Can we meet?'

'If you'd like to come here, to the hotel.'

'Sure. I can't get away till around five.'

'Right-oh, I'll meet you in the lobby a bit after five.' With *my* cohort, Daisy thought. 'I hope you'll bring news of Mr Thorwald. Cheerio till then.'

'Uh . . . ? Oh, *ciao*,' said Pascoli.

Chow? Daisy puzzled over it for a minute before deciding that either Pascoli had misheard her, or it was the American pronunciation of cheerio.

Daisy finished the letter to Belinda, then handwrote a brief note to Mrs Fletcher, who would undoubtedly object to a typed personal letter. So would Daisy's mother, to whom she next composed a note almost as brief. The Dowager Lady Dalrymple would complain about its brevity but would be equally displeased if forced to wade through pages of Daisy's handwriting. Somewhat longer letters to her sister and Lucy, her former housemate, left her satisfied with having done her duty by all.

In none of her epistles had she mentioned the murder. She had managed almost to forget it herself, for over an hour.

Feeling rather an ass, she rang down to the switchboard and asked to be put through to Lambert's room. 'I'm going downstairs,' she told him, 'to see if they have any postage stamps at the desk and leave some letters to be posted, and then I'm going to pop in to see the Misses Cabot. I *don't* need an escort, but I promised to let you know.'

'But what if they don't have stamps?' Lambert said in alarm. 'You mustn't go out looking for a post office.'

'I'll send Stanley.'

'Who?'

'The buttons. Bellhop.'

'OK. I guess. I'll meet you down below at the elevator.'

'It's really not necessary,' Daisy protested, but he had rung off.

He was waiting for her, when she stepped out of Kevin's lift. 'I came down the stairs,' he panted, 'to get here before you.'

Daisy sighed.

He accompanied her to the Cabots', where Miss Cabot was much too tenderhearted to make him wait outside. Daisy told Miss Genevieve about Mr Thorwald being hauled off to police headquarters.

'As long as he has his lawyer with him,' Miss Genevieve assured her, 'he won't come to any harm.'

Daisy wondered just what sort of harm her editor might come to if he had gone without his lawyer. The police in America seemed to be quite as dangerous as the criminals. She wasn't sure whether to be more afraid of Gilligan or the suppositious assassin who might or might not be after her.

Miss Genevieve eagerly agreed to be with Daisy in the lobby when she met Pascoli. 'Not that I believe you have anything to fear from him,' she added.

'Nor do I,' Daisy agreed.

'Better safe than sorry,' Lambert said firmly.

'Oh yes,' said Miss Cabot, 'so very true!'

'Poppycock,' Miss Genevieve snorted. 'If everyone thought like that, we'd still be living in caves. Or at least walking everywhere, instead of riding in trains and automobiles.'

'Oh dear, those newfangled automobiles, so dangerous! Papa would never set foot in one.'

'But you have frequently travelled with me in a motor taxi-cab, sister and have come to no harm,' Miss Genevieve pointed out. 'Now, what I could bear to do is go up in an airplane. Have you ever flown in an airplane, Mrs Fletcher?'

'No, but Alec has promised to take me up one day. He was a pilot in the Royal Flying Corps in the war. He flies an aeroplane now and then to preserve his skills. My stepdaughter, Belinda, has flown with him more than once, I believe, much against her grandmother's will.'

'Oh dear!' Miss Cabot shuddered. 'A little girl up in the air, it doesn't bear thinking of.'

'Have you ever flown?' Daisy asked Lambert.

'Who, me? In one of those kites? Oh boy, not hardly! An airship, now, that's different. You can understand why a dirigible stays up, helium being lighter than air. That's where the future of flight is, you betcha.'

'Oh dear, it's simply not natural. If God had intended us to fly before we get to heaven, he would certainly have given us wings here below instead of trains.'

Daisy blinked and decided this curious proposition was not worth refuting. 'I'm quite looking forward to it,' she said, 'if Alec ever has time to take me when we get home. The view must be breathtaking.'

'As long as you don't do it while I'm trying to take care of you,' said Lambert.

'That'll soon be over,' Daisy reminded him. No doubt he'd be almost as happy as she would when Alec arrived.

They stayed with the Cabot sisters until it was time to go down to the lobby. Miss Genevieve, struggling to her feet, suggested she should be the one to give Pascoli information on the case, assuming that was really what he came for.

'Please do,' said Daisy. 'You'll know what he should be told, much better than I.'

'And what's better not told,' Miss Genevieve agreed.

Kevin took them down. 'This Pascoli guy,' he said sternly to Daisy, 'you know him?'

'I've met him.' How on earth did Kevin know Daisy was meeting Pascoli?

On second thoughts, that was an easy question to answer. The hotel switchboard girl had told him. Pascoli was right to be wary of eavesdroppers.

'Well, you be careful, you hear? I got my people watching, but if he pulls a gat, there ain't nuttin much they can do. Hey, Mr Lambert, sir, you maybe better frisk him soon as he gets here.'

Lambert's jaw dropped, but he managed not to say, 'Who, me?' 'I – I guess so,' he stammered instead.

'Frisk?' Daisy asked.

'Check to see is he packing heat,' Kevin explained. 'I'll see you get some "Irish tea" right away, sir. What you need's Dutch courage.'

'I guess so,' Lambert agreed gratefully.

Kevin ushered them out of the lift and through to the lobby. There he seized Stanley – his inferior in age, size, and cheekiness – by the ear. 'Here, you order tea for the ladies and a spot of the Irish for Mr Lambert. And put some pep in it!'

'I always do!' Stanley buzzed off to the restaurant to pass on the order, and Kevin, seeing the desk clerk coming in to take over from the manager, dashed back to his lift.

Only one other couple was in the lobby, and they left after a few minutes. A waiter arrived, his tray laden with two teapots and the cakes and biscuits for which the Misses Cabot must have a standing order. 'Indian,' he said, setting the large pot before Miss Cabot. The small one was deposited in front of Lambert. 'Irish. I'll need cash for that.'

While Lambert fumbled for his wallet, Daisy reached for her handbag, saying, 'Let me treat you both, Miss Cabot.'

'So kind!'

'No, no,' said Miss Genevieve. 'My dear Mrs Fletcher, you eat like a bird. It can go on our tab.'

Daisy had never in her life been told she ate like a bird; in fact her mother had frequently castigated her for eating like a horse. She smiled and gave in gracefully.

Miss Genevieve regarded Lambert with disapproval. 'You're a federal agent,' she reminded him as he picked up his cup and took a gulp of whiskey.

He choked, coughing and spluttering while tears came to his eyes. When he had recovered his breath, he begged, 'You won't report me?'

'Do I look like a police nark?' Miss Genevieve demanded in outraged tones.

'Something's been puzzling me,' Daisy put in quickly. 'The first time I saw Carmody, he took a nip of spirits from a flask. Yet I'm sure he was interested in Kevin's arrangements from the muckraking reporter's point of view, not as a source of supply for himself. If he drank himself, why would he want to expose someone dealing in drink?'

'What makes you think so?' asked Miss Genevieve.

Daisy thought back. 'We were in the elevator. Kevin whispered to me that he could get me genuine Irish whiskey and it was quite safe because all the "right people" had been paid off. I don't know how much Carmody overheard, but at the very least he heard "paid off". Kevin cleverly pretended he'd been telling me his brother was laid off.'

'That's it, then. Carmody wasn't interested in bootlegging as such, only in the police accepting bribes to ignore it.'

'Oh yes, that's much more—'

'Here's Pascoli,' said Lambert, who was facing the door. 'Do I really have to frisk him?'

'No,' said Daisy.

'Yes,' said Miss Genevieve.

'Better safe than sorry,' said Miss Cabot brightly.

Lambert stood up, squaring his shoulders. 'Aw, gee,' he said, 'Mr Thorwald's come, too.'

'Don't you dare frisk Mr Thorwald!' said Daisy. 'He'd never buy another article from me. And he won't be happy if you frisk his colleague, either.'

'Oh dear,' said Miss Cabot, 'but better safe than sorry, you know.'

However, Daisy's protest resonated strongly with Miss Genevieve. When Lambert looked at her she shrugged, sighed, and nodded. The two editors were permitted to approach unfrisked, though Lambert observed them closely as if trying to spot unnatural bulges.

This constant vigilance and endless suspense were very wearing on the nerves, Daisy thought. What with one thing and another, she thanked heaven that Alec was not an American policeman!

CHAPTER 15

Daisy went to meet the editors. 'Hello, Mr Pascoli,' she said. 'Mr Thorwald, I'm frightfully glad to see you're safe and sound.'

Thorwald took her hand in both his. 'My dear Mrs Fletcher, I'm most sincerely obliged to you for your advice and encouragement in a situation in which I felt myself at a considerable disadvantage.'

Now Daisy felt herself at a considerable disadvantage, due to her upbringing. Miss Genevieve, no doubt, would have seized the moment to request an increase in her remuneration. Daisy could only murmur, 'It was nothing,' and hope his gratitude was long-lasting.

'What did they want?' she continued, leading the way back to the others. 'Gilligan and Rosenblatt, I mean.'

'Exactly as you suggested, Rosenblatt wanted my narrative reiterated, and Gilligan desired me to scrutinize a person whom he held in custody.'

'Barton Bender. You didn't recognize him, did you?'

'Certainly not. While circumstances may upon occasion require one to be in proximity to such individuals, I don't hesitate to affirm that no male acquaintance of mine would adorn his person with such a quantity of gold and gems, to say nothing of the excessive and disagreeable effluvium of bay rum which remained in the atmosphere after his departure!'

Daisy didn't think Thorwald had quite understood the purpose of the exercise, but as she was quite certain Bender had not himself shot Carmody, she held her peace. 'Miss Cabot, Miss Genevieve,' she said, 'may I introduce Mr Thorwald and Mr Pascoli?'

'So happy to meet you,' twittered Miss Cabot. 'Will you take tea?'

Miss Genevieve regarded the gentlemen with interest as they bowed, Pascoli dismayed, Thorwald with a look of foreboding. 'Sigurd Thorwald,' she pronounced, 'so you're an editor now. I suppose it was inevitable.'

'I'm most obliged to you, ma'am,' said Thorwald in surprise, taking off his pince-nez and polishing the lenses vigorously.

'Always did use half a dozen words where one would suffice, but I dare say you're quite capable of cutting other people's words to good effect.'

In the meantime, Pascoli drew Daisy aside and said, 'I hoped for a word with you in private, Mrs Fletcher. I'd like to discuss the Carmody case and the old ladies won't want to talk murder.'

'On the contrary. Miss Genevieve knows just as much about it as I do,' Daisy assured him, 'and she's positively eager to discuss it. Maybe you've heard of Eugene Cannon?'

'Sounds familiar,' said Pascoli, puzzled. 'Oh, you mean the crime reporter? Yes, his writing was held up to me as a model when I started in the business, but he was pretty near retirement then. I never met him. Why? Just a minute, there was something odd about him. I can't remember . . .'

'He was a she. Eugene Cannon was Genevieve Cabot.'

Pascoli swung round to stare at Miss Genevieve. 'This lady here? Oh boy!'

Miss Genevieve stared back, critically.

'Mr Pascoli is interested in Carmody's murder,' Daisy said to her. 'You've been in the news business. I'm sure you know much better than I what information will be useful to him.'

'*Town Talk*?' Miss Genevieve's eyes gleamed. 'I expect I can give you a few pointers, young man. Sit down.'

Daisy left them to it, turning to Thorwald, while Lambert divided his attention between the two conversations.

'Tell me what happened at police headquarters and the DA's Office,' Daisy invited.

'I consider myself exceptionally fortunate that my profession has never required me to frequent Centre Street,' Thorwald began. 'In actual fact, today was the occasion of my first visit to that abominable place.'

'And you went as a witness, not a journalist,' Daisy said sympathetically.

'Indeed! The headquarters building I cannot bring myself to describe to a lady of refinement. Suffice it to say that I was escorted to an apartment of the most sordid aspect, which my lawyer later informed me was one of the better rooms. There Detective Sergeant Gilligan interrogated me in an unpleasantly hectoring fashion, demanding a repetition of the narrative with which I obliged him immediately after the crime.'

'I'm afraid the police practically always want to hear one's story at least twice. One often recalls later details which seemed insignificant at the time.'

'My description of the scene did differ in significant

respects from the original of yesterday,' he admitted, 'according to the sergeant, that is. He made no allowance for the fact that I was at that time ... ahem ... indisposed. He appeared to believe that I had deliberately misled him!' Thorwald took off his pince-nez again and blotted his forehead with his handkerchief. 'I cannot say, my dear Mrs Fletcher, how inestimably grateful I am for the advice you gave me over the telephone, to insist upon my lawyer's attendance.'

'It seemed a sensible precaution. In England, the police have to warn suspects that their words may be used against them, and that they have a right to legal representation. I suppose there's nothing like that here?'

'If so, it is, I believe, "more honoured in the breach than the observance", but I am unacquainted with criminal law. Certainly Sergeant Gilligan never made any such communication to me.'

'I expect it's just because you're a witness, not a suspect,' Daisy said soothingly. 'Your lawyer put an end to the harassment, I take it.'

She paused as the waiter returned with tea for the two editors – two small pots. Pascoli must have given Stanley an order for the real thing for Thorwald and Irish for himself. Thorwald poured himself a cup, the rising steam confirming half Daisy's guess.

'By the way,' she went on, 'did you recall anything helpful about the crime? Were you able to tell Gilligan where the shot came from?'

'I'm convinced it came from beyond the elevators.' Thorwald sounded confident. 'However, when I so declared to the sergeant, he became abusive. If I understood him correctly, he is hoping for evidence which will implicate Mr Lambert, who, like us, approached from the opposite direction.'

'Who, me?' asked Lambert, aghast. 'He wants to send me up the river? What about Barton Bender?'

'If Barton Bender is the person bedizened with gold and diamonds whom I was asked to identify, then I believe he has been released, there being no grounds to arrest him. My impression was that he is still under extreme suspicion. Detective Sergeant Gilligan's interest in Mr Lambert, on the other hand, is of a purely sanguine nature. He little expects to succeed, but should he find credible evidence against Mr Lambert, it will enable him to – as he expressed it – get the feds off of his back.'

'But it won't!' Lambert squawked. 'I *told* him Washington is sending another agent. A guy called Whitaker's going to arrive this afternoon.'

'Perhaps Gilligan hoped Mr Whitaker would be too taken up with exonerating you to delve into the police department's or Tammany's misdeeds,' Daisy suggested. 'Anyway, you needn't worry. Mr Thorwald is sure the shot came from the opposite direction. Which makes me think: what if the man on the stairs was neither the murderer nor a frightened witness but actually the intended victim?'

'Gee whiz,' said Lambert, impressed, 'that would sure explain why he ran away.'

Daisy pursued the idea. 'And if he was Wilbur Pitt, it would explain why no one has seen him since then.'

'Who is Wilbur Pitt?' Thorwald wanted to know.

'Otis Carmody's cousin. He has a room here at the Chelsea, but he hasn't come in since yesterday.'

'Might the attack possibly stem from some species of primitive feud?' Thorwald proposed hesitantly. 'That is, the murderer is an individual with animosity towards both Carmody and his relative?'

'Gee, yes, a grudge against the family! After all, they come from the sticks, like the Hatfields and the McCoys.'

'Capulets and Montagues.'

'Hardly,' Daisy deflated them. 'There was only one shot. There's no reason to suppose more than one victim was aimed at. But there is reason to suppose the shooter was a rotten shot – otherwise why wasn't Carmody killed outright? He could very well have aimed at Pitt and hit Carmody by accident.'

'*If* the man on the stairs *was* Pitt,' Lambert said a bit sulkily. He had rather fancied his Hatfields and McCoys, whoever they were, and whatever the sticks were. 'How do you know Pitt hasn't come in since yesterday?'

'Actually, I don't,' Daisy was forced to concede. 'All I know is that Kevin – the lift boy – hasn't seen him since yesterday, and there's not much escapes that lad's eye.'

'He's only here days,' Lambert pointed out. 'Besides, if Pitt's fleeing a would-be murderer, he could always come in the back way like we went out.'

'The man in the bowler hat!' said Daisy triumphantly.

Thorwald blinked at her, looking thoroughly bewildered. 'You said his name was William?'

'At that time, I'd only heard him referred to as Willie. Oh, never mind, that's all conjecture. Did you learn anything of substance when you saw Mr Rosenblatt? Tell me about that interview. Did you see him in the same place as Gilligan?'

'No, no, the Criminal Courts Building presents quite a

different ambiance. Though distinctly shabby now, it was once an elegant edifice, with marble pillars and balustrades and ornate iron scrollwork. Mr Rosenblatt's office has beautiful golden-oak woodwork and a bronze and porcelain chandelier depending from the high ceiling. The view from the window, however, is unpleasant, not to say sinister.'

'How so?'

'It looks out on to the Tombs,' pronounced Thorwald in a voice of doom.

'Whose tombs?' Daisy asked.

'The Tombs is a prison. I believe it was constructed on a graveyard, hence the appellation. Its round grey tower cannot but bring to mind those ancient castles whose dungeons were the scene of unspeakable torments.'

'I'm glad you only saw it from the outside. Rosenblatt didn't threaten you with incarceration, did he?'

'Happily, no. He questioned me closely about you, my dear Mrs Fletcher. Naturally I was able to assure him most fervently that your antecedents are well known to me and of the utmost respectability.'

'Thank you!'

'Not to say *nobility*.'

'Please, Mr Thorwald, I allowed the use of my courtesy title on my articles, but we did agree it was not to be mentioned otherwise. You told Mr Rosenblatt about the direction the shot came from, I assume? Was his reaction as extreme as Sergeant Gilligan's?'

'By no means. He declared himself satisfied to have the problem solved.'

'So the DA's not looking to frame me?' Lambert said in relief.

'Frame?' Daisy asked. 'Is that the same as send up the river?'

'Not exactly. It's fixing the evidence to make it look like your fall guy's guilty.'

'Fall guy? Scapegoat, I suppose.' Daisy sighed. 'I was beginning to think I understood American! Surely the police wouldn't do that?'

'You can betcha sweet life they would,' said Lambert gloomily.

'Not to a federal agent,' Thorwald said, 'not when it would undoubtedly induce an even closer scrutiny of New York police practices than will already eventuate from this disgraceful affair.'

'In any case,' Daisy reminded Lambert, 'Mr Thorwald's evidence exculpates you, so you have nothing to worry about. What I want to know is whether I have anything to worry about. Is there really a chance some bullyboy is after me because I'm the only witness who saw the murderer's face?'

'Jumping jiminy!' Thorwald exclaimed, appalled.

This outcry from his undemonstrative colleague drew Pascoli's attention. 'What's that?' he queried.

Both Daisy and Lambert started to explain. Before they had sorted out who was going to speak, they were interrupted.

Balfour burst through the glass swing doors from the street. 'Miz Fletcher, ma'am,' he cried, 'a man headin' this way and he walk like he totin' a gun!'

Lambert jumped up. 'Get under the table, Mrs Fletcher,' he ordered incisively.

'It's glass!' Daisy pointed out. 'He's probably not coming

here anyway. Besides, how can one possibly tell from the way a man walks that he's got a gun?'

'You can tell,' Lambert, Pascoli and Miss Genevieve all affirmed at once. Balfour elaborated, 'He kinda swaggerin', like he not afeared o' nuttin. You better hide, Miz Fletcher, ma'am! I'll go slow him down.'

'I'm sure he'll walk on past, but if not, don't put yourself in danger, Balfour. And thanks for the warning.'

As she spoke, Daisy was being hustled across the lobby by Lambert and Pascoli, both breathing whisky. Lambert opened the door leading to the passage to the ladies' sitting room, thrust Daisy through, and shut the door behind her.

It was dark – what Daisy had assumed to be a fanlight with iron tracery above the doorway admitted no gleam of light. Daisy promptly opened the door again, just an inch or two, and peered through the crack.

Kevin arrived on the scene, alerted by Stanley. He and Pascoli and Lambert stood in agitated consultation. Beyond them, Miss Genevieve waved her stick and demanded to take part. Sheer force of personality had the little group drifting towards her when a large man in a brown overcoat and soft felt hat bulled through the glass doors and strode across the lobby.

Daisy's friends fell silent. Kevin hurried after him, towards the registration desk.

Though Daisy couldn't see the desk, she heard the impatient ting-ting-ting of the bell. She thought she recognized Kevin's Irish-American twang, presumably offering assistance. The stranger's voice was louder. Even so, Daisy only made out a couple of words, those most easily distinguished by any listener's ear: her own name.

CHAPTER 16

As soon as Daisy heard the stranger pronounce her name, she eased the door shut with barely a click. So she actually was in danger! She hadn't truly believed all the fuss had any basis in reality.

She felt cold and shaky and much in need of Alec.

What would he advise her to do? Instinct said, creep down the passage to the sitting room and find a window to climb out of. But where would she go then? It was getting dark outside. Common sense said she was safer here with all her friends to protect her.

Common sense went on muttering in her head. Wasn't it rather odd that a man who had come to kill her because she might recognize a face should walk into a hotel and show his own face to any number of people? Surely, even in America, he couldn't hope to get away with killing everyone who saw him!

On the other hand, who else could he be? Could Gilligan have sent a plain clothes man to take her to police headquarters? That prospect was almost as alarming as the notion of a hired assassin stalking her.

A tap on the door made her jump. She held her breath as it opened. Though neither an assassin nor a policeman was likely to knock before coming after her, if he had somehow discovered her whereabouts, she was relieved to see Lambert. Behind him stood Thorwald and Pascoli, their backs turned, keeping watch.

Lambert had brought Stanley with him. The boy was hopping from foot to foot with excitement. 'I heard 'em!' he blurted out. 'I snuck up an' listened. "Whatcha want?" says Kevin. "I wanna see Mrs Fletcher," says the guy, real sharp. "Mrs Fletcher checked out," says Kevin, but Mr Blick the desk clerk comes out an' hears him an' up an' says, "No she ain't; her key's not here so she oughta be in but our residents ain't always careful 'bout handing in their keys when they go out."'

He was forced to pause for breath, and Lambert put in, 'Because there's never anyone at the desk.'

Stanley brushed this remark aside as the irrelevance it was. 'An' the guy says, "Call up an' see is she in," so Mr Blick called an' there wasn't no answer, course, an' Mr Blick says, "Mrs Fletcher's out," an' the guy says, "Mebbe she just don't feel like answering the phone I'll go up an' knock," an' Mr Blick, he makes Kevin take him, so I come an' tell the gennelmen.'

'Good for you, Stanley!' said Daisy.

'So we've got to get you away from here,' said Lambert, 'before he comes down.'

'Where could I go? I haven't even got my hat and coat.' Daisy had an inspiration. 'Wouldn't the safest place be the Cabots' suite?'

'Maybe, but it'd be mighty risky getting you up there. If we have to wait for the other elevator—'

'I'll go up the stairs. It's only the second floor –

third to you. But let's not waste any more time. We'll have to ask Miss Genevieve's permission and get her key, and I don't want to be halfway across the lobby when that chap comes down again and gets out of Kevin's elevator!'

Pascoli swung round. 'You go get the key, Lambert. Thorwald and I will take Mrs Fletcher to the stairs, where she'll be outa sight. Come on, let's hustle!'

So Daisy was hustled to the stairs, and then up them at a breathtaking pace which left Mr Thorwald far behind. Lambert, youth on his side, overtook the *Abroad* editor and caught up with Daisy and Pascoli as they paused on the stairs just below the third-floor level.

'Here's the key,' he panted, dropping it into Pascoli's extended hand.

'Bully! Now you better go check the elevator isn't passing by just when Mrs Fletcher gets to the top of the stairs.'

'OK.' Lambert sped off, to reappear a moment later on the landing above them. 'It's just coming down now.'

'You watch and see is the bullyboy in it.'

In the waiting hush, Daisy heard the lift mechanism's perpetual complaint. Its sudden cessation startled her and she took a step backwards. She had to grab the rail to save herself from a tumble, so that though she was aware of the clang of lift gates and then Lambert speaking in the passage above, she missed his first words.

'I left him knocking on Mrs Fletcher's door.' That was Kevin's anxious voice. 'I wasn't gonna wait and bring him back down not knowing where she is. You guys get her away safe?'

'She's going to hide out in Miss Genevieve's place. Keep the elevator here while she goes past, OK?'

'Sure.'

Thorwald arrived from below as Lambert appeared again above to announce in a whisper from the side of his mouth, 'All clear!'

Daisy and Pascoli went on up, followed by Thorwald, huffing and puffing. Passing the lift, she waved at Kevin. 'You OK now, m'lady?'

'Right as rain.'

'Hot dog! I'll go on down now, keep an eye on what's going on,' he said.

Moments later the door of the Cabots' suite closed behind Daisy and her escort. Lambert stationed himself by the door, presumably to repel boarders. Daisy and Thorwald sank into chairs, while Pascoli started to read the framed newspaper articles hanging on the walls.

'Oh boy, Eugene Cannon sure was some dame!' he exclaimed admiringly.

'In her heyday, she used to terrify me,' Thorwald admitted.

Daisy had expected 'Eugene Cannon' and Miss Cabot to be hot on her heels, but the minutes ticked past and they didn't come. Lambert started to twitch.

'Maybe I better go see what's happening,' he muttered.

'No!' said Pascoli. 'The less coming and going the better. I bet Miss Genevieve's waiting downstairs so she can tell us when the big galoot leaves.'

'What shall I do if he doesn't?' Daisy fretted. 'Suppose he finds out somehow where I am and comes knocking on the door?'

As if in response to her words, someone knocked. Everyone froze.

'Who's there?' Lambert enquired cautiously.

'Who do you think? Let me in, you fool. You have my key.'

Miss Genevieve lumbered in, her sister fluttering after her. Behind them came Kevin, sporting one red ear and waving two envelopes.

'He left a message for you, ma'am, and one for Mr Lambert. Warning him to stay outta the way, you betcha. I went and got 'em for you, but Mr Blick caught me and gave me a thick ear. I tol' him you asked me to get it for you, only he said it's Stanley's job running errands and I oughta be in my elevator. So I got Stanley to give 'em to me,' he ended triumphantly, handing one note to Daisy and the other to Lambert. 'Whassit say?'

Though she gave him a severe glance, Miss Genevieve seconded his question. 'Do please read it out, Mrs Fletcher. We are all agog. Mr Pascoli, you will find a paper knife on my desk.'

With the utilitarian steel blade, Daisy slit the envelope – hotel stationery – and took out a single sheet, which she handled gingerly by the edges. 'Fingerprints,' she explained, unfolding it.

The writing was large, at first glance straight from a copy-book but actually quite difficult to decipher. '"Dear Mrs Fletcher,"' Daisy read with a frown of puzzlement. 'How odd to be so polite if his aim is to . . .' Her eyes flew to the end. 'And it closes, "Yours truly." It's signed! I can't read the signature, but underneath he's printed . . .' A half-hysterical giggle escaped her. 'It says, "Agent, Bureau of Investigation, US Department of Justice."'

'Agent Whitaker!' groaned Lambert, studying his note.

'Aw, punk!' said Kevin in tones of deep disgust.

'Yes, that could be a W,' Daisy said, examining the signature. She turned back to the body of the letter and managed to make some sense of it. 'My husband asked him to drop by when he reached New York, to make sure I'm all right.'

'But I'm to stay on the job till Mr Fletcher arrives,' said Lambert.

'He's putting up at the something Hotel – I can't make out the name – and will come back tomorrow morning when he's talked to the local police.'

'My dear Miss Dal ... Mrs Fletcher,' said Thorwald, 'do I understand correctly that the immediate jeopardy is averted? Permit me to congratulate you most sincerely.'

'It don't mean there ain't some other creep after her,' Kevin said hopefully.

'Very true,' Miss Genevieve agreed.

'Oh dear! Surely, sister ...'

'I hope, young man, that you and your colleagues will continue to keep a watch for suspicious characters.'

'I gotta go home soon, ma'am,' Kevin deplored, 'but I'll sure get the night shift on the job.'

'Kevin,' said Daisy warmly, 'you're an angel. If Mr Whitaker had really been out for my blood, only your organization would have saved me.'

Behind the freckles, Kevin blushed rosy red. 'Aw, geez, m'lady, it wasn't nuttin.'

'Indeed, we are deeply indebted to your vigilance, my boy.' Thorwald slipped him a crackling green note, which disappeared with a practised ease.

'Tell you what,' said Pascoli, 'you ever need a job, you

come to me. The news business can always use a kid with get-up-and-go. Here's my card.'

'Yes, sir! I gotta get back to work now, or Blick'll have conniptions.' Kevin's hand went up protectively to his ear as he departed.

'Gosh,' said Daisy, suddenly exhausted, 'I want to thank all of you for coming so nobly to the rescue. And now I think I'll go and lie down for a bit after all the brouhaha.'

Though she left the bedside light on, intending to read, Daisy actually dozed off. Through her dreams floated faces from Gilligan's mug book, with Barton Bender's broad, greasy face looming over them in the guise of a dirigible. In the basket dangling below the airship, a scarlet-and-white cat with Mrs Carmody's face preened itself with long, painted talons. It kept fading, like the Cheshire cat, leaving a sharp-toothed grin. On the ground, a figure in a bowler hat and a bandit's bandanna mask aimed a crossbow at the airship and shot it. Deflating, Barton Bender whizzed around madly, growing smaller and smaller until he disappeared. Meanwhile his lady love turned into a winged crocodile, weeping copiously, and flew away. 'Rats!' said Detective Sergeant Gilligan. 'Angels and ministers of grace defend us!'

'That's Hamlet's line,' murmured Daisy, waking up.

Not long ago, a dream had helped her solve a murder, so she lay for a few minutes pondering the images. Nothing significant emerged from her ruminations, however, and pangs of hunger began to gnaw at her vitals. What with one thing and another, her tea had been skimpy. It was time for dinner.

Dinner with Lambert, she supposed, but she'd soon be rid of him. She resolved to be extra nice to him.

He was waiting in the passage outside her room. Thorwald and Pascoli were both waiting in the lobby below.

'Better safe than sorry,' said Pascoli cheerfully, 'and the more the merrier. Thanks to you, Mrs Fletcher, I've gotten some swell copy. Dinner's on *Town Talk*.'

The ebullient news editor took them to what he called a 'joint', where a furtive waiter provided a water carafe filled with white wine, which they drank from tumblers. After half a glass, Daisy stopped worrying about what the AC (Crime) would say to a headline reading 'Joint raided, Scotland Yard 'tec's wife pinched'. She stopped at half a glass, though, as she didn't want to risk getting tiddly and missing Alec at the station.

The wine only made her more determined to meet his train, in spite of Lambert's disapproval. Penn Station, he pointed out, was an ideal spot for any skulduggery instigated by Tammany or Bender.

'You needn't come,' she said.

'We'll *all* come,' said Pascoli. 'There won't be any shenanigans with three of us to guard you.'

Whether or not they averted shenanigans and skulduggery, Daisy was glad of her triple escort. Beneath the Roman pillars of the Baths of Caracalla and the lacy Victorian ironwork of the vast railway terminal, spread a netherworld, a Greek labyrinth of cavernous halls and gloomy tunnels. Not so very different from the London Underground, perhaps, but Daisy knew the Tube like the back of her hand and had always felt perfectly safe there.

Here, it was all too easy to imagine an assassin around every corner, or someone creeping up behind her, unheard in the constant din of loudspeaker announcements, rumbling luggage trolleys, and locomotive whistles. Besides, she was sure she would have got lost had not Pascoli and Thorwald steered her straight to the right platform.

The editors and Lambert clustered about her, keeping a lookout in every direction, as the train chugged in. Daisy had eyes only for the passengers as they swung or clambered down the steps from the high train to the low platform. Though Alec's dark hair was hidden by his hat, she spotted him as soon as his head appeared through a door.

Waving madly, she started walking towards him. The walk turned into a run, and she dodged between travellers and porters, one hand holding her hat on. He dropped his attaché case and Gladstone bag to catch her in his arms.

'Darling,' she said, smiling so hard it hurt, 'I've missed you most frightfully!' And then she astonished herself and him by bursting into tears on his chest.

Alec was horrified. 'Great Scott, Daisy, you never cry! Hush, love. It's not these wretched New York police that have upset you, is it? I've been hearing stories about them which would make your hair stand on end.'

'I've heard them, too, darling.' Sniffing, Daisy pulled away enough to straighten her hat and blink up at him. His hand went to his pocket. 'No, I don't need your hankie. I'm all right, honestly. Only don't let's talk about the police, or the murder, or anything like that tonight. I'll tell you all about it tomorrow.'

'OK by me, as they say.' He looked tired, Daisy noticed. 'Let's get back to your hotel.'

As he reached for his bags, Lambert said eagerly, 'I'll take those, sir!' Daisy's escort had caught up with her.

'This is Agent Lambert, darling, my guardian angel.' In response to Alec's darkly lowering eyebrows, she hurried on, 'And my editor, Mr Thorwald, and his colleague, Mr Pascoli. They kindly accompanied me here so that I wouldn't get lost.'

'And so . . .' Lambert began, but Daisy's frown cut him short. 'Uh, yes, I guess you want a cab, sir?'

Outside the station, they parted from Thorwald and Pascoli. Much as she wanted to be alone with Alec, Daisy was too well brought up to leave Lambert to take a separate cab to the Chelsea. As they set off, Alec said witheringly, 'So you're my wife's guardian angel, are you, Lambert?'

Though the street lamps shed little light inside the cab, Daisy was certain the young agent's ears were red. 'Gee, sir,' he stammered, 'I'm mighty sorry I didn't . . .'

'It's not your fault,' Daisy interrupted. 'He couldn't help it, darling.'

Alec sighed. 'No, who am I to find fault? *I've* never managed to keep you out of trouble. I beg your pardon, Lambert. You must explain to me exactly how it all came about.'

'Tomorrow,' Daisy said firmly. 'You promised we wouldn't talk about it till tomorrow. Let's meet for breakfast and get it all over with before Mr Whitaker turns up.'

'Good idea, love.'

'Not in the hotel dining room,' said Lambert, in what Daisy recognized as his cloak-and-dagger voice. 'You never know who's listening.'

True, Kevin would undoubtedly find out somehow what was said, but he knew most of it already. It wasn't worth the effort of reminding Lambert that practically no guests at the Hotel Chelsea came down for breakfast, and in any case no one but the Misses Cabot had shown the least interest.

'Right-oh,' said Daisy.

After breakfast and explanations, Daisy, Alec and Lambert returned to the hotel to find the Misses Cabot lying in wait in the lobby, commanding a view of the entrance. Daisy had told Alec about Miss Cabot's kindness and Miss Genevieve's part in protecting her from Sergeant Gilligan. Doffing his hat, he submitted to being introduced in his full glory: Detective Chief Inspector Fletcher of New Scotland Yard.

Miss Cabot was thrilled. 'Now that you're here, Chief Inspector,' she declared, 'this terrible business will be cleared up in no time.'

'I'm afraid not, ma'am. I have no access to the police investigation.'

'I explained all that, sister!'

'Oh dear! Well, at least dear Mrs Fletcher will be quite safe now.'

'I intend to make sure of that, ma'am, though I confess I find it difficult to believe that complete strangers are out after her blood!'

'You do not know America, Mr Fletcher,' said Miss Genevieve grimly.

'As I have frequently been reminded these past few days,' Alec admitted with a smile.

Miss Genevieve grinned. 'All too frequently, I dare say. Do you want me to see what strings I can pull to let you involve yourself in the official investigation?'

'Great Scott, ma'am, no thank you! I'm only afraid Whitaker, the agent from Washington, is going to drag me in further than I want to go. Mr Hoover, the heir apparent of the Bureau of Investigation, instructed him to make sure I have every facility.'

'This Hoover, now, tell me about him. A relative of Herbert Hoover, the Secretary of Commerce?'

'I think not. J. Edgar Hoover's an odd little man. Literally little: to compensate, he wears shoe lifts and has his desk set on a platform. He's a bully, I'm afraid, and a bit of a bounder, but I believe he's sincere, obsessive even, in his intention of setting up an incorruptible national police force. Sincere and probably competent.'

'Incorruptible, ha!' snorted Miss Genevieve. 'That I'll believe when I see it with my own eyes, and even then ... But to return to Otis Carmody's death, let me impart what I have learned from young Rosenblatt. Add it to what Mrs Fletcher has undoubtedly told you, and I should value your opinion of the case.'

As she spoke, a man turned away from the reception desk and headed for the main door at a rapid stride. He carried a shabby cardboard suitcase in one hand, his hat in the other.

A bowler hat – 'Gosh!' said Daisy, her glance flying to his face as he hurried past. The features were nondescript, yet recognizable. 'Gosh, it's him! It's the man in the bowler hat.' She jumped up. 'Alec ...'

Kevin dashed up. 'Mrs Fletcher, that guy's Mr Pitt, that you asked about. He came down the stairs or I'da tol' you sooner. He just checked out.'

Wilbur Pitt, of course! That face was memorable because it was a blurred replica of Carmody's distinctive looks. His clothes explained the discrepancy between Daisy's and Lambert's description to Gilligan: he wore a thigh-length overcoat which looked less like a fashionable motoring coat than something cut down from an ancient frock coat.

He was out on the pavement by now. Daisy grabbed Alec's arm. 'Darling, we've got to stop him. Come along, quick. You, too, Mr Lambert.'

'Who, me?'

'But Whitaker's coming, Daisy,' Alec expostulated, even as her urgency made him rise to his feet, 'and anyway, you simply can't detain a stranger going about his lawful business!'

'You don't understand, he's the man in the bowler hat.' She practically dragged him towards the door. 'The man on the stairs. At least we must follow him so we can tell the police where to find him. We can't just let him get away. Now I know the man in the bowler hat is Carmody's cousin, I'm absolutely positive he's the murderer!'

CHAPTER 17

Daisy rushed out to the street, followed by Alec, still remonstrating, and Lambert, bleating plaintively.

'We can't just let him get away,' she repeated, stepping back up on to the doorstep to scan the scene. 'Maybe it *is* meddling, but by the time we find a policeman and persuade him ... Balfour, which way did he go, the man who just came out?'

'That way, Mrs Fletcher, ma'am.' The doorman pointed towards Seventh Avenue.

'Oh yes, thanks, I see him.' Of the few bowler hats among the swarms of soft felts moving in every direction, only one was heading east. 'Come on, you two.'

To her relief, Alec came. 'But only to follow him, Daisy,' he insisted, jamming his own grey felt on his head. 'You are absolutely not on any account to approach him! Promise, or we'll stop right now.'

'Right-oh, I promise, darling. Hurry!'

'Don't get too close,' Lambert warned. He too had scooped up his hat as they deserted the Cabots. As the opportunity for doing his cloak-and-dagger stuff dawned on him, he pulled it down over his eyebrows and went on buoyantly, 'That's the first rule of tailing a suspect.'

A tram rattled past them to the stop near the corner. Pitt darted towards it and disappeared.

'Oh blast!' said Daisy, starting to run.

A bell clanged and the tram set off again.

'Lost him,' Alec observed hopefully.

'We'll catch the next streetcar,' Lambert proposed.

'That's no good,' Daisy objected. 'He could get off anywhere. Maybe he's going to the elevated railway on Sixth Avenue. If we run . . .'

'There he is!' exclaimed Lambert, pointing. 'Over there, just stepping up on to the sidewalk. He only crossed the street. After him!'

A sudden rush of traffic held them up. Daisy was on tenterhooks, sure they would lose Pitt. Even on tiptoe, she could see no sign of him among the crowds on the opposite pavement. But when at last the policeman on point duty let them cross, Lambert swore he still saw their quarry ahead.

'Alec, can you . . . Oh, I see him. Just a glimpse between all the people. Where *is* everyone going at this time in the morning?' she demanded crossly, narrowly avoiding another pedestrian.

'Perhaps they're all pursuing suspected murderers,' Alec suggested dryly. 'You do realize, Daisy, that I have no authority whatsoever to arrest your man whatever crimes he may have committed.'

'I know. That's why I asked Mr Lambert to come.'

'Who, me? I can't arrest him!'

'You could if he crossed into another state, couldn't you? You said something about crossing state lines to escape the police being a federal offence.'

'Um, sort of,' Lambert said cautiously. 'To escape prosecution, though, not just questioning. I think. Gilligan and Rosenblatt may want to grill Pitt, but we don't know for sure that he's committed an indictable offence.'

'*I'm* sure.' Daisy would have explained her deductions, but she needed her breath and her attention for the chase. At least, however unconvinced, Lambert and Alec were keeping pace as the bowler hat continued north on Seventh Avenue at a fast walk.

They crossed Twenty-sixth, Twenty-seventh, Twenty-ninth, and Thirtieth Streets. Daisy spared a thought for the missing Twenty-fourth, Twenty-fifth and Twenty-eighth. If they must have such a dull, though logical, system of naming streets, at least they ought to be consistent about it. But as they neared Thirty-first, her guess as to Pitt's aim turned into a certainty.

'He's going to Pennsylvania Station!' she said. 'He's leaving New York. I bet he's going home. All we have to do is get on the same train, and as soon as he gets to the next state you can arrest him.'

'I don't have a warrant,' moaned Lambert. 'All I'm supposed to be doing is looking after you, not arresting people.'

'Have you got your credentials on you?' Alec asked.

Lambert felt his inside breast pocket. 'Ye-es.'

'Then you can at least request assistance from the local police, wherever we run him to ground, until you've consulted Whitaker, Washington, or the New York authorities. Come on, having come so far, we ought at least to try to stand close enough to him in the ticket line to overhear his destination.'

'You are a sport, darling!' Daisy told him.

He gave her a rueful grin. 'I must be mad.'

'That's all right. You haven't got Mr Crane or the AC overlooking your every move here.'

'Thank heaven!' said Alec fervently.

They were crossing Thirty-first Street when Wilbur Pitt paused on the steps going up to the station and looked back. Daisy instinctively ducked her head.

She didn't think he would recognize her. This morning in the lobby he had marched straight ahead, intent on leaving the hotel, glancing neither to left nor right. In the Flatiron Building, though he had turned his head her way when she called out to him to stop, he had appeared far too distraught to take in what he was seeing. If they had passed each other in the hotel before she knew who he was, he might remember her, she supposed, but to catch sight of a fellow resident crossing a street not far from the hotel ought not to alarm him. Still, it seemed better not to let him glimpse her face.

When she looked up again, he was gone.

'What if he already has a return ticket?' she exclaimed, hurrying her step. 'He'll go straight to the platform and we'll never find him.'

Lambert broke into a run, dodging through the crowds approaching and leaving the station. He hurdled the steps and disappeared between two of the grandiose pillars.

'He's hot on the trail,' said Alec.

'Yes, he seems to have decided the pleasure of the chase outweighs the terror of actually catching Pitt and having to do something about it.'

'Can't we just leave him to it?'

'Alec!' Daisy tugged him onward.

'Why not?'

'Because I'm the only person who can identify him as the man who ran off down the stairs just after Carmody was shot. We told you, Lambert had his specs knocked off and couldn't tell Pitt from Adam.'

Alec snorted. 'Young whippersnapper. I wish I'd heard the story before I met your Mr Thorwald. I'd have liked to shake his hand.' He paused at the top of the steps, where Pitt had stopped before. 'You are absolutely certain of your identification, aren't you? A wild-goose chase would be bad enough, but great Scott, Daisy, the prospect of harassing a perfectly respectable citizen makes me shudder.'

'I'm positive.' As they moved on into the immense, echoing spaces of the upper station, she guiltily confessed, 'That is, I'm positive he's the man on the stairs, and he's more than likely the murderer, but it is remotely possible he's just a frightened witness.'

'Remotely possible?' Alec sighed. 'In that case, I shouldn't dream of letting Lambert attempt an arrest. We'll try to discover where Pitt is off to and notify your friend Rosencrantz.'

'My friend! He's not as ghastly as Guildenstern, but only because he has better manners. Here comes Lambert. What's up?'

'Pitt's in the ticket line. There's lots of people ahead of him but only a couple behind him so far, so I figured I'd better find you and put you wise.'

'Quite right,' Alec told him.

Lambert positively glowed. 'I'll go and get in line behind him now,' he said eagerly, turning back towards the ticket office. 'I'll get three tickets to wherever he's going.'

'Have you got enough money on you?' Daisy asked. 'He may be going clear across the country.'

'I guess not,' Lambert admitted, crestfallen.

'Let's first find out what his destination is,' said Alec. 'Then we can decide what to do next.'

'OK.'

'You should be the one to stand in line, darling. He might have seen either of us around the hotel and wonder what we're doing close behind him.'

'Possibly, but there's no earthly reason why Lambert shouldn't be buying a railway ticket. He's more likely to recognize the name of some obscure American city than I am.'

'I'll go!' Lambert went.

'If you ask me,' Daisy said darkly, 'you're just trying to avoid getting any more involved than absolutely necessary.'

'You're absolutely right,' Alec agreed, 'though whether any of this is necessary in the absolute sense . . . No, don't tell me again! I'm still with you, am I not?'

'Only because you don't trust me out of your sight.'

'With good reason,' Alec pointed out dryly.

'Just think, darling, how simply spiffing it would be if Scotland Yard and I between us caught the murderer. Wouldn't that be one in the eye for Rosencrantz and Guildenstern!'

'When you put it like that, my love, how can I resist? Ah, here comes . . . Something's gone wrong. Come on!'

Lambert was gesturing frantically at them. Beyond him, Daisy caught a glimpse of a bowler hat rapidly disappearing down one of the stairways to the lower level. Seeing he had their attention, Lambert turned and plunged after it.

Their pursuit was brought up short by a porter pulling a trolley laden with baggage across in front of them, followed by a massive woman with a nursemaid and three children. The whole lot stopped right there for the porter to patiently assure the woman, 'Sure, lady, I got the blue grip. Here, see? OK?'

'Not that one. The dark blue.'

Alec cut round in front of them. Daisy dashed the other way, just as one of the children dropped a ball. All three ran to retrieve it. The littlest toddled right into Daisy's path. To save herself from falling over him, she clutched the nearest support – the biggest child's shoulder.

'Mommy, she grabbed me!'

Alec was already at the top of the steps. No time for explanations. Daisy sped on, praying she would not hear a hue and cry of 'Kidnapper!' raised behind her.

CHAPTER 18

As she started down the steps, Alec reached the bottom. Gazing around, he apparently caught sight of Lambert, for he glanced up at Daisy, gave her a brief wave, and strode off.

'Blast!' If she went down any faster, she would risk breaking her neck. What if she couldn't find Alec in the maze of tunnels? She'd have to retire ignominiously to the hotel and wait to hear from him. No doubt he'd be delighted to have her well out of the affair.

Just when he seemed to have realized her pursuit of Pitt was worthwhile!

At the bottom, Daisy turned in the direction Alec had taken. She saw no sign of either him or Lambert. Ahead of her, gaped the mouths of several tunnels. A bewilderment of signs directed her steps, none of which helped as she didn't understand them and didn't know where she wanted to go, anyway.

Nor did she dare stand still, in case the fat woman above had summoned a policeman. What if she were arrested for attempted kidnapping and had to appeal to Sergeant Gilligan to vouch for her? Not only would it be horribly humiliating, but she'd miss the chase after Pitt.

She moved uncertainly towards the tunnels. Just as she reached the point where she would have to decide which way to go, and probably lose Alec and Lambert altogether, the latter appeared.

'This way, Mrs Fletcher. Quick!'

'What's happened?' Daisy asked, joining him and hurrying down a tunnel at his side.

Lambert blushed. 'I guess it was my fault. I pulled my hat down at the front, like you told me not to, and turned my coat collar up. Pitt got kind of twitchy standing in line and kept looking around. I guess he noticed me watching him, and then next time he looked around, there I was watching him again.'

'With those glasses lurking between hat and collar, you must have been rather conspicuous.'

'I can't take off my glasses. I can't see a thing without them,' he reminded her anxiously.

'No, but with your collar down and your hat in a normal position – push it a bit further back and tilt it at a jaunty angle. That's better.'

Lambert was dubious. 'I'm not exactly a jaunty sort of person.'

'Pitt doesn't know anything about your character. Think of it as a disguise?'

'Oh, a disguise! OK. Mr Fletcher took over tailing Pitt and sent me back to find you.'

'Where's Pitt going?'

'The subway, I guess. I have to admit, I haven't figured out their system. All the signs seem to be the names of companies, not where the trains are going.'

'No wonder I can't make head or tail of them. I wonder whether Pitt can?'

'Gee, not likely. He's a backwoodsman, isn't he? Maybe he's just chasing his nose.'

'I'm sure his aim *was* to get back to his backwoods, but now he's simply trying to escape us. You, anyway. With any luck, he hasn't caught on yet to Alec and me.'

'Do you think I ought to quit?' Lambert asked wistfully.

'No! We need you. You're the only one with official standing. But I thought you weren't frightfully keen.'

'That was before. Look, there's Mr Fletcher.'

Alec was standing on the platform just beyond the barrier, facing their way. Seeing Daisy and Lambert, he gestured urgently. Daisy heard the rumble of an approaching train.

Hastily she and Lambert paid and passed through the barrier as brakes screeched.

'Don't look to your right,' Alec muttered. 'Head straight for the train, but don't get on till I say.'

The train came to a halt. Doors opened. Alec glanced casually to his left, and then to his right, as if looking for an uncrowded carriage – not that much was visible through the filthy windows.

'Right-oh, he's got in. Let's go.'

The New York business day started early, in conformity with the motto 'Time is money'. At this time in the morning, the subway was well patronized but not crammed with passengers. They found three seats together, next to a door.

'How will we know when Pitt gets off?' Daisy asked as the train rattled into motion.

In the echoing din, compounded by the bellowed conversation of their fellow travellers, Alec's reply was inaudible. It wasn't something he could shout to her, unlikely as it seemed that anyone could conceivably overhear.

The racket lessened somewhat as the train slowed for the next station. Alec leant over to Daisy and said in her ear, 'Don't get up, but be ready to hop off, both of you.'

Daisy leant over to Lambert and passed on the message.

Alec joined the group of passengers waiting by the door. As soon as it opened, the surge carried him out on to the platform. Keeping a close watch on him, Daisy saw him look to the rear of the train, where Pitt had got on. He took a step back towards the door and beckoned.

Daisy and Lambert jumped up and pushed out against the inward flow of boarders.

'"Times Square",' Daisy read the station sign. 'I wonder if he can change lines here, or if he'll just go straight back to Pennsylvania Station.'

Alec did not respond but put out an arm to stop the others following Pitt's receding figure too closely.

'The announcement said, "Change here for . . .",' Lambert told her. 'But I didn't get for what.'

'I didn't even catch the "Change here",' Daisy said.

'Lambert, tie your shoelace!' Alec suddenly ordered.

Lambert glanced down and protested, 'It's not untied!' Then Daisy caught a glimpse of Pitt. The mass of people ahead were parting to pass around him as he paused in the mouth of the exit tunnel to stare back.

The crowd hid him from Daisy again, but Alec snapped, 'He's spotted us – unless something else has alarmed him. Come on.'

'I guess he spotted me,' Lambert said humbly, striding along after Alec with Daisy trotting to keep up. 'I guess that's why Mr Fletcher said to tie my shoes. I guess I got a lot to learn about tailing.'

Somehow Alec kept Pitt in sight. They followed the fugitive to Grand Central Terminal, where they almost lost him, and then on to another subway train. The next leg of the chase seemed to go on forever, to the point where Daisy began to wonder whether they were doomed to travel through subterranean tunnels for all eternity.

She also had time to wonder whether Wilbur Pitt had really been the man on the stairs. The horrid possibility dawned on her that she might have recognized his likeness to Carmody rather than to the face briefly seen in the Flatiron Building. How ghastly if Alec was right and they were harassing a respectable citizen!

But why should Pitt flee if he was perfectly respectable?

Daisy recalled her own frightened efforts to escape the thugs who had never materialized. Pitt's cousin had been murdered, and he was being followed relentlessly by two men he didn't know. In his shoes, she would have done her utmost to shake off her pursuers, she acknowledged – to herself.

To acknowledge to Alec that she could be mistaken was another matter. After all, she was no more sure she was wrong than sure she was right. If she breathed the slightest doubt, he was bound to abandon the pursuit at once.

And she might be right.

It wouldn't hurt to find out where Pitt was going, she considered. Time enough then to decide what to do next.

The next station was taking a very long time to arrive. Returning to an awareness of her surroundings, Daisy heard one of her neighbours shouting to his companion, 'Yeah, under the East River, right this minute, you betcha. Wunnerful what modern science can do!'

Since she had passed beneath the Thames innumerable times, Daisy was not impressed. She was trying to work out where one would get to by crossing the East River, when she noticed that Lambert's eyes had widened and his face paled.

'Under the river!' he gasped, staring upward in horror. 'Gee whiz!'

'Don't worry. There have been tunnels under the river in London for ages, and nothing's ever gone wrong.'

Unconvinced, but his shoulders relaxing a little, Lambert pointed out, 'There's always a first time.' His gaze stayed fixed on the roof of the carriage, as if he expected water to trickle through at any moment, until it became obvious the train was labouring uphill.

Daylight seeped through the grimy windows, and then they were above ground, pulling into a station lit by pale, wintry sunshine.

Alec went to the door. It opened and a nasal voice shouted, 'Brooklyn! Everybody out!'

Standing aside, Alec let the other passengers descend first, watching over their heads. Daisy and Lambert joined him.

'I have a good view of the exit,' he explained, 'and Pitt has no choice but to get off here.'

'I'm a bit vague about the geography,' Daisy said, 'but isn't Brooklyn on an island? He'll have to go back to the city to get anywhere.'

'There he goes,' said Lambert, and crouched to untie and retie a shoelace.

'Keep back in the shadows, Daisy,' Alec said sharply. 'With any luck, he'll think he's lost us.'

'Everybody off!' The official reached them. 'Everybody off, sir. You wanna go back to the city, you gotta get off and get on again. Or there's streetcars and cabs outside if you wanna go anyplace else.'

'Cabs!' Alec looked worried.

'Where can he go?' Daisy said. 'He has to get back to the city.'

'There are probably other ways. Other tunnels, bridges, ferries perhaps. Come on. Pitt's gone through the gate.'

Pitt was lurking on the pavement between the row of taxicabs and a hoarding advertising five-cent cigars. He spotted them the instant they stepped through the gate. He jumped into the nearest taxi, which immediately pulled out of the row and turned towards the yard exit.

Daisy, Alec and Lambert piled into another cab. 'Police!' snapped Alec. 'Follow that cab! Double your fare if you keep it in sight.'

'Sure thing, boss!' said the young driver eagerly, starting the meter running with one hand as he wheeled away from the kerb with the other. 'You want I should catch up to him? You gonna make a pinch?'

'No, we just need to know where he's going.'

'OK. Say, you a limey?'

'Yes, I'm a limey cop'

'I ain't got nuttin against limeys.'

'I'm glad to hear it. But my colleague here is American, a federal agent.'

The driver looked back with an ominous frown. 'Geez, you Treasury?'

'US Department of Justice, Investigation Bureau,' intoned Lambert.

'Oh, that's OK. Say, you feds got lady cops now? Or is it the limeys got lady cops?'

'I'm a limey,' Daisy told him, 'but I'm a witness, not a cop.'

'Tough! Hey, look, that crook's heading outta town, that you're tailing. He better be going someplace I can get a fare back.'

'We're paying double,' Alec reminded him, '*if* you don't lose him.'

The driver concentrated on driving.

The countryside was not very different from parts of England, with trees and fields, occasional villages, and parkland with glimpses of mansions. The smaller houses were mostly weatherboarded – or clapboard, as Daisy had learned to call it in Connecticut – instead of brick or half-timbered. Churches were also clapboard, whitewashed, with funny little pointed steeples hung with bells. Many trees were already leafless, but here and there a maple still blazed with a scarlet rarely seen in English woods, brilliant in the autumnal sunshine.

All very pretty, but where on earth was Pitt going? 'I didn't realize Brooklyn was on such a big island,' said Daisy. 'Or is it Bronx that's on an island?'

'Nah, this here's Long Island. Hunnert and twenny miles end to end. Geez, I hope your crook ain't going all the way to the Hamptons!'

'If the Hamptons are at the other end of the island, so do I! Alec, do you think Pitt has friends somewhere here, who he hopes will hide him? I can't imagine why else he's running all over the country.'

'Maybe.' Alec glanced at the ticking taximeter. 'We can't go on chasing him forever. When he stops, Lambert and I had better approach him and see if we can't persuade him to go back to New York with us, while you, Daisy, go on to find a telephone to report his whereabouts.'

'But, darling . . .'

'Hey, boss, he's turning off the highway. You figure he's trying to shake us?'

'Let's hope he's nearing his destination.'

For a few suspenseful minutes, they lost sight of the taxi ahead. Their driver swore, afraid of losing his double fare. Then there it was again, turning off the road towards a farmhouse and two huge barns, on the edge of a large, flat, empty field.

On top of one barn a wind stocking floated from a flag-pole, and nearby stood several aeroplanes: three bi-planes, a monoplane and an unwieldy triplane.

'An aerodrome!' Alec cried. 'Great Scott, don't tell me he's hoping to escape by air!'

In front of the farmhouse, a single-engined biplane was preparing for flight. The four-bladed wooden propeller turned idly, and a helmeted man in the cockpit was leaning out to call something to a couple of men on the ground.

Even before the first taxi had braked to a halt twenty yards from the aeroplane, Pitt jumped out. His suitcase in his left hand, he brandished a pistol in his right. Then he took careful aim, and a shot rang out.

The aviator ducked. The men on the ground threw themselves flat, while several others emerged from the house and hangars. Pitt ran towards the aeroplane.

'Holy cow!' breathed the second cab driver, swerving as he jammed on his brakes.

Lambert sprang out, automatic in hand.

'Don't shoot, you fool!' yelled Alec, diving after him as he squeezed the trigger.

The gun failed to fire. Alec hit Lambert behind the knees and he measured his length on the grass, losing both his weapon and his spectacles.

Daisy perched on the running board for a better view. She saw Pitt reach the aeroplane, drop his suitcase, and clamber into the open cabin in the rear of the fuselage. He leant forward to hold his revolver to the pilot's head. The pilot cried out to the ground crew. One of them chucked the suitcase up after Pitt.

The engine roared, the propeller speeded to a blur. The men on the ground crept to the wheels, pulled away the chocks and scampered clear. The aeroplane started to move, then gathered speed across the tarmac.

After it lumbered the first taxi driver, bellowing, 'Hey, what about my fare? What about my fare?'

CHAPTER 19

His spectacles restored to him, Lambert was almost weeping with frustration. 'Gee whiz, why did you stop me? I could have arrested him. That was US Government property he was shooting at.'

'Government property?' Daisy queried, shading her eyes to gaze after the ascending biplane.

'You can't go shooting towards a plane!' Alec expostulated. 'Hit the fuel tank or lines and the whole thing goes up in flames. Anyway, your pistol misfired.'

'I dropped it eighteen storeys,' Daisy reminded him. 'Government property?'

'Didn't you see the post office insignia on the side?' Lambert shook his head angrily. 'They shouldn't have given in to him so easily.'

'He had a gun,' said Alec, 'one which didn't misfire. If he had started shooting again, your precious government property would more than likely have become an inferno, and the government employees incinerated with it.'

'Air piracy, by George!' said an exhilarated and very English voice behind them. 'Bally bad show! I say, what was all that about, if you don't mind my asking?'

They turned to see a tall, thin man in flier's leathers, a

helmet dangling from his hand and a pipe from his mouth. He had a splendid handlebar moustache, a Roman nose, and very blue eyes, which widened as he saw Alec's face.

Alec's mouth dropped open. 'Great Scott, it's Dipper!' he exclaimed, just as the other said, 'By *George*, if it isn't the Arrow! What ho, old chap!' They wrung each other's hands and slapped each other on the back.

Lambert interrupted this touching reunion. 'Say, Mr Dipper, do you have an airplane? I guess you're not an American citizen, but the US Government would sure make it worth your while to chase that air pirate.'

The blue eyes lit up. 'By George, there's an idea. Not that I need the bally rhino, but what a lark! As it happens, I've got a four-seater just about ready to take off. Let's go!'

The next quarter of an hour was utter confusion. Alec made hasty introductions – Dipper turned out to be Sir Roland Amboyne, a friend from RFC days. But Alec considered the whole notion of chasing the fugitive through the skies crazy.

He was overborne by Sir Roland's enthusiasm, aided by Lambert's insistence that the kidnapper of a federal employee must not be allowed to disappear into the blue vastness.

'While you follow him, I'll alert the federal authorities,' he said importantly.

'Oh no,' said Alec, 'you're coming along. You're the only one of us with the official standing to arrest the miscreant, if by some miracle we catch him. Daisy's perfectly capable of notifying whoever needs to be notified.'

'Me!' Indignation overruled both grammar and pleasure at this unwonted compliment. 'I'm going with you. Darling, you said you'd take me up in an aeroplane one day.'

Alec's dark eyebrows lowered forbiddingly. 'Not on a crazy wild-goose chase with gunfire possible.'

Daisy didn't bother to argue. She was not going to be left behind. She hurried after Sir Roland, who, as soon as Alec agreed to pursue Pitt, had loped towards the group by the farmhouse, calling out instructions and requests.

As she followed him into the building – it had a sign over the door saying HAZELHURST FIELD – someone thrust a leather flying suit into her arms and pointed her towards a door at the rear of the big front room. Finding herself in a sort of scullery turned into an office, she scrutinized the outfit. Though it was several sizes too large for her, she decided reluctantly that she couldn't stuff her skirt inside. Her petticoat would fit, and might help to keep her warm even if it made her bulge around the bottom, and her jacket and blouse could stay on under the top. She started to undo buttons, fingers fumbling in her haste. She was *not* going to be left behind.

A plump girl bounced in, carrying a pair of trousers and a pair of smart leather boots. 'Hi, I'm Leora. I do the record keeping around here. Jake – he's one of the mechanics and on the small side for a guy – he says you can borrow his pants and he'll go home in his overalls. You'll need something under that suit. And I brought you my boots.'

'Gosh, thanks, Miss . . . Leora.'

'I guess they'll about fit you. Your feet'll freeze if you go up in those shoes, but I'd kinda like them back sometime if you can. Here, lemme give you a hand. You don't hafta wear that helmet in the cabin, but you may want it when it gets cold. And take your coat to tuck around your knees. It won't go on over these.'

As Leora efficiently inserted her into the flying suit, Daisy heard Alec in the next room dictating telegrams. Still speaking as he tied his bootlaces after changing, he didn't see her when she and Leora entered. She was careful to keep out of his sight.

Lambert, shaking too much to dress himself, was being stuffed into his borrowed kit. He ventured a last feeble protest: 'But Rosenblatt said not to leave New York!' No one took any notice.

One of Sir Roland's flying colleagues came in through another door, his arms full of paper bags, boxes and other small containers. 'Anyone else have a lunch pail or Thermos flask to donate to the cause? OK, I'll take these out to the plane.'

Daisy sneaked out with him. She helped him store the supplies in the cockpit and minuscule cabin of the biplane, and he helped her squeeze into one of the seats and fasten the safety belt. A short man in greasy dungarees gave her a grin and a thumbs-up. Lambert was marched out by two more men and inserted beside her, moaning quietly. One of them handed Daisy a couple of folded paper bags.

'In case of airsickness,' he said.

'I don't get seasick,' Daisy said hopefully.

Hooking a wordless thumb at Lambert, he lowered the wood-framed canvas roof over the passenger compartment.

Sir Roland was already in the open cockpit, going over a checklist with a second mechanic. Alec came out of the house and strode across the tarmac, looking frightfully romantic in the flying suit, a green silk scarf around his neck and goggles perched on top of his helmet. Glancing around, he saw Daisy's face as she peered at him through the celluloid side panel of the cabin.

He scowled, eyebrows meeting, then raised brows and eyes to heaven, shrugged, and scrambled up into the cockpit with Sir Roland.

He strapped his safety belt and helmet, lowered his goggles over his eyes, and pulled on his gauntlets. 'Right-oh, Dipper, take her up.'

'Goodbye!'

'Good luck!'

'Go get 'em!'

Through streaky glass, Daisy saw one propeller begin to turn, and then another. The muted hum of the engines rose to a rumble, and the aeroplane began to taxi.

She was actually going up in an aeroplane!

Beside her, Lambert huddled with his eyes shut and his hands over his ears. For a moment, Daisy was tempted to follow his craven example. Curiosity saved her from the ignominy. What a subject for an article!

They bumped across the grass and turned into the wind. The rumble became a deafening roar as they picked up speed. Daisy saw Dipper press the stick forward, and the tail rose so that she was sitting upright instead of leaning back. With the skid off the ground, the joggling lessened. Faster and faster they raced across the airfield.

Then Dipper eased the stick back. Daisy's stomach lurched as the hard vibration of wheels on earth suddenly ended. They were airborne.

Lambert clutched his mouth and middle and began to sweat.

Handing him a paper bag, Daisy turned away, giving all her attention to the blurred view beyond the celluloid. Engine bellowing with effort, the biplane swung upward in a wide spiral. The ground tilted below.

Proud of her sangfroid, Daisy gazed down. The white farmhouse, the group of people still standing on the tarmac watching, the motionless planes, the hangars, the field, trees and bushes, all grew smaller beneath her. Long Island spread out, its greenness seamed with roads and streams, patched with leafless woodland and villages.

The aeroplane levelled off. Relaxing, Daisy discovered how tense she had been.

She couldn't see much out of the window now. The engine noise had lessened slightly with the end of the climb, though it was still a terrific din. Now she could distinguish the sounds of the wind as it whistled through the forest of struts stiffening the wings and twanged the wires. It played the taut canvas of the wings like timpani, half a dozen different booming notes at once. The fabric sides of the cabin flapped in and out, slap, slap, slap, like a housemaid beating a carpet.

Daisy realized, too, that the apparent smoothness of flight was merely in contrast to the jolting acceleration across the grass. A constant vibration set every loose oddment to rattling. She only hoped no vital gadget was going to fall off.

She and Lambert would have to shout if they wanted to converse. Fortunately, she had no great desire to communicate with him, even if he were in a condition to speak. She cast a quick sidelong glance his way. At least he didn't appear to have actually been sick, but the way he was curled around his inner workings reminded her of Alec on the Atlantic crossing.

Looking forward through the glass pane separating the cabin from the cockpit, she saw Alec leaning sideways to peer around the edge of the windscreen, binoculars in hand.

As she watched, he straightened, pushed up his goggles, undid his safety belt, and to her utter horror stood up.

If her determined pursuit of Wilbur Pitt led to her husband performing such risky stunts, Daisy wanted nothing more to do with it. She banged on the glass.

'Alec! Sit down!'

He and Dipper either didn't hear or ignored her. Alec scanned the skies, shading his eyes with his hand, while the aeroplane droned steadily onward. Suddenly he stopped, stiff as a pointer scenting prey. He raised the glasses. For a long moment he stared, then sat down with a sharp nod. Pointing, he said – or rather, shouted something – to Dipper, which Daisy couldn't hear but assumed to be on the lines of 'That's him!'

Dipper altered course slightly. The chase was on.

Now Daisy had the leisure to contemplate what she had wrought. Her recognition of Pitt as the man on the stairs in the Flatiron Building had brought them to this fragile craft sailing through emptiness, high above Mother Earth. How certain was she of her identification? What if she was wrong?

She tried to picture the pale, frightened face of the man who had run from the scene of Carmody's death. It was vague in her memory, eclipsed by Pitt's face as she had last seen it at the Brooklyn station yard. Had she imagined the likeness? The face beneath the bowler hat had been nondescript, as she told Gilligan and Rosenblatt. So was Pitt's, but for his distant resemblance to his cousin.

Daisy acknowledged reluctantly that she just might be mistaken.

What was worse, even if she was right, she had no proof

that Pitt had shot his cousin. Of course he *had* behaved suspiciously, galloping off down those stairs, playing least in sight, then doing his utmost to evade her and Alec and Lambert. But suppose he had fled in fear of his life, perhaps because of a family feud as posited by Mr Thorwald?

Still, though maybe he had not shot Carmody, he had most certainly pirated the air mail aeroplane. A dozen or more witnesses could swear to that. He was a criminal.

A horrid thought struck Daisy: what if her relentless pursuit had driven a previously innocent Pitt to the desperate step of kidnapping a federal employee? If he had recognized her and Lambert from the Flatiron Building, he could reasonably believe that they had killed his cousin and were now after his blood.

At that moment, had she been able to communicate with Alec, she would have called off the chase and let the poor man try to escape the forces of the law without her interference.

The force of the American law she had brought with her, in the shape of Lambert, cowered at her side, in no state to arrest anyone. His eyes were still determinedly shut and his hands once again covered his ears, the threat of sickness apparently past. The thrill of flight was not for him.

In fact, the thrill of flight was definitely wearing off for Daisy. The take-off had been exciting, but for what seemed like hours she had been stuck in this cramped, vibrating, fearfully noisy box. She couldn't even see much because the celluloid blurred the distant view. In spite of numerous draughts (less than a handsbreadth is a draught, more than a handsbreath is fresh air, her nanny had always said when flinging up the sash in midwinter), the air was growing stuffy.

The man who had helped her into the cabin had shown her how to open the side window. Daisy followed his instructions.

The air blasting in was more gale than draught, cold but exhilarating. It roused Lambert from his unhappy apathy, but after one glance at the open window he shuddered and returned to contemplation of his misery. It made Daisy's eyes water. She pulled on and buckled the helmet she'd been lent, and fastened the goggles over her eyes. Now she could see out.

They were floating over rugged, wooded hills, not far above the treetops. Daisy saw a hawk hovering below, intent on its next meal, oblivious of the aeroplane passing overhead. She saw the aeroplane's shadow moving across the landscape – a hillside of tree stumps and a logging camp where tiny figures looked up and waved; a valley of scattered farms with small, irregular fields, in one of them a man and a horse ploughing; a village with a motorcar and three horse buggies in its single unpaved street; a curve of railway line with a train of coal wagons puffing along.

Gervaise would have liked to see that, Daisy thought. Her brother's clockwork train had been a favourite toy, back in nursery days.

This was fun! No wonder Alec had given in so easily to Dipper's persuasion, in spite of not being at all keen on following Pitt. She had never thought before that he might actually miss flying. She had always pictured him dodging German shells and fleeing German fighters in his single-seater observer aeroplane.

Turning to Lambert, she shouted, 'This is fun! Do open your window and have a look. There's a spiffing view.'

He opened his eyes just long enough to give her a look of terrified entreaty before huddling still lower in his seat.

Daisy returned to the view, but soon her cheeks and nose began to grow numb with cold. Wishing she had borrowed a muffler, she closed and fastened the window. In front of her, Dipper and Alec were shouting to each other, inaudible as far as she was concerned. For want of anything better to do, she speculated on the reason for Sir Roland Amboyne's nickname. Alec's obviously had something to do with his surname: Fletcher, a maker of arrows; but Dipper was obscure.

The flight became a test of endurance. As the chill penetrated Daisy's flying suit, her bottom grew numb and her limbs cramped from immobility. A meal provided a brief respite from boredom when she saw Alec and Dipper eating sandwiches and sharing a flask and remembered the stores in the cabin. Lambert refused to eat but drank some coffee – fortified with spirits, as Daisy discovered when she took a swig from the same Thermos.

How long could this go on? Surely soon they must run low on petrol and descend to refuel. Or had Dipper been prepared for a transatlantic flight when they diverted him?

Daisy knew from the sun that they were heading westward. Pitt came from somewhere in the West, some-where with mountains and forests, in which he could disappear. If he was used to mountains, she thought with a momentary excitement, that might explain how he managed to run down flight after flight of stairs. Another scrap of evidence.

She couldn't remember the name of the place he came from. Miss Cabot's many guesses swirled in her head. It began with an O – or ended with an O. San Francisco? Leora, back at Hazelhurst Field, had told Daisy the post office plane was bound for San Francisco, officially.

No longer, Daisy was sure. Gilligan had referred to Pitt's home as a little 'hick' town, which San Francisco definitely was not, from all she had heard. Gilligan had mentioned the name of the town. What on earth was it? Beginning with an O or ending with an O?

Daisy tried to recreate the scene when Pitt's provenance had been discussed. The town's name was on the tip of her tongue when she realized they were heading downward.

She gasped as the aeroplane suddenly plunged, pressing her back in the seat and leaving her stomach behind. She had just time to realize that the still roaring engines had not failed – so Dipper was presumably doing this on purpose – when they pulled out of the dive.

As the aeroplane levelled off, she peered out of her window. Just a few feet below her was the post office aeroplane, on the ground beside a shed with a wind sleeve on a flagpole. Flashing by, she thought she saw two men by the shed, and a horse and cart, and Pitt standing in the aeroplane's rear compartment, his gun trained on the pilot, who was climbing into the cockpit.

Dipper pulled back the stick and they ascended again, circling in that dizzying, wing-tilted way. Then the engines muted to a rumble and they glided down towards the field.

'I think we're landing,' Daisy said to Lambert. 'At last!'

He opened his eyes and glanced out of his window. 'That's when most crashes happen,' he croaked, gripping the edge of his seat.

'Pitt's down there. I can't see quite what Alec and Sir

Roland hope to do. It's the same situation as back at Hazelhurst Field.'

'Except that we're in the air this time and we're all going to die.'

'No, we're not,' Daisy said crossly. 'Sir Roland came through the war without crashing and . . . Oh!'

The engines bellowed as the aeroplane's nose pulled up sharply. Looking out, Daisy saw Pitt's aeroplane taxiing across the field right where they had been about to land.

Whatever his reasons, he was obviously absolutely desperate to escape.

CHAPTER 20

Dipper circled the field again, giving Daisy an excellent view of the post office aeroplane taking off. She expected that they would follow, but instead they came in to a gentle landing, bumped across the grass, and came to a halt near the shed.

Alec folded back the cabin's roof. 'We have to refuel,' he said. 'That crazy stunt was Dipper's attempt to frighten Pitt into staying on the ground. There are clouds ahead he's going to disappear into. I'm afraid we'll probably lose him.'

'No, we shan't,' said Daisy, standing stiffly and taking Alec's hand to help her down. She saw Dipper striding over to the shed, from which two farmers were cautiously emerging. 'I'm pretty sure I know where he's going. The name of the place is on the tip of my tongue.'

'I'm not going any farther.' Lambert's adamant tone left no room for argument. He jumped down beside Daisy, colour beginning to return to his cheeks, and felt in his pocket. 'Here, you can have my identification papers if they're any good to you. I quit. I'm going to find me a train station and catch a train home and go into Dad's insurance business.'

Alec regarded him with sardonically raised eyebrows. 'I shan't stop you. But before you quit, you can send a couple of telegrams for me at the Bureau's expense.' He took out the notebook he was never without.

'At the Bureau's expense?' said Daisy. 'Darling, send one to Miss Genevieve, will you? Ask her to pass on the news to Kevin. And one to Mr Thorwald and Pascoli, at the Flatiron Building. They'll all want to know what's going on.'

Leaving them, Daisy went to join Dipper.

'What ho,' he greeted her. 'This is one of the air mail service's emergency landing fields. Arrow was right as usual: we're in Ohio.'

'Oregon!' Daisy exclaimed, her memory jogged by the plethora of O's. 'That's where Pitt's going. It's in the West somewhere.'

Dipper laughed. 'That's the direction he's heading. I was wondering how we're going to find him again, but if you know his destination, we can't miss him. These admirable gentlemen have petrol for us,' he added as the two men, farmers by the look of them, each carried two large petrol cans from the shed. 'Jolly good show, fellows.'

They took the fuel to the biplane. Dipper and the older farmer started pouring petrol into the tank.

The younger man, returning for more cans, said shyly to Daisy, 'You're British, ain't you, ma'am? I was over there.'

'In the war?'

'Yes, ma'am. You know that song, "How you gonna keep them down on the farm, now that they've seen Paree"? That's me. Only it was Lunnon for me. I mean, Paree's gay, like they say, but heck, they don't even try to speak English. At least you guys try.'

'We do our best,' Daisy said solemnly.

Alec came over. He nodded to the ex-doughboy and said, 'Have you got a telephone?'

'No, sir. Ain't none for twenty miles.'

Alec glanced at the horse and cart. 'Too bad. Daisy, Lambert's agreed to escort you back to New York, or Washington if you prefer. I'll join you there as soon as this business is wrapped up.'

'Then you're going on? I was sure you'd be ready to give up.'

He came as close as she had ever seen to a blush. 'I suppose Lambert's put me on my mettle,' he conceded ruefully. 'And Dipper's still keen as mustard. We'll be off as soon as the tanks are full.'

'So will I,' said Daisy. 'Darling, you really can't abandon me with *Lambert* for an escort, dressed like this, here in the middle of nowhere!'

'The middle of nowhere, ain't that the truth!' The young man sighed. 'I guess I better go help Pa and your pilot. You gotta get going if you're gonna catch that screwball that was waving his gun around all this gasoline.'

Alec was going to argue with Daisy, but Dipper called him for a consultation. While they had their heads together over a map, Daisy managed to climb into her seat and strap herself in. Loath though she was to return to the torture chamber a moment sooner than necessary, she wasn't about to give them a chance to leave without her.

Lambert, standing disconsolate by the shed, waved to her but made no move to come anywhere near the aeroplane. Daisy waved back, wondering whether she would ever see him again. She would have liked to say goodbye properly, to thank him for his efforts to protect her from the foe, however chimerical. He obviously was not going to budge, though, and nor was she. She hoped he'd get home safely.

At last, Alec climbed into the cockpit and stood looking down at her, shaking his head. 'Daisy, there's nasty weather ahead, we can't tell how nasty. It could be dangerous.'

'I'll call it quits if you call it quits.'

He threw an exasperated glance at Lambert, and another at Dipper, but his exasperation was mostly for himself. 'I can't, love.'

'Then I shan't. You really can't expect me to face your mother with the news that I deserted you in the middle of America and you've disappeared.'

'It does sound rather difficult.'

'Much more difficult than disappearing with you, darling.'

'I don't anticipate disappearing.'

'Well, then,' said Daisy, 'that's that, isn't it? Besides, without me you don't know where to go.'

'Dipper said you told him Oregon.'

'Yes, but that's a state. I know I've heard the name of his home town, if I could only think of it.' She frowned. 'There's some connection in my mind with Miss Genevieve. I can't quite pin it down. Unless it's just that she was there when I heard it.'

'Great Scott, Daisy, if we don't know his destination, this whole mad jaunt is pointless! I'm not flying clear across the country only to humour you and Dipper.'

'I'll remember,' Daisy said determinedly. 'Anyway, with any luck you'll see him when we take off, so that we can follow again.'

This time, as Alec was flying the aeroplane, it was Dipper

who stood up in the cockpit to peer around the windshield. To Daisy's relief, he spotted their quarry.

It wasn't very long, though, before he stood up again. This time he balanced there, scanning the sky ahead, for what seemed an age. When he sat down, he was shaking his head. Alec shrugged. They shouted back and forth a bit, then Daisy felt the aeroplane gradually ascending.

She soon saw why. They were sailing above a blanket of cotton-wool clouds. Wisps floated about them, insubstantial as dreams, but the mass below was quite solid enough to hide Pitt's biplane, whether he was forcing his unwilling pilot to fly through it or under it. Daisy imagined the poor man's quandary as he weighed the probability of Pitt shooting him if he disobeyed, against the dangers of flying blind through what she guessed must be a pea-soup fog.

If the pilot died, Pitt would also die, of course. Did he not fear death? If not, what was he fleeing? Not someone who had killed his cousin and might kill him. Which suggested that he had in fact been responsible for Carmody's death, intentionally or not.

Was he afraid of imprisonment? Daisy wondered if that fate might seem worse than death to someone used to roaming the forests and mountains. Or perhaps he was not so much running *away* as running *to* – to those forests and mountains which he had, according to Miss Genevieve, described in Proustian detail in his book.

With a sigh, she decided she'd never understand the motivation of someone whose background was so utterly different from her own, especially as she had never even talked to him.

She ought, however, to be able to remember the name of

the Oregon town he and Carmody came from. What was the connection with Miss Genevieve? She worried away at the riddle but was eventually driven to the conclusion that the direct approach would never work. Perhaps, as with an acrostic, the answer would suddenly come to her when she was thinking of something else.

Outside the window, occasional rifts in the clouds showed a rain-drenched countryside below, but no sign of the post office aeroplane. With nothing to hold her attention, and slightly more room to stretch her legs since Lambert's departure, in spite of noise, cold and vibration, Daisy drowsed off.

What roused her was a change in the note of the engines. The cloud tops were tinged with pink and the sun was a blood-red globe dead ahead. Then the aeroplane plunged into the clouds.

It wasn't like a pea-souper after all, more of a ragged mist streaming past the windows. Daisy held her breath, half expecting to run into a hillside, or a tall building, or even the tail of Pitt's aeroplane. She did not have to hold it long. The cloud layer was not thick, and when they emerged beneath, it was not raining.

Rosy sunlight slanting through a gap to the west revealed to Daisy's astonished gaze flat farmland divided neatly into squares like a chessboard, as far as the eye could see. *Alice Through the Looking Glass*? Curiouser and curiouser, thought Daisy.

They flew on below the clouds, which grew sparser and fell behind. Then Daisy saw Dipper point ahead and consult a map. He and Alec exchanged a few of those infuriating shouts which she couldn't hear. The aeroplane tilted as they turned northward. Now the pattern of squares was broken up by a great river, whose course they followed, cutting across its meanders.

The sun had set by now and the light was fading fast. Daisy wasn't at all sure she wanted to experience a night landing, especially at a field unfamiliar to both pilots. If they actually found an airfield. What on earth had possessed her to insist on chasing Pitt?

Because she had been convinced that he had killed his cousin, and that Rosenblatt and Gilligan were incapable of catching him, she reminded herself. And once begun, the excitement of the chase was added to reluctance to admit she might be wrong and refusal to give up as long as anyone else continued.

It was not quite dark when the engines throttled back and the aeroplane began to descend. The lights of a town appeared below. Wherever it was that they were going, they had apparently arrived. They circled above the town, while Dipper consulted his map with the aid of an electric torch. He pointed at the ground, and he and Alec exchanged shouts. Down they went again.

The landing was decidedly bumpy, not to say bouncy. Daisy was just grateful to be down in one piece, especially when she realized Alec had landed by the light of a row of paraffin lanterns hung on a fence.

The field was very like their last stop, but with no friendly farmers at hand. Whoever lit the lamps had already left.

'Sioux City, we think,' said Dipper ruefully, helping Daisy to the ground. 'We were aiming for Omaha. Should have turned south when we struck the Missouri River, dash it, as Arrow said. Still, no bones broken, what?'

'Sioux City!' Daisy exclaimed. 'As in "Little Indian, Sioux or Crow"? We're in the Wild West, then. It can't be much farther to Oregon.'

'Awf'ly sorry to disappoint you, Mrs Fletcher, but we're not even halfway across the country, as near as I can reckon it. The maps I've got only go as far as a hundred and five degrees west.'

'This is crazy,' said Alec, stretching wearily. 'I don't suppose you've remembered yet, Daisy, where in Oregon Pitt comes from?'

'No, I'm afraid not, darling. Actually, I fell asleep while trying to think of the name of the town. But I *will* remember, I promise.'

He groaned. 'I suppose it's no good walking into the town. The telegraph office will be closed, and anyway Washington will be shut down for the weekend. If only I knew what was going on, whether there's a general alert out, whether the federal authorities have found out where Pitt's from and where he's going.'

'I can't see Lambert getting close enough to tell them. So it would take cooperation from Rosencrantz and Guildenstern,' Daisy pointed out. 'Most unlikely.'

'Rosencrantz and Guildenstern?' queried Dipper, intrigued.

'It's a long story,' said Daisy.

'We've got time. We can't take off again until the early hours of the morning unless we want to land at an unknown field in the dark.'

'Always assuming there's fuel in that shed,' Alec said gloomily.

'If there isn't, darling, we're stymied, which ought to please you. Let's go and see.'

There was fuel. In the last of the twilight, Alec and Dipper refuelled the aeroplane. Daisy scavenged the last of the food supplies from inside and, by the light of the torch, arranged a meagre picnic within the petrol-smelling shelter of the shed. The men brought in a couple of the paraffin lanterns, which made things more cheerful and perhaps slightly warmer, though adding to the overall effluvium.

They sat down cross-legged – much easier in aviator's gear than a skirt, Daisy noted – to curling sandwiches and lukewarm coffee.

'First,' said Daisy, 'before I explain everything, would you mind telling me, Sir Roland, why you're called "Dipper"? And also why you call Alec "Arrow", unless it's just because he's Fletcher?'

'That's part of it, of course. But it's largely because he was the best navigator of all the observer pilots in the RFC.'

'Spare my blushes!' said Alec.

'By George, it's true, though,' Sir Roland insisted. 'Always flew straight as an arrow to his target. Some of the chaps used to ramble over half of France and come back never having set eyes on whatever they'd been sent to take a dekko at. Arrow always got the goods. Comes of being a copper, I dare say. Always get your man, do you, old man?'

'Not quite always.'

'Jolly nearly,' said Daisy. 'What about "Dipper"?'

Sir Roland laughed heartily. 'That's another story! Thing is, I was shot down two or three times, and ran out of fuel now and then, and then there were mechanical problems – nothing out of the ordinary, by George, nothing that didn't happen to most of the chaps, sooner or later. But somehow

I always came down in the water, the Channel, a river, a reservoir—'

'A duck pond,' Alec put in.

'Dash it, that one I prefer to forget, old man! Ever taken a dip in a duck pond, Mrs Fletcher? I can't advise it.'

'At least you didn't drown,' said Daisy, appalled by his list of mishaps.

'True enough. I was lucky.'

'We both were,' said Alec.

'True,' Dipper said soberly. 'We came through. Most of the chaps didn't. I say, is that the last of the sandwiches?'

'I'm afraid so. There's just an apple left. Darling, let me have your penknife and I'll slice it. What brought you to America, Sir Roland?'

'Oh, a couple of chaps and I decided to pop over just for fun. Gives a chap something to do, don't you know?'

'You flew across the Atlantic?'

'Nothing to it these days,' said Dipper mournfully. 'People doing it all the time since Alcock and Brown showed the way in 1919. We fitted an extra petrol tank in the rear, where you've been sitting. Took it out when we got here, to lighten the load – that's why our range is only six hundred miles or so – but it's easily reinstalled when we need it. Let's have your tale now. Rosencrantz and Guildenstern, eh, what?'

As the lamps burned lower, Daisy told Sir Roland the story, from the quarrel she had overheard in the next room the day before the murder to recognizing Wilbur Pitt in the lobby.

'That was just this morning!' she said in astonishment. 'It feels like a month ago.'

'So the chap we're chasing bumped off his cousin as well as pirating a plane?' said Sir Roland. 'Ripping!'

'Ye-es.'

Alec pounced on Daisy's hesitation. 'You're not sure, are you?' he demanded.

'I'm sure I saw him in the Flatiron Building,' Daisy temporized, persuading herself as much as Alec. She really was pretty certain. She remembered telling Rosenblatt and Gilligan the man had seemed familiar, which could only be because of his resemblance to Carmody. 'It's just that I can't help wondering whether he ran because he was afraid he might be shot, too. By someone else, of course.'

'Poppycock,' Sir Roland snorted. 'If your chappie was so easily scared, he wouldn't have been running around waving a gun at the aerodrome.'

'I think he's right, love,' Alec agreed, to Daisy's enormous relief. 'I rather doubt that shrinking violets are bred in those farms and mines and logging camps, however civilized the Wild West may have become in these degenerate days.'

'In any case,' said Sir Roland, 'we can't let air piracy flourish unpunished. We've got to go on, by George, on the off chance that we might catch him when everyone else fails. Time for beddy-byes, now. We'll take off about two ack emma. Don't want to waste any time.'

With that, he stretched out along a wall and apparently fell asleep straight away. Daisy, with Alec to warm her and pillow her head on his shoulder, managed to doze fitfully. She was not so comfortable, however, as to mind much being woken in the middle of the night.

They took off under a waning moon and a million brilliant stars. Daisy slept on and off as they droned westward. Again the changing note of the engine roused her.

In the light of dawn, the aeroplane was circling above a large city. And as it turned, Daisy saw that the way to the west was barred by a wall of mountains, their towering, snowy peaks tinted pink by the approaching sunrise.

CHAPTER 21

Two wind sleeves in the northeast corner of the city announced the presence of rival aerodromes. Dipper chose the one which displayed the most activity. As they landed, three small biplanes were being prepared for take-off.

Pilots and mechanics stopped to watch as they taxied across the grass towards the tarmac. Dipper stopped near a petrol pump, not far from the group, who all strolled over to the new arrival. Daisy was interested to note that one of the people in flying dress was a woman, a black woman.

Someone folded back the hood over Daisy's cabin. She stood up stiffly, and hands reached out to help her down.

'Denver!' Alec was saying. 'I've lost my touch, Dipper. Too far north last night and too far south this morning. We were aiming for Cheyenne.'

'Lowry Aviation Field, Denver, Colorado,' said a short wiry man in airman's leathers. 'You're heading west? The Cheyenne route's generally easier flying.'

'That's the way the air mail planes go, isn't it?' said Dipper.

'It's not quite as high, and more of a plateau, without the big peaks. But the radio weather man said it's gonna be snowing that far north today. You better go the southern route.'

'We haven't got a map from here on.'

'Ah guess we can find you a spare, cain't we, Hiram?' the woman put in. 'Where're y'all going to?'

Alec and Dipper looked at Daisy.

She stared at the short, wiry pilot. 'Hiram,' she said. 'That's it. Not quite, but that's nearly it. Now hush a moment while I think. It's one of those names which sound as if they ought to be English, but one just doesn't come across them at home. Hiram, Caleb, Elmer, Chester, Floyd – and Miss Genevieve? Of course, her pen name was Eugene Cannon! Eugene City, Oregon, that's where we're going.'

'At last!' said Alec.

'Well done, Mrs Fletcher,' said Dipper.

'Ah know Eugene,' the black woman said. 'Ah did a show there last summer. Nice little airfield they have.'

'That's good to know, madam,' said Dipper, 'always supposing we can find it.'

'Jack, go see what maps we can spare,' Hiram ordered one of the others.

'Madam!' The black woman laughed. 'Ah don't get called that too often. Bessie's my name, Bessie Coleman.'

'How do you do, Miss Coleman.' Dipper introduced himself and Alec and Daisy, and Miss Coleman introduced her colleagues. They were barnstormers, they explained, who had just put on a show in Denver and were moving on to fresh pastures.

Daisy and Dipper left it to Alec to explain their arrival in Denver at dawn on a Sunday.

Daisy did not hear how much he revealed, as Miss

Coleman said to her, 'Ah expect you'd like to wash up, Miz Fletcher. They don't have a little girls' room here, but Ah'll stand outside the men's room while you go in.'

'Gosh, thanks! I've been making do with bushes. Real plumbing will be sheer heaven.'

'It's not elegant,' Miss Coleman warned, leading the way towards the buildings. 'Y'all are English, aren't you? Ah learnt to fly in France. Ah was always crazy for it, and Ah couldn't find anyone over here who'd teach me. Then Ah came back to show people what a coloured woman can do if she puts her mind to it.'

'Good for you! I'm not exactly sure, what are barn-stormers?'

'Fools who risk their lives to give the rubes a thrill because that's the only way they can make a living flying airplanes, and that's the only thing they want to do. Gypsies, they call us. We put on an air circus to attract the crowds. Ideally they pay to see us loop the loop and walk the wings and so on. Hiram has a great new stunt where we fly in formation and he climbs down by rope ladder from the top plane to the one in the middle, and then to the bottom one. But of course anyone who wants can see it from outside.'

'I suppose so,' said Daisy.

'The real money comes from taking people up for joyrides. We make enough to buy gasoline and food and keep the Jennies more or less in flying condition, and maybe a bit over.' She shrugged. 'We get by, and we're doing what we want. Ah guess that's about as much as anyone can ask for.'

'That's how I feel about writing,' Daisy told her, 'or I did, till I got married. I'm going to write an article about flying.'

'Flying's been in the Denver papers the last couple of

days. Some guy was arrested in Ohio for flying over a city and dropping leaflets. They're more forward looking here in Denver – the citizens are going to raise money for a municipal flying field, and they're going to put up an airplane lighthouse on Pikes Peak. There was a column about a new record air speed, too. Two hundred fifty-nine miles per hour, think of that!'

'It's not so long since they said the human body couldn't survive travelling at thirty miles an hour!' Daisy exclaimed as they reached the men's room.

It was not the most salubrious place Daisy had ever found herself in, but it was definitely an improvement over bushes. She emerged feeling a bit less grubby, at least about the face and hands.

'Ah missed what your husband was saying about why y'all are here,' Miss Coleman said as they walked back towards the aeroplane.

'We're chasing an air pirate.'

'Is that right? That makes those train bandits they're hunting over in the Siskiyous look real old fashioned! And you think he's heading for Eugene?'

'That's where he's from. It's only a guess that he'd make for home, though,' Daisy admitted. 'He knows the mountains and forests, so he'd find it easy to disappear if we don't get there in time to stop him. At least, the police may be on the lookout, but we've no way of knowing, and they're not likely to pay any heed to a telegram from people they know nothing about.'

'So you're in a hurry,' said Miss Coleman thoughtfully.

'Rather. Oh dear, Alec's not looking very happy.'

Alec was frowning over a couple of maps spread out on

the lower wing, with Hiram beside him explaining something, while Dipper was supervising refuelling.

'What's up, darling?' Daisy asked.

'Mountains,' Alec said briefly. 'Dipper, have you any experience flying through high mountains?'

'Not me.' Dipper came over. 'Nothing higher than the Alleghenies we crossed in Pennsylvania. Trouble?'

'Flying due west, we'd have to cross at least one pass at nearly twelve thousand feet, but going round by the south makes it considerably farther. I suppose we'll have to go the long way.'

'Waste of time, dash it. Let's go . . .' Dipper smothered a huge yawn. 'Let's go for it. Where's that coffee?'

A fit of yawning overcame Alec.

'Coffee's not gonna make you guys fit to fly through mountains you don't know,' said Hiram bluntly. 'Better grab a bit of shut-eye first, whichever way you're going.'

'They're in a hurry,' Miss Coleman pointed out. 'We let this air pirate get away with it, there'll be others deciding it's a good way to make a getaway, and it's us they'll be coming after. Why don't Ah take them over? Leastways—' She asked Dipper some technical questions about his altitude meter, ceiling, range and maximum speed. 'Sounds just fine. Miz Fletcher, ma'am, can you read a map?'

'On the ground,' Daisy said dubiously, amused by Alec and Dipper's flabbergasted expressions, but not at all sure that they were wrong to be incredulous.

'That's OK, honey. It'll be mostly watching out for roads and railroads and rivers. Ah've flown it before and the weather forecast's fine this far south. Hiram, Ah'll join up with y'all in New Mexico soon as I can get there, OK?'

'I guess,' said Hiram laconically.

'At least take her up for a practice run!' Dipper blurted out. 'Get the feel of her.'

Miss Coleman beamed at him. 'Good idea. Stand clear, boys!'

As she swung up into the cockpit, the mechanics pulled out the petrol pump nozzle, capped the fuel tank, and backed away. The engines, still warm, burst into life. With a cheerful wave, she taxied across the tarmac, turned into the wind, and started her take-off run across the grass.

'Oh Lord!' groaned Dipper.

'She's a mighty good pilot,' Hiram told him. 'Watch.' The boy who had been sent to buy them breakfast turned up at that moment. Distracted, Daisy missed the take-off. She only looked up from a rather disgusting fried-egg sandwich – which she was happily devouring, being ravenous – when she heard a horrified unanimous gasp from Alec and Dipper.

For a moment she couldn't see anything wrong. Then she realized that the aeroplane was upside down.

With difficulty, Daisy suppressed a gasp of her own. She ought to have more faith in Bessie Coleman. The others must know she was a stunt pilot. They wouldn't be worried if she were a man. Hiram and the others didn't look at all worried.

The aeroplane's nose turned downward, diving towards the hangar. Daisy's fingernails bit into her palms. But Miss Coleman pulled up and flew right side up a few feet above the hangar, waving to the spectators. She zoomed up, did a few barrel rolls, and came gently down for a perfect landing.

Ten minutes later, the refuelling completed, Daisy found

herself in the cockpit buckling her safety belt, with Alec and Dipper unwillingly stowed in the cabin behind.

Miss Coleman spread a map on Daisy's knee. 'See here, Miz Fletcher, ma'am, this here's the road we want to follow, via Glenwood Springs and Grand Junction. It's going to be hard to see sometimes, in the high passes where there's snow, and down in the canyons among the trees. Some places it'll be easier to spot the railroad lines or a river or creek, so you take note where they run together or at least the same direction.'

'Right-oh,' said Daisy, determined not to get them lost so they'd have to crash land in snowy mountains. 'I'll keep my eyes peeled.'

'And hang on to that map. It gets mighty windy. Most all of the time Ah'll be looking, too, but there's places Ah'll have to concentrate on flying. We'll be going up to about twelve thousand feet. That's our ceiling, as high as the plane can fly. The air's getting thin up there. You feel dizzy, you put your head down between your knees and don't worry about where we're going, you hear?'

Daisy had an uneasy feeling that Alec had said one of the passes was twelve thousand feet, but she nodded. 'Right-oh, Miss Coleman.'

'Bessie.'

'Daisy, then.'

They smiled at each other. Bessie taxied towards the take-off position, while Daisy concentrated her entire attention on the map in her lap.

Daisy didn't raise her head until the aeroplane levelled out after taking off. She was stunned by the view from the cockpit, so much clearer than from the cabin. The city of

Denver spread out below, scarcely beginning to rouse so early on a Sunday morning. She had expected the mountains ahead to look smaller once she shared the sky with them. They didn't. They looked bigger. And they grew as the city slipped away behind.

The road west from Denver was easy to see, heading for the foothills as straight as a Roman road. Though unpaved, it appeared to be made of well-packed gravel, and if snow had fallen here, it had melted. When the road reached the hills, it narrowed and began to wind between slopes of evergreens, but it was still clearly visible from above. They followed it, cutting across the curves.

The hills grew more rugged, too steep in places to support trees. Daisy assumed they were also higher, and that the aeroplane was constantly ascending. She thought it was getting colder, though that might have been her imagination. The road was harder to see, and sometimes they had to fly high above it as it wound through a narrow valley. Bessie followed its course closely, afraid to lose it if she cut across. They were flying between the hills now, not above.

Daisy found it curiously disorienting to see trees and rocks when she looked straight out sideways. There were patches of snow, too, on the north-facing slopes.

The valley branched ahead.

'Which way's the road?' Bessie shouted, fighting gusts of wind which shook the plane.

A shoulder cut the view ahead. Daisy reached for Dipper's binoculars and stuck her head over the side, hoping she wouldn't have to stand up. The goggles protected her eyes, but the icy blast stung her cheeks above the scarf Alec had passed on to her. Catching a glimpse of the road climbing along a hillside, she pulled her head in and pointed.

Bessie nodded.

They were forced ever higher by the narrowing valley. Snowy peaks rose about them and ahead, and then the road reached the snow level. Someone had driven it since the snow fell, though. Daisy saw the double track black against the white as they curled around the mountainside.

Down went the road into a valley wide enough for what looked like a farm and a few fields. But ahead rose a great ridge and more, higher peaks. The road climbed again, and they climbed with it, until it disappeared into the shadow of a sheer cliff.

This time there didn't seem to be much choice about where to go. A few minutes later the road reappeared, still with those tyre tracks without which it would have been invisible. To follow it between the rocky buttresses and near vertical slopes, Bessie flew at an angle, one wing up and one wing down. Only a stunt pilot could have done it, Daisy was sure.

At intervals the road vanished, but somehow they always found it after a minute or two. Daisy's heart was beating nineteen to the dozen, and breathing was difficult. She didn't know if it was the altitude or sheer terror.

She must have been stark raving mad to think catching Wilbur Pitt was worth the risk of crashing in this frozen white wilderness.

CHAPTER 22

The snowy peaks seemed to go on forever, yet when Bessie shouted to Daisy that they had passed the worst, the sun had not yet cleared the mountains behind them. As long as the weather remained fine, she said, as predicted by the radio forecast, and no mechanical failure forced a landing in the desert . . .

'Desert!' Daisy shouted back. 'I didn't know there was desert ahead.'

Bessie nodded. 'Most of the way to Salt Lake. Desert and sagebrush.'

Picturing hundreds of miles of rolling sand dunes, Daisy was stunned by the stark beauty of cliffs and canyons and mesas. The colours ranged from almost white through greys, near black, buff and brown, pale pink to brick red. The rock formations were extraordinary. One rust-red massif stretched for miles like a fortified castle, with curtain walls, battlements, bastions, turrets and buttresses.

There were long miles of dull, flat or rolling sagebrush where the road and railway ran straight as an arrow. Then both would disappear into a wooded gorge carved into the plateau by the Colorado River. There the aeroplane followed the winding gash in the land, with glimpses of the river at the bottom.

Whenever Daisy was not too busy looking out for road, rail, or river, and working out which was best to follow, she and Bessie talked, shouting in abbreviated sentences. She heard about Bessie's childhood in Texas, her half-Negro, half-Indian father who had left his wife and thirteen children when Bessie was seven.

In spite of helping pick cotton and do the laundry her mother took in, Bessie had finished high school and even gone on to a term of college, though she could not afford more. Determined to better herself, she had then headed north to Chicago. Working as a waitress and manicurist, she had saved every penny and then, her heart set on flying, she applied to aviation schools, only to be turned down.

'Ah want to open a school anyone can attend,' she said. 'Ah'm saving up every penny Ah can spare again. And every chance Ah get, Ah talk to people about what a coloured girl can do.'

In return, Daisy described growing up on her father's country estate, with all the privileges of a viscount's daughter – and all the restrictions.

'Girls just didn't go to university,' she explained. 'And they didn't work, either.'

The war had enabled her to avoid finishing school and the social season, but it had also killed her brother, so that when her father died, the estate had gone to a distant cousin.

'No one left to stop me working,' she shouted. 'Mother tried! Tried to stop me marrying Alec, too. He's a policeman, a detective.'

Naturally Bessie wanted to know what had brought them to America and how they found themselves chasing an air pirate across the country. By the time Daisy had satisfied her curiosity, they were both hoarse.

'Sounds like you're just 'bout as crazy as Ah am,' Bessie croaked with a grin.

There was another mountain range to cross, but they were able to fly round to the south of the highest peaks. They descended over a vast, flat, fertile plain surrounded by barren mountains. The blue waters of the Great Salt Lake sparkled in the distance. Shortly before noon, they landed in Salt Lake City.

From the air, the great city looked deserted. The airfield was one of the regular stops on the coast-to-coast air mail route, but it too was oddly quiet.

'Sunday,' Bessie said curtly, when Dipper asked where everyone was. 'This is the Mormon capital. They'll all be in church.'

Alec groaned. 'I suppose it's no use trying to find out what's going on, then, or conversely to tell anyone what we *think* is going on.'

'Let's refuel as quick as we can and get moving,' said Dipper cheerfully. He claimed to have been unable to close his eyes for fear of his life, but both he and Alec were much restored. He left a bank draft for the petrol, made out to the City Fathers, and they took off again.

Dipper was pilot, with Bessie beside him to navigate, so Daisy and Alec were together. Since his comment about 'what we *think* is going on', all her doubts had returned.

What if Pitt wasn't heading for Eugene City, and she had dragged everyone across the country for nothing? Was it really Pitt she had seen in the Flatiron Building? If so, was he the murderer? If not, was it fear of the murderer that had made him run and hide? If so, was it her pursuit that had driven him to steal an aeroplane and kidnap the pilot?

If he reached Eugene City safely, that meant the pilot was unhurt. What harm had been done, apart from a minor disruption of the air mail service? Ought she to persuade Alec and Dipper to give up the chase and let Pitt escape in peace?

But what if he *was* his cousin's murderer?

In normal circumstances, she would have nerved herself to discuss these questions with Alec, whatever he thought of her vacillations. She couldn't bring herself to shout about it.

He held her hand as they took off. 'Not scared?'

'Not after those mountains. Scared me half to death! Not you?'

'I slept through them,' he confessed.

'Oh, darling, what you missed. Utterly spectacular as well as utterly terrifying.'

'More ahead, I gather, though not so high. I'll stay awake now.'

He may have, but Daisy did not. She woke several hours later to find herself leaning against his shoulder, even colder and stiffer than before, and with a pain at her waist where the safety belt had cut into her. She groaned as she straightened.

Alec couldn't hear her groan, of course. He smiled and shouted at her, 'Sleep well? We're going down.'

Ahead, the sun was low over white-topped mountains. The peaks were widely spaced, Daisy noted hopefully. With luck, crossing the range would not require stunt flying.

After a low pass to inspect the ground, they made a bumpy landing in a field on the outskirts of the little logging town of Bend. Several horse-drawn carts – buckboards, Bessie called them – which had been headed out of town altered course to come and inspect the aeroplane. Each carried several men, and not a one wore a fedora or a trilby. Those not in caps or cowboy hats – Stetsons – had on bowler hats. Daisy felt vindicated.

They were loggers returning to the forests after spending their Sunday off in town. With Dipper promising largesse, they willingly agreed to transport gasoline.

'Will a little place like this have enough to spare?' Daisy wondered.

'We don't need a full tank. Only eighty miles to go, as the crow flies,' Bessie told her.

Alec went off to the railway depot, determined to find a telegraph operator and let the authorities in Eugene know they were coming, and why. 'Helpful chap,' he reported when he came back. 'I signed off with my full title, including "Scotland Yard", which isn't exactly correct but is more likely to be recognized than "CID Metropolitan Police". I hope it will get someone's attention.'

As soon as they took off, to a great cheer from the loggers and townspeople, Daisy's worries returned. The fact that bowlers like Pitt's were common here did not actually mean anything, she realized. The one thing she had no doubts about was that Eugene was his home.

'Darling, what if Pitt's already got there and disappeared?'

Alec shrugged, grinning. 'Whole trip makes no practical sense,' he shouted back. 'We should have stayed in New York and started a hue and cry. Not my job to chase American crooks.'

'If it was, you'd have done it the practical way. You did send off those telegrams before we left.'

'I asked someone to send them. Dipper says his friends aren't keen on paperwork, so who knows?'

'Lambert will have reported what happened.'

Shaking his head, Alec said, 'My guess is Lambert will have done a bunk. He'll send in his resignation from home.'

Daisy had to admit it wouldn't surprise her.

The last of a glorious sunset reflected rosily off the river as they landed at the Eugene airfield. Though the town had looked quite small from the air, it had a proper aerodrome, with well-kept grass, a hangar with a wind sleeve, tarmac and a petrol pump. There was a small building, from which a man in uniform emerged as they taxied towards it. He stood with hands on hips, watching.

Bessie had been flying the aeroplane. She stopped on the tarmac and blissful silence fell as she switched off the engines. The man came over.

'Detective Chief Inspector Fletcher?' he called up to Dipper.

Alec had folded back the cabin's hood as they rolled across the grass. Standing up, he said, 'I'm Fletcher.'

'Judkins, Chief of Eugene City Police. You send a cable?'

'I did. I'm glad it reached you.' Alec started to climb down.

'You got identification?' the police chief asked, rather truculently. Though he could have had no way of knowing if Alec's credentials were genuine, he studied them carefully. 'OK,' he said, handing them back, apparently satisfied, 'so what's the story, Chief Inspector?'

Alec explained that the previous day they had witnessed

the theft of a US post office aeroplane and the kidnapping of its pilot. 'We have reason to believe the pirate intended to make his way to Eugene City.'

'Oh yeah?'

'My wife recognized him as someone known to her to have come from here.' Alec glossed over the fact that Daisy hadn't remembered the name of the place until they reached Denver. 'I take it the plane hasn't landed here yet?'

'Nah. Only person to land here last coupla days is our local aviator, Mr Simmons, back from a business trip to Portland. I'da heard for sure if an air mail plane came in. I ought to've heard it was expected.'

'We did our best to notify the proper authorities,' Alec assured him, 'but we thought it best to come ourselves to make sure he would be apprehended.'

'The proper authorities, huh? Well now, this here's a federal offence. We got two federal agents in town, but they're Prohibition men. I don't know that they'd have the authority to arrest this here . . . You didn't give me a name in your cable, Chief Inspector.'

'Pitt,' Alec told him. 'Wilbur Pitt.'

'Can't call him to mind,' said Judkins, shaking his head.

'He's Otis Carmody's cousin,' said Daisy.

Suddenly alert, Judkins exclaimed, 'Mr Carmody's boy? He was shot in New York City.'

'I saw him shot. Wilbur Pitt was there and he ran away.'

'Pitt shot his cousin?'

'I didn't say that,' Daisy protested, suddenly exhausted and certain she had misinterpreted everything, from Pitt's presence at the Flatiron to his intended destination.

'So you didn't, ma'am. But I guess that's enough for me to hold him on, pending New York State requesting extradition. I'll need you to take a look at him when he lands and make a statement.'

'He's not likely to land in the dark,' said Alec. 'My wife's had a tiring two days, Mr Judkins. If you don't mind, we'll go and find a hotel for the night.'

'I'd like for you to stick around for a bit, Mr Fletcher, talk 'bout how we're gonna do this without everything going up in flames.'

'I'll take the ladies to a hotel, old man,' said Dipper, returning with Bessie from hauling the plane into a hangar, with the aid of a mechanic.

'Streetcar's over that way,' said Judkins.

'I'll call for a cab,' said the mechanic disapprovingly. Daisy guessed Dipper, whose funds seemed inexhaustible, had rewarded his help with a lavish tip. 'It's the Osburn you want, sir.'

The taxi took them to the Hotel Osburn. As they entered, it dawned on Daisy that, dressed in flying suits and with no luggage, they would not appear to the management as desirable guests. She relied on Dipper to cope.

Dipper might have succeeded if it hadn't been for Bessie. 'No coloureds,' said the desk clerk, stony faced. 'There's a rooming house the other side of the river.' Tired as she was, Daisy wasn't going to stand for that.

'If Miss Coleman can't stay here,' she snapped, 'I shan't. Come on.' And she marched out to the pavement.

The others followed. They stood in a cold, weary, disconsolate group under the winking hotel sign. Somewhere a train whistled mournfully.

'There's bound to be another hotel in the town,' said Dipper with forced cheeriness.

'It'll be the same, honey,' said Bessie dispiritedly. 'Ah'll go find the rooming house and y'all go on back in there.'

'Never!' Daisy and Dipper declared as one.

CHAPTER 23

Almost dropping on her feet by now, Daisy wondered where on earth they were going to spend the night. Perhaps Chief Judkins would give them a bed in a cell.

'I'll find us somewhere,' Dipper said confidently. 'I hate to leave you, ladies, but first I'll have to find someone to ask.'

'Looks like that might be an all-night drugstore over there,' said Bessie, pointing.

As Daisy and Dipper turned to look, a young man strode up to them. 'Miss Coleman?' he asked Bessie eagerly. 'You're Miss Bessie Coleman, ma'am?'

'Ah sure am.'

'Haycox, Ernest Haycox, *Eugene Daily Guard*. At least, I'm not a regular reporter – I'm a student at the university – but I happened to be talking to Mr Fisher when some guy out at the airfield called in that you'd just flown into town. Mr Fisher said would I like to interview you. Would that be OK, ma'am?'

'Sure thing, but first we have to find a place to stay, me and my friends. This here's the Honourable Mrs Fletcher, and this gentleman's Sir Roland Amboyne, the British war ace. And Mr Fletcher's out at the airfield consulting with your police chief. He's a Detective Chief Inspector at Scotland Yard.'

'Whew!' Haycox whistled. 'There's gotta be a big story here. Say, ma'am, sir, can I interview you, too? And Mr Fletcher? But aren't you staying here at the Osburn ...? Oh, no, don't tell me. You just wait, I'll fix things. Come on in and sit in the *lobby* while I get to a phone.'

Daisy sank on to a sofa by a roaring fire, doubting that she'd ever be able to get up again. Bessie sat beside her, tensely upright, while Dipper leant against the mantelpiece, taking out his pipe. Haycox went over to the reception desk.

They couldn't hear what he said, but he persuaded the clerk to lend him the telephone. He spoke for a few minutes, then came over to them, grinning.

'It's all fixed,' he announced. 'Mr Fisher, the owner of the *Guard*, will be happy to host you, Mrs Fletcher, and your husband, of course. And Mr Earl Simmons, our local aviator and owner of E. C. Simmons Motor Company, would be thrilled to death to have you stay, Miss Coleman, and you, sir. They're both motoring over to fetch you.'

Daisy did not think Alec would be thrilled to be staying with a newspaperman, but she was beyond caring. When the desk clerk came over to say he had consulted Mr and Mrs Osburn and there were rooms free after all, she was almost tempted just to stay put. The man had obviously overheard Haycox crying them up on the phone. But to accept would be to let down Bessie, and to disappoint Mr Fisher, who was expecting to put up a Scotland Yard detective.

Mrs Fisher took the unexpected guest in her stride and asked for no explanations. While her husband drove off to the airfield to find out what was going on and to bring back

Alec, she lent Daisy a nightdress and dressing-gown. It was utter bliss to get out of the flying suit and Jake's trousers, and into a hot bath.

Food completed the transformation: Daisy was beginning to feel almost human again when Mr Fisher returned with Alec. He had apparently been told enough to satisfy him for the present, for he let Alec eat in peace.

Daisy didn't like to ask Alec what plans had been made for her to identify Pitt – always supposing he actually landed in Eugene – in case she let slip something Mr Fisher had not been told. Her thoughts turned to Miss Genevieve, ex-crime reporter, who must be dying to know what was going on, might even be worrying. After all, Daisy, Alec and Lambert had dashed off without a word of farewell.

Lambert might have sent her a telegram, as Daisy requested, but he was not to be relied upon. Moreover, if he *had* sent one, it would have worried the Cabot sisters still more to know Daisy had embarked on a perilous cross-country aeroplane flight.

'Mrs Fisher, would you mind awfully if I sent a telegram? Just a short one, to reassure a friend. If Alec hasn't enough money to pay for it, I'm sure Sir Roland will.'

'Pay for it?' cried Mr Fisher. 'Nonsense! It's a business expense. Make it as long as you like.'

So to the brief message that she had arrived safely in Eugene, Oregon, Daisy added a request to notify Mr Thorwald – and Kevin, she tacked on as an afterthought. She did not want the Misses Cabot roused in the night, so she told the Western Union clerk to deliver the telegram in the morning.

By the time they read it, Pitt might have landed. Or he might not. Daisy was too sleepy to care.

*   *   *

Having gone to bed early, Daisy woke early the next morning. It was still dark outside, but the luminous hands of her wristwatch told her it was after six o'clock. She slipped out of her bed and tiptoed across the rag rug to squeeze into Alec's bed with him.

It wasn't nearly as tight a fit as the bunk they had shared crossing the Atlantic. Plenty of room for what she had in mind.

Daylight was seeping through the curtains an hour or so later, when they heard domestic noises from below. 'That sounds like breakfast preparations,' said Daisy. 'I'm starving. Gosh, I hate to get back into Jake's trousers.'

'Mrs Fisher seems to possess the imperturbability necessary to a newspaperman's wife – or a policeman's. I don't suppose she'd mind you going down in that dressing-gown she lent you. I'll pop out as soon as the shops are open and see if I can find a frock for you. Judkins will just have to wait.'

Daisy kissed him, so it was a few minutes before she got up. She found Mr Fisher at the breakfast table, studying the competing *Morning Register*.

'They haven't even a mention of your arrival,' he said with satisfaction. 'Good morning, Mrs Fletcher.'

'Good morning. I hope you don't mind this.' She indicated her déshabillé, just as his wife came through from the kitchen.

'That's just fine, honey,' said Mrs Fisher. 'I ran you up a dress last night on my sewing machine. You can try it on after breakfast. Ingrid's making waffles.'

'Spiffing!' Daisy assured her. 'It's awfully kind of you to make me a frock, I can't tell you ...'

'A cable came for you,' Mr Fisher interrupted, flipping through a heap of letters beside his plate and fishing out a yellow Western Union envelope.

'Heavens! Who on earth ... ? Oh, it must be from Miss Genevieve. I'd forgotten the time difference. She's the only person who knows where I am.'

Mr Fisher handed her a paper knife. He didn't resume his perusal of his competitor's newspaper but watched as she slit the envelope, no doubt hoping for something newsworthy. Alec came in as she unfolded the form.

'A cable from Miss Genevieve, darling. She *was* feeling extravagant. It's miles long.' Daisy started to read. 'Oh *no!* How too, too dreadful! Gilligan's arrested Barton Bender for murder, and Mrs Carmody as an accessory. So it wasn't Pitt, after all.' Despairingly she gazed at Alec over the telegram. She had hounded an innocent man into committing a crime!

'Great Scott!' Frowning, Alec leant across the table and twitched the telegram from her fingers. He read it, then looked up at her with a wry grin. 'Buck up, my love. You didn't read far enough. Gilligan's arrested that precious pair, yes, but Agent Whitaker has arrested Lambert.'

Daisy stared at him incredulously. '*Lambert*? For murdering Otis Carmody?'

'Let me see if I can make this out. Her telegraphese is so brilliantly ingenious, it takes some working out. She learnt some of this information from your young friend Kevin. Lambert apparently returned to New York and sneaked into the Chelsea to pick up his stuff. Whitaker had asked the management to notify him when any of the three of us returned, which they duly did. Lambert going out met Whitaker coming in and took to his heels – Miss Genevieve witnessed that bit. But I didn't think Lambert knew Whitaker.'

'He may not have known him, but he saw him when Whitaker came to see me at the hotel. We took him for a villain, remember, and they hid me, he and Mr Thorwald and Pascoli, with Kevin's help, of course, after Balfour warned us. Maybe Lambert got muddled and thought he really was a villain. It would be like him.'

'Very,' Alec agreed wholeheartedly. 'Hmm, what does Miss Genevieve mean by "Washington"?'

'The Washington connection,' said Daisy. 'I bet she thinks Whitaker thinks Lambert was sent by someone in Washington whom Carmody upset, to assassinate him. What utter bosh! No one in his right mind would send Lambert to accomplish *anything*!'

'No one who knew him, certainly.'

'And as for Barton Bender, his arrest doesn't necessarily mean there's any real evidence against him. Rosencrantz and Guildenstern just want a scapegoat until after the election.'

Mr Fisher had listened avidly to every word in silent fascination, but this was too much for him. 'Rosencrantz and Guildenstern?' he asked.

Daisy looked at Alec, suddenly aware that they had been spouting all sorts of things which he might not want the newspaperman to hear.

'It's all right,' he said. 'Mr Fisher has promised not to publish the story until Chief Judkins gives him the word.'

So Daisy explained how Hamlet's courtiers had worked their way into the adventure in spite of her efforts to keep them out. 'I was constantly afraid I'd use those names to their faces,' she confessed. 'They already considered me an unreliable witness. They would not have been amused.'

Mr Fisher laughed heartily, but he went on to ask, 'And who exactly are the other people you mentioned?'

'Not now, Chuck,' Mrs Fisher chided. 'Let them eat their waffles while they're hot.'

Chief Judkins arrived while they were still eating. Daisy was embarrassed to be caught in a dressing-gown, but he was either too polite to appear to notice or too preoccupied to notice. He was persuaded to sit down to a waffle and a cup of coffee. Then he and Alec put their heads together, and Daisy went to change into the dress Mrs Fisher had made her. It was a rather ghastly mustard yellow wool, clashing horribly with her blue costume jacket, but it fitted reasonably well and she was far too grateful to quibble. Anything rather than Jake's trousers.

Judkins drove her and Alec out to the airfield in a Model T with police insignia. (Mr Fisher swore he would join them there after calling at his office.)

On the way, Alec told Daisy the Chief had made some telephone calls and discovered that news of the pirating of the post office plane had been circulated to Investigation Bureau field offices all over the country. 'But no one seems to have made the association of the pirate with Eugene,' he said. 'They had a report from a farmer somewhere in Illinois of it landing to refuel at an emergency airfield.'

'That's all? Isn't Illinois somewhere in the middle of the country?' Daisy asked.

'Midwest,' Judkins confirmed over his shoulder.

'But it must have come down more than once, mustn't it, darling?'

'Yes, if he's coming all the way to Oregon. But remember how few people we saw. Pitt would force the pilot to stick to emergency fields well away from towns.'

'I suppose all he had to do was threaten to shoot him if he landed at a proper aerodrome. Unless he decided to stop somewhere else and come home by train. Or just stay somewhere else.'

'I sure hope not,' said Judkins. 'I got a federal agent coming down from Salem just to pinch this guy.'

'If Pitt had hopped off somewhere en route, the pilot would have reported by now,' Alec argued.

'Not if Pitt made him fly to Mexico,' Judkins pointed out. 'Or shot him.'

Daisy shivered. It would be bad enough if Pitt just didn't turn up, after all the fuss. But what if Rosenblatt and Gilligan were right that Bender was Carmody's murderer, and her pursuit of Pitt had caused the death of the pilot?

Alec put his arm around her shoulders. 'There's plenty of time yet for him to arrive,' he said comfortingly. 'The pilot had no one to relieve him, so they would have had to stop for him to rest.'

They drove up to the airfield building and stopped beside a large and gleaming Packard. Two police officers came over to salute Judkins. As Alec and Daisy got out of the Ford, Dipper, Bessie, the reporter Ernest Haycox, and another man – Earl Simmons, Daisy guessed – emerged from the hangar.

Those who had not met were introduced. Simmons

wanted to tell Daisy about his wife, who often flew with him. 'I dropped Mrs Simmons off by plane Saturday in Salem to visit with relatives,' he said. 'She'll be real sorry to have missed you. She'd have been mighty pleased to meet the real English aristocracy seeing she married a fake earl! And you a flyer, too.'

'Not really,' said Daisy, smiling at Haycox, who hovered at her side, notebook in hand, anxious to interview her. 'I'm not a pilot.'

'No more is Mrs Simmons. But Miss Coleman's been telling me how you helped her navigate through the mountains. Now I gotta admit, I never flew across the Rockies. Miss Coleman's gonna take me up for some stunts while she's here. Before Mrs Simmons comes home,' he added with a wink.

They turned to look at Bessie, to find her standing quite still, staring into the northern sky. 'There's a plane coming,' she said. Squinting against the glare, Daisy made out a distant dot. Everyone fell silent, and a faint buzz came to her ears. 'Sounds like it's a DH-4,' said Bessie. 'That's what the post office flies.'

Dipper swung up his binoculars. 'It is. That's him.'

'Everyone under cover,' snapped Chief Judkins. His men herded them into the building.

All except Alec, who stayed outside conferring with Judkins, to Daisy's dismay. The two officers joined them, then all four moved out of sight.

Daisy was on tenterhooks. Dipper was indignant. 'Dash it!' he exclaimed, standing behind her at the window, 'I could have helped if they'd just told me what to do.'

'Me too,' said Haycox.

'Don't go out now, for heaven's sake,' said Daisy. 'If Pitt sees people around he might decide not to land. Or you might put Alec and the others in danger.'

For what seemed an age, nothing happened. Then the drone of the approaching plane penetrated the walls. It grew louder, and suddenly the biplane appeared, a few feet above the grass, crossing in front of the building. The post office insignia was plain on its side. It really was the pirated aeroplane. Daisy exhaled on a long sigh. She had not quite believed it until that moment.

The wheels touched down, bounced, settled again. As the plane slowed, the tail came down and the skid slid across the grass. Just before the plane moved out of Daisy's field of view, the pilot turned his head for a quick glance behind him.

That was when she realized there was no figure sitting in the rear with the mailbag.

Where was Pitt? If he had abandoned ship before reaching Eugene, why had the pilot come here? Was it a different aeroplane after all, perhaps the first of a new air mail service to Oregon?

Where was Wilbur Pitt?

The plane taxied back into view, close enough for the engine noise to make the window panes vibrate. It stopped on the tarmac. Silence came as a shock. The pilot clambered down with what looked like weary haste, and started towards the building at a lumbering run.

As one, Dipper and Haycox moved towards the door, but Alec and Judkins intercepted the pilot. They exchanged a few words. Judkins waved his arms and headed for the plane, while Alec and the pilot came on towards the building.

Daisy was torn between watching what happened outside and going to meet Alec. She stayed at the window long enough to see Judkins and his officers approach the biplane, crouching beneath the illusory protection of its canvas-covered wings. Then she turned away as Alec and the pilot came into the room.

'Let the man sit down,' said Alec as everyone crowded around, babbling questions. 'Yes, Pitt's on the plane. He's asleep.'

'And not likely to wake without he's shaken,' said the pilot in a gravelly voice, flopping into a chair and taking off his helmet. He looked badly in need of sleep himself, his eyes red-rimmed, his hands trembling. The urge to tell his story was stronger. 'He's stayed awake two nights, holding a gun on me. I didn't sleep too good, I can tell you, and every time I woke up, there he was with his eyes wide open and that goddamn gun pointing at me. He threatened to burn the mail, too. And he talked, boy, did he talk. Say, anything to eat and drink around here?'

'There's usually something in the icebox,' said Simmons, hurrying out.

'What did Pitt talk about?' Daisy asked. All she really wanted to know was whether he had shot Otis Carmody.

'Pitt's his name? He didn't tell me. Mostly he went on about his book. He's written this goddamn – excuse me, ma'am – this book, see, and he quoted me miles and miles of it. Geez, what a load of bull!'

'Here.' Simmons returned, carrying a box and a bottle. 'It's not much.' He opened the box to reveal several semi-mummified doughnuts. 'And a root beer. I can put on coffee.'

'That'd be dandy, thank you, sir.'

'And I'll take you into town and buy you a good meal soon as Chief Judkins gives the OK.'

The pilot was already devouring doughnuts before Simmons finished speaking. He paused only to wash down the crumbs with root beer, whatever that might be. Simmons went off to make coffee; Dipper, Bessie and Fisher returned to the window; Alec, Daisy and Haycox stayed with the pilot.

'What else did Pitt say?' Alec asked as the pilot finished off the bottle.

'He was shooting off his mouth about his cousin. Seems he had this cousin born with a silver spoon in his mouth, who was always putting on side. The guy laughed at his book, and that really got his goat, but if it wasn't for the bad blood between 'em going way back, I guess he wouldn't have shot him.'

'He shot his cousin?' Daisy demanded, wanting confirmation but already feeling tension drain from her. Everything she had done, and persuaded other people to do, was justified, after all.

'Yeah, didn't I say? That's why he was on the run. Said he didn't mean to kill him, just show him he was serious and make him stop saying the book was baloney. Only he – the cousin – fell down an elevator shaft and broke his neck. Pitt was sure he did it just to louse him up, like he was always doing when they were kids together. Nutty as a fruitcake, if you ask me.'

'Darling,' said Daisy, turning to Alec, 'you'd better go and cable Whitaker and tell him to release poor Lambert!'

Judkins brought Pitt in, looking like a sleepwalker between the two burly officers. He looked harmless enough, and they had not bothered to handcuff him. He was carrying his suitcase, clutched to his chest with both arms.

'It just has a bunch of papers in it,' Judkins said to Alec. He patted his pocket. 'I got his gun. Mrs Fletcher, ma'am, this is the man you saw kill Otis Carmody?'

Closing her eyes, Daisy took her mind back to the lift lobby and her brief glimpse of a fleeing man's face. When she opened her eyes, that face was in front of her, blinking back at her unseeingly.

'This is the man I saw running away in the Flatiron Building in New York City just after Carmody was killed,' she said with confident precision.

'And he told me he shot his cousin,' the pilot affirmed.

'Well, that about wraps it up,' Judkins said with a sigh of relief.

At that moment, Pitt focused on Ernest Haycox, busy with pad and pencil. 'You're a writer?' he croaked, thrusting the suitcase at him. 'Here. Take this. My book. You understand, don'cha? You'll see it gets published?'

'Gosh,' said Daisy as the police led Pitt away, 'I think maybe I don't want to write a novel after all!'

EPILOGUE

Earl C. Simmons swept into the Hotel Osburn's lobby with Bessie at his side. The day desk clerk opened his mouth – and closed it again. It wasn't for him to question the actions of so notable a citizen. Daisy was not sure she approved of patronizing the place, but Bessie turned and winked at her.

With Alec, Dipper and Jeffries, the post office pilot, Daisy followed Simmons and Bessie through to the restaurant. Jeffries was soon tucking into a vast plate of eggs, sausages, fried ham, hashed brown potatoes and toast, while awaiting his order of hot cakes. The others contented themselves with coffee, except Daisy, who, after her early awakening decided it must be time for elevenses. The Danish pastries looked simply too scrumptious to resist.

Dipper, Bessie and Simmons still had only the sketchiest notion of what had been going on. Alec told the story, with sticky interpolations from Daisy.

'So you see,' he finished, 'I was a latecomer to the whole nasty business. Daisy was in it from the start, and I don't suppose the murder or the piracy would ever have been cleared up if not for her insight and persistence.'

'Gosh, darling, I never thought I'd hear you say that!' Daisy exclaimed, startled. She explained to the others, 'Alec generally tells me off for meddling when I get involved in his cases.'

'But this case was yours, honey,' said Bessie, 'right from the get-go. A girl's gotta fight for every scrap of credit she's earned. Don't you let anyone do you out of it.'

'She won't,' said Alec, and everyone laughed.

Jeffries finished his last pancake and his fourth cup of coffee. 'Oh boy,' he said, leaning back, 'that was swell. Thank you, sir. I feel almost human again, fit to get the mail down to San Francisco.'

'What, today?' said Alec.

'"Neither snow, nor rain, nor heat, nor gloom of night stays these couriers from the swift completion of their appointed rounds",' Daisy quoted.

'I guess they forgot to put piracy in that,' said Jeffries, 'but I don't reckon it excuses me for being any later than I can help. I'm off.' He yawned. 'Hey, mebbe I better have another cup of coffee first.'

'Miss Coleman and I have a sort of plan,' said Dipper. 'I'm going to fly her to New Mexico to join her friends. Apparently San Francisco is on the way. How would it be, old chap, if one of us flew your kite?'

'Now that's a scheme!' Simmons applauded. 'I'll drive you over to the airfield.'

Jeffries obviously wasn't keen on entrusting his precious mail to either a woman or a foreigner, but he was too tired to put up much of a fight.

'What about you, Arrow, Mrs Fletcher?' Dipper asked. 'Are you coming with us?'

Alec looked at Daisy. 'Whatever you want, love.' Daisy weighed the terror of flying through the mountains, the boredom, the noise and cold and constant vibration, against the thrill of her first flight and the stupendous scenery she had seen. What tipped the balance was the thought of climbing back into Jake's trousers.

'No, thanks,' she said. 'I'm glad to have done it, but if it's all the same to you, darling, I'm going back by train.'